MATTHEW PRITCHARD

SCARECROW

Matthew Pritchard worked as a journalist in Spain for ten years, mainly for the ex-pat press, but also for UK nationals (at which he has some good connections). While resident in Spain he perfected his craft as a writer. Now living in the UK once more, he plans to write full-time.

MATTHEW
PRITCHARD

SCARECROW

CROMER

PUBLISHED BY SALT PUBLISHING
12 Norwich Road, Cromer, Norfolk NR27 0AX

Salt Publishing 2013

Printed in Great Britain by Clays Ltd, St Ives plc

Typeset in Paperback 9/10

ISBN 978 1 907773 60 0 paperback

1 3 5 7 9 8 6 4 2

To my sister, mother, father and friends
– without you, impossible

A Loli, Mari Carmen y a mis hijos – siento que
este libro nos haya costado tanta mierda

CONTENTS

PROLOGUE

1

Mamá was fast, considering her size: Tommy never saw the blow coming.

'¡Imbécil! I told you to go downstairs.'

His face stung as the cellar door slammed and he peered into sudden darkness. He felt for the wall, tried to remember what he'd overheard his sister telling her friend: four steps forward, duck, two more steps and bend, then feel for the loose board in the wall.

He stumbled once, feared he'd lost his place. But the torch was exactly where it was supposed to be; spare batteries, too. She was smart, his sister.

Little bitch.

The torch lit mildewed walls, cobwebs, musty furniture covered with sheets. Spiralling motes of dust fell through the beam of light as Mamá moved across the floorboards above. Tommy heard a gruff voice, then Mamá answering with her funny English: 'It's true I pissed off. Someone stealed my cat.' A pause. 'You pay now.' The voices faded as they headed upstairs.

Now he was safe. He shone the torch into the hole, exploring the treasures his sister had hidden there, picking them out one by one.

Doll.

Lipstick.

Mascara.

The doll's hair was matted. Lipstick and mascara filled the creases of the face where it had been applied, then wiped off. So this was what she did down here: it was she Mamá normally locked in the cellar. Mamá hated the slut.

Something behind the board in the wall stank. Tommy knelt, played the torch beam over a carrier bag at the back of the hole. It took him a moment to realise what it was; the red smears on the see-through plastic had dried to a dark brown mess but patches of ginger fur were still visible.

It was funny: after all the hissing and clawing, Mamá's cat was so stiff and still now. That had been fun, fun to slice and peel the animal into silence. He didn't care that it was her *idea. HE had done the real work.*

A rhythmic thudding began somewhere far above. Tommy swung his legs in time as he took the plastic doll's head and began to smear it with make-up. He cradled the doll, traced a finger from breast to belly, then moved onward to the smooth plastic between the legs. He frowned. That wasn't right.

Little girls weren't like that.

Tommy yanked the legs apart, fished in his pocket for the knife.

2

Nineteen years later

He pulled the duvet cover to the top of the stairs with a final heave and toed the mass that lay within with the point of his shoe; a muffled whimper emerged, but nothing stirred.

Good. The sedative was still working. Like the rest of the house, the stairway was half-finished, a zig-zag of concrete rectangles in the centre of the building site. He'd never used this house before. The old place was no good; not since they'd built above it. Caution and patience: that was how he'd avoided capture all these years.

He walked to a windowless hole in the exterior wall and checked that he had not been followed.

Nothing. Wind rustled the palm trees; somewhere a dog barked. Lights – distant and stationary – sparkled against the mountain foothills.

Time to work.

He'd wanted to be rid of the thing ever since it lost its nerve: blubbering about nightmares, sticky red hands that clutched at its throat. He'd needed to exert all his influence to make it comply the last time. Best to be rid of it.

As always, he'd built the first half of the wall the week before. He put his hand atop the waist-high row of bricks and wobbled it. Solid as a rock. He unpeeled the duvet cover and stared at the pale expanse of naked goose-flesh curled within, knelt for a moment, and cupped the cold-shrivelled genitals in his hand. There was a knife in his tool kit.

Tempting.

But no. The thing did not deserve the honour. He could wait. Caution and patience. The dark did not scare him.

Not anymore.

He used the winch to raise the thing from the ground. Once suspended, he bent the legs backward from the knee, fed them into the tiny space between the interior and exterior walls. As he did so, the thing moved, barked its shin on the edge of the bricks. Sentience returned and with it a groggy presentiment of danger. It began to struggle feebly as it dangled above the wall. He traced a finger over the tight black mask that covered the thing's head. 'You've displeased me. You things always do. Now it's time for us to part.'

He watched, expressionless, as the thing raised a feeble arm; then he released a handle on the winch. The thing slumped, disappeared into the foot wide gap between the walls.

He turned to the pile of loose bricks, looking for his trowel.

PART I – LA PAYASADA

1

Sunday, March 28th, 2010

Danny Sanchez arrived at 10:27.

It was already bedlam; hundreds of people covered the dusty patch of waste ground beyond the white walls of the property, shouting, pushing, arguing among the cacti and scruffy palms. The excavator's arm loomed menacingly above the roof of the two-storey villa.

The demolition had been scheduled for nine a.m., but frantic negotiation had earned the elderly expat owners a three-hour stay of execution while the house was cleared. The whole neighbourhood turned out to help, Briton and Spaniard alike. A stream of people walked back and forth along the edge of the unpaved road, carrying everything and anything they could salvage – doors, windows, even the kitchen work surface. The problem now was where to put it all. An incongruous pile of household items was collecting around the trunk of a fan palm. Danny watched as a negligée blew free from a box and wrapped itself around a cactus.

Christ, what a mess.

In eighteen years of journalism Danny had witnessed dozens of horrors – people cut from the wreckage of car accidents, a woman leap from a burning building, a suicide on a railway track – but this was something new. They were going to demolish Peggy and Arthur Cookes' house and *nothing* could be done to avert it. He'd seen the paperwork. Nearly every penny the poor old duffers had was invested in the villa; a lifetime's equity would be smashed to rubble. It was like waiting for an execution.

The *Junta de Andalucía*, southern Spain's regional government, had sent a woman in her mid-thirties to oversee the demolition. *Crafty*, Danny thought; people found it harder to get angry with a woman, especially an attractive one. Her hard hat and fluorescent bib bobbed at the centre of a tightly-knit group of people. *Guardia Civil* officers in green boiler suits formed a protective ring around the *Junta* woman. Then came the leaders of the protestors, waving documents and trying to argue over the shoulders of the Guardia officers.

Behind them was the press pack, two dozen strong, cameras and microphones waving above the crowd as it surged and rocked. Gawkers and curious children milled at the edges, wondering what all the fuss was about.

For her part, the woman from the *Junta* looked genuinely distraught at what she had to do. Danny had no idea whether she could follow the English words being bellowed at her, but it was obvious she understood the gist. She kept pointing to the paperwork on her clipboard, raising hands and shoulders in shrugs of helplessness. Someone, somewhere had decreed the demolition must go ahead; it was her job to get it done.

The Cookes were inconsolable. Peggy sat on an armchair that had been dumped among spiky clumps of esparto grass. Tears carved streaks through the dust that had settled on her face. Danny recognised the armchair; he'd sat in it when he'd interviewed them a year before, when the demolition orders were first served. Arthur Cooke had looked dapper and defiant as he posed for the cameras back then; now, every one of his seventy-three years weighed upon him. He stood with his hand on his wife's shoulder and turned moist eyes as Danny approached. 'Not now, mate,' he said, shaking his head. 'The bastards are about to ruin us.'

Danny nodded, glad he'd been spared having to ask the obligatory '*How do you feel?*' It was amazing how dumb those four words could make you feel sometimes. Peggy Cooke wanted to speak, though. 'Why us?' she said, her voice shrill. 'Out of all the hundreds of people, why does it have to be us? I want you to print that. It's not fair.'

Why us? That had been everyone's first reaction in March 2009 when the judicial demolition orders were delivered to eleven different families dotted around the municipality of Los Membrillos. It seemed so monstrously unfair, given the scale of the problem in Almeria, the province that occupies Spain's south-eastern tip. A Junta survey had uncovered more than 12,500 irregular constructions in just *ten* of the worst affected municipalities. But the Spanish legal system was a Heath-Robinson contraption manned by characters from Kafka: immense and baffling in its complexity, arbitrary in the decisions it dispensed and spitefully prescriptive when it did so. It was one of the dangers of emigrating to Spain, the flipside to all the sunshine, fiestas and good living.

Not that it had worried the tens of thousands of Britons who had flooded the Almanzora Valley at the turn of the century, buying up villas and plots of land for self-builds, breathing life into the moribund rural communities that nestled below the *Sierra de los Filabres* mountain range. But the rush to expand had left thousands caught in the legal quicksand between the local and regional government of Andalusia. Local councils could grant licences to build, but the regional government had the right to challenge those licences. The catch-22 was that no one would stop you from *planning* to build a house; the house actually had to be built – and the money spent – for it to come to the Junta's attention and challenge its legality.

Why us? Danny knew the answer to Peggy Cooke's question; he'd interviewed the mayor of Los Membrillos. 'We had so many applications for building licences, we were swamped,' the mayor had said, unlocking a cabinet and indicating three large cardboard boxes leaking paperwork. 'We only got round to processing eleven.' That was the bitter irony of it; by trying to follow the rules, these unlucky eleven home owners had created a paper trail that Junta officials could follow back to specific properties.

Time was ticking on. The crowd was getting angrier, the shouting louder. More Guardia officers arrived. Danny phoned everyone and anyone he could think of who was involved with the case.

It was the usual pass-the-parcel.

The council blamed the Junta, the Junta blamed the courts, the courts blamed the council; all down the line, each link of the chain shrugged its shoulders and pointed to someone else. Arthur Cooke watched Danny in action, hoping that this man who spoke such perfect Spanish could somehow work a miracle. Danny finished the phone call, shook his head. The flicker of light in the old man's eyes dulled.

Paco Pino arrived at 11 a.m., yawning and scratching at his chest. 'My one day off,' the photographer said, screwing a lens onto one of three cameras dangling from his neck, 'and this has to go and happen. Just my luck.'

Danny was glad the Cookes couldn't speak Spanish; crass comments like that were the last thing they needed to hear. Not that Paco was a bad person; experience had simply made him blasé, like everyone who made a living reporting other people's misfortunes. Truth be told, Paco was a saint in comparison with some; Danny had spoken to one of the journalists sent by a UK red top to cover the announcement of the demolition orders the previous year. 'We won't be interested again now until they knock the things down,' she said as she left, nodding toward the cloudy March sky. 'Let's hope they do it in summer, eh? I might get a bit of a tan.'

The pile around the palm tree grew: beds, sofas, lampshades, mirrors, cardboard boxes stuffed with clothes and crockery. Danny looked at his watch. Not long now.

At ten to twelve, uniformed officers of the *Policia Local* cleared the last of the protestors from the garden and checked no one was left inside the house. There were more scuffles on the white gravel outside the villa, more insults in English and Spanish. The property's black gates had been lifted from their hinges earlier to allow the excavator through. Having shoved a final protestor outside, *Guardia Civil* officers formed a human barrier in the space between the gateposts. Protestors waved paperwork at the Junta woman as she looked at her watch and waved toward the workers.

The sudden roar of the excavator's engine caused everyone to freeze and fall silent. The crowd turned as the engine revved and the excavator's mantis arm uncoiled and rose above the house. For a moment, time seemed stilled . . .

. . . and then the air thundered as the excavator's claw drove down through the roof. An angry moan emerged from the crowd as the arm rose and hundreds of dislodged tiles showered and smashed on the ground. The excavator arm dipped once, twice, three times more, prising the roof apart before ripping backwards and pulling free a ragged-edged section of brickwork. Looking through the jagged rent it created was surreal: the neatly-tiled interior walls had been exposed, giving a view inside a giant dolls' house.

The Cookes stood holding each other: Peggy sobbing; Arthur straining to keep her on her feet, his face stoic. They were tearing his house down, but he wouldn't show a flicker of weakness. Another huge section of wall tumbled away; it fell to the ground with a thud. Dust rose, people coughed, choked, began walking back along the road. Danny pulled his jacket up to cover his mouth.

The Spanish woman atop the ridge didn't really care about the foreigners; their house was illegal; it had to come down.

She was only there for the spectacle, to have something to tell her friends tomorrow at the market.

She was the first to see it.

Her mouth gaped; then she began to scream and point toward the corner of the house. People looked to see what the noise was but the sounds were rendered unintelligible by the rumble of falling brickwork and the excavator's diesel chug.

But the dust was settling now; people were following the woman's outstretched hand, squinting as they too noticed the thing wedged in the narrow gap between exterior and interior wall.

A *Guardia Civil* officer rushed to the excavator, banged on the window. The machine fell silent. Other people had noticed the shouting woman now and were pressing closer, shading their eyes, unsure of what they were seeing. For the second time that morning, asudden silence halted the crowd.

Danny thought it was a mannequin at first. And then the corpse fell forward, bending from the waist, its blackened head rocking back and forth. Some people screamed; others stood open-mouthed; some turned to run.

Arthur Cooke's face remained expressionless as he stared at the semi-skeletal corpse lolling from the broken wall of his house. Then, without moving a single muscle of his face, he toppled forward and fell heavily to the earth.

2

Police cleared the area as quickly as they could – which wasn't very quickly at all as they had to contend with hundreds of panicked people screaming, pointing, taking photos and fainting. As they pushed the nearest members of the crowd back, more people elbowed their way towards the house, eager to see what the sudden excitement was about. The dun-coloured ridge that ran behind the house was lined with spectators, hands held to their brows as they leant forward to gawp at the dead body dangling from the ruined wall.

The press pack ran haywire, unsure what the hell to concentrate on: the body in the wall, the guy on the floor, the demolished house? Cameras clicked everywhere; microphones waved; reporters accosted the police chief, eye witnesses, protest leaders, anyone who might give them an angle on the story. Paco and Danny took their time, Danny seeking out scenes that would make good copy, Paco finding unusual shots for pictures.

The ambulance had to force its way through in order to collect Arthur Cooke. There was almost a fight after a Spanish cameramen tried to film the old man lying on the dirt in the recovery position, a folded jacket beneath his head. Danny made sure he put camera and notebook away before approaching the couple to offer Peggy Cooke his help: he owed them that much. Arthur Cooke was still breathing as he was lifted into the ambulance, his skin deathly pale. Peggy made as if to go with him, but looked round in confusion when a young policeman stopped her and said in Spanish that she would need to be questioned.

'Jesus, you can question her at the hospital,' Danny said, not hiding his irritation. 'It's not like she's going to make a run for it, is it? Besides, she probably needs a doctor, too, with all she's been through this morning.'

The policeman hesitated, then climbed into the ambulance with her. The vehicle began its tortuous return journey through the crowd, siren wailing. More police cars arrived. Scene-of-crime tape was wrapped around the gates of the house. Policemen kept pushing at the crowd, forcing it back along the dirt track. Above them all, the corpse dangled, wedged between the walls, a silent spectator with the best seat in the house.

Danny got a last few quotes from eye witnesses and then he and Paco walked to a nearby bar, set up their laptops on the table and got to work, uploading the images from Paco's camera. Although, technically speaking, the two men were rivals – Paco worked for EFE, a Spanish news agency, Danny for the expat newspaper, *Sureste News* – together they had developed a lucrative sideline when major stories broke on their patch. They sold such stories as exclusives to national newspapers in Spain and the UK using the pseudonym Alan Smithee. By rights, the exclusives belonged to their employers, but both Danny and Paco had learned to put professional ethics to one side. A modern newspaper was a business, just like any other. Certainly it hired and fired as ruthlessly. The old rules no longer applied.

They ordered beers – it was Sunday after all – and plates of *carne con tomate*, pork in tomato salsa. Tapas came free in Almeria – it was the principal reason why Paco weighed three stone more than he should.

'OK, what are we looking at?' Danny said as they clicked through the dozen or so usable shots that Paco had taken with a zoom lens.

'Looks like a man's body.'

'Really?'

'Look at the muscle structure. Been there a while, hasn't he?' The body was dark brown in colour; the skin clung to the skeleton like paper.

'Yes, that figures.' Danny was flicking through his notes. 'The Cookes started living there January 2008. That means the body's been there at least fourteen months, probably more.'

'That is, assuming they didn't put it there themselves.'

'C'mon, Paco. You saw the Cookes. Do you seriously think they killed someone then walled the body up inside their own house? Plus the property's been under threat of demolition for a year. If they knew about it, why not move it?'

Paco shrugged. 'It must have been the builder, then.'

'That's more probable. But I still don't buy it. Why not bury it in a secluded corner of the plot? And why wall someone up in a house you're linked with? Remember, all sorts of legal and financial wrangles held up the construction; it was a building site for the best part of two years. Someone could have sneaked in there, put the wall up themselves.'

Danny had written a hundred words when his mobile began ringing; it was one of the Fleet Street redtops, asking whether the wild rumours were true. 'Every word,' Danny said. 'You want an exclusive?'

Paco mopped salsa with a slice of bread. He was squinting at the laptop. 'Could decomposition have done that to the head?' he said, zooming in on the blackened mass, turning his own head to one side as he examined it. 'Looks like he was wearing a gimp mask, no?'

The comment was not as flippant as it sounded. Close up, it was obvious that the entire head was covered in a tight black substance – like a rubber mask but without any holes for eyes, nose or mouth. Danny leant closer. It didn't seem to be a single piece: the surface comprised multiple layers. He leant closer still, his attention drawn by something protruding from the lower part of the face. 'What does that look like to you, Paco?'

'It's a tube, isn't it?'

That's what Danny had thought: a length of clear plastic tubing silhouetted against the black background. Then he knew.

'It's gaffer tape.'

Paco swore softly as he realised that Danny was right; the entire head was swathed in black gaffer tape. It covered eyes, nose, hair and ears to form a type of mask. The tube had been placed there to allow the victim to breathe.

'Why do that to someone?' Paco said. 'Could it be a sex game gone wrong?'

The same thought had occurred to Danny. There was no time to ponder the question, though. Other journalists would be phoning newspapers, making their own offers to cover the event. Forty minutes later, the Alan Smithee article had been despatched, 600 words of copy plus six photos.

The two men shook hands outside, Paco anxious to get home to the wife and daughters he hardly ever saw. 'They're being a right pain today. They've got some kids' entertainer coming to their nursery tomorrow. They've been like things possessed the whole weekend.'

Danny was about to head home, too, when his phone rang: William Fouldes.

Sureste News's editor wasted no time on pleasantries. 'Is it true?'

'About the dead body? Yes.'

'Brilliant,' Fouldes said in a way that made Danny imagine him punching the air. 'Oh, that's great. We've not had anything decent to put on the front page for weeks.'

Danny was tempted to say, 'I'm sure Peggy and Arthur Cooke will be over the moon,' but he bit his lip. He'd been trying to improve relations with his editor recently, more for the newspaper's sake than anything else.

'I want you to get over to the hospital, interview Peggy

Cooke.' Fouldes's voice could hardly be heard over the background babble of conversation. It was Sunday: Fouldes was probably hosting one of his barbecues, wining and dining every provincial bigwig he could persuade to attend. Social climbing didn't begin to describe Fouldes's ambitions.

'Bit tough at the moment, William. Arthur Cooke's been rushed to hospital and the police are there interviewing Peggy about the dead body. I've got her mobile number, though.'

Fouldes tutted as if the complication were Danny's fault. 'Try that. If not, go along to the hospital tomorrow.' The editor hung up without saying goodbye.

William Fouldes was not an easy man to like.

3

The sun was setting when Danny reached home. He poured Lucky, his dog, a bowl of water, before taking down the sheet of paper pinned to the fridge door with an *I ♥ Toledo* magnet.

A curious feature of his mother's written messages was that the less important the information, the more words she used. Basically, the note said that she was spending the night with a friend; yet she had managed to cover an entire side of A4. One month earlier she'd needed just nineteen words to drop an atom bomb on Danny's life: *Things over with Christopher for good so need place to stay for a few days. See you on Thursday.*

Christopher being her husband of the last seventeen years, the man she'd lived with in New York for the last nineteen. No mention that, at fifty-nine (she claimed less but Danny had checked her passport) she was getting divorced, moving country or expecting Danny to put her up.

Of course, she hadn't turned up on that Thursday. Not at Danny's house, anyway. She went to visit friends in Malaga first, leaving Danny to fret until Saturday evening when a taxi had dropped her off, giggly drunk. They'd argued that first night. 'I'm not *getting* divorced,' she said when Danny scolded her for not keeping him abreast of events, 'I already bloody *am* and that's all there is to it. But don't worry; my lawyer did a nice job alimony-wise, so I shan't be a financial burden.'

What could he do? Adriana Sanchez was an unstoppable force of nature, just like her own mother, the *abuela*, the woman who had cared for Danny while he was growing up in the UK. That was the only similarity between the two women, though: if the *abuela* was a fast-flowing river – purposeful, focused – Adriana Sanchez was a flash flood.

Danny screwed the note up, tossed it into the bin. The door to his mother's bedroom was open. The room's interior was acquiring worrying signs of permanent residence: a calendar on the wall, silk drapes placed over the wall lamp. And three framed photos of Danny, placed in a conspicuous semi-circle on the bedside table: one of him as a baby, one at junior school, a third as a teenager.

It was curious that those photos had survived all her travels. So curious, in fact, that Danny decided to check his own photo album and quickly realised that they hadn't been the constant companions of her colourful career after all; they were *his* photos, taken from his own album.

Christ, he was going to be on holiday soon, the first time off he'd had this year. How the bloody hell was that going to work out with Mother in the house?

The obvious solution was to go away somewhere. He'd always dreamed of visiting the First World War battlefields. The trouble was that it would be anything but relaxing, and relaxation was what he craved: five days drinking wine, strumming his guitar, eating too much and reading something other than bloody press releases.

Balls, he'd decide when the moment arrived. And he was a long way from being on holiday yet. Danny went outside with a glass of wine, a cigarette and his laptop and sat where he always sat in the evenings, on the edge of the patio. From here he could see the sun sink behind the final snow-capped mountain of the Sierra Nevada and listen to the chirrup of cicadas coming from the olive trees that surrounded his house. Lucky bounced happily across the dry earth, chasing birds.

Danny looked at the photos he'd taken of the demolition that morning. They weren't a patch on Paco's – that was the difference between a pro and a journalist with a camera – but they still captured the horror of the moment. Spanish had a word, *dantesco,* to describe grotesque or calamitous situations. Taken literally, it meant "worthy of Dante's Inferno". It might be applied to the Cookes. Their fortune was beyond bad luck now, it was . . . *dantesco.*

He phoned Peggy Cooke.

'How's Arthur doing?'

'Better, thanks,' she said in a voice ragged with worry. 'But I really don't think I'm up to answering any questions at the mo – '

'You've answered the only question I wanted to ask, Mrs Cooke. If you need help with anything, give me a bell. I know people at the hospital that can help. And if the language proves a barrier, say the word and I'll hop into the car.'

'That's very kind, but they're doing a grand job, thanks.' She spoke with more warmth now. 'Touch wood, it was just a scare.'

'I'll be touching wood, too, then. I'll phone again tomorrow, if that's OK?'

It was.

Speaking to her reminded Danny of the reality of the situation. Sure, the discovery of the dead body was a big, drum-banging front page story, but the real tragedy was the demolition itself. An elderly couple who'd tried their damnedest to follow the rules and, for their troubles, were going to be left penniless and without a roof over their heads. It was easy to lose sight of that in the furore.

He began writing the event up as two articles: one described the discovery of the dead body; the other concentrated on the demolition.

Having spent an hour writing, he'd built up such a head of steam that he phoned *The Guardian* and asked if they wanted a piece for their comment section. The woman at the other end ummed and ahhed, but brightened when Danny offered to do it for free.

What did Danny care? They paid bugger all for comment pieces, anyway, and it would take him only an hour.

He did it in forty-five minutes; after eight years of reporting the same ruddy story – legal snarl-ups, bewildered Brits and mealy-mouthed refusals by Spanish authorities to admit that it was the system itself that was really at fault – the 300-word piece just flowed.

Keep up the pressure on the bastards: that was all he could do. Spanish politicians didn't like their country looking bad in the foreign press. Or rather, Spanish politicians didn't like *themselves* looking bad – most of them didn't give a damn about Spain or the people that lived in it.

After he'd sent it, he searched for a copy of the interview he'd done with the Cookes the previous year. Danny kept digital copies of all the interviews he conducted; you never knew when someone was going to sue. He opened his March 2009 folder and found the interview he'd done with the Cookes. It had taken place just after the demolition orders had been served.

'So . . .' Danny's recorded voice said. He'd let the words hang; it was his technique for beginning interviews on painful subjects. The Cookes had known why he was there; he'd let them choose how to approach the subject and then he'd run with it.

Arthur Cooke answered. 'I suppose you want to know how we feel.'

'If you're able to tell me.'

'Fucking terrible.'

Peggy tutted at the language. Danny remembered him shrugging her hand away. 'No, Peggy, I'm going to tell it how it is. I'm sure this young chap's heard worse in his time. We've been shafted left, right and centre: council, regional government, lawyers, builders, architects. It was a bloody shambles from start to finish. September 2005 we were supposed to move in. Do you know when we finally started living here? January 13th, *2008*! The bloody developer went bust when the thing was half finished and they stopped building work for close on two years while the financial mess was sorted. And now that it *is* finished they want to knock the ruddy –'

Danny paused the recording. There had been a part further on when the Cookes were showing him round the house. Danny found it, listened to Arthur Cooke make disparaging comments about the quality of the building work. 'There's not a single right angle in the whole house. And nothing's the right bloody size. Everything's smaller than they said it would be.'

This was the comment that most interested him. He'd been sure that Cooke had said something about the rooms being too small. Danny had dismissed it at the time; it was a common problem in Spanish self-builds. Agreements were signed that specified the total floor space of the finished house in square metres. Homeowners expected this to be the interior measurement, but unless this was expressly stated constructors measured from the outside, with the result that the floor space was reduced by the width of the walls. It was a way of screwing a little extra profit out of a job.

'I reckon they diddled us out of a good twenty square metres, all told,' Cooke's voice said. 'Look at this bathroom. It's two square metres smaller than shown on the floor plans. And look at the damp up –'

Danny paused the recording, looked at the photos of the demolition. Through the rent in the wall behind the corpse's shoulder he could make out blue and white tiles. It was the bathroom, the same one that Cooke had been talking about.

Of course the room had been too small. There'd been a false wall.

Danny examined the image. The interior wall was built of the same grey breeze blocks as the exterior. Whoever had put the body there had not wanted it to be found; Spanish builders normally used lightweight red bricks for interior walls. Was it possible that someone could have built the wall without the builders knowing? Arthur Cooke had said that the building work was stalled for close on two years. How much space did a body need? Fifteen inches or so? Plus the width of the bricks. If the wall was the same colour as all the others, who would spot that it had crept forward a half-yard or so?

Danny looked more closely at the photo, wondering why a swift shiver of unease had gripped him. Something was wrong. One of the corpse's hands was visible, dangling over the splintered brickwork. He zoomed in on it, saw the picture blur. But he knew now what had caused him to feel chilled.

He phoned Paco, asked him to look at the same image on his big 30-inch monitor. Danny heard Paco chasing his two young daughters out of the room. 'You're right,' the photographer said eventually. 'The fingernails *are* all scratched and broken. What does it mean?'

Danny's mouth was dry. 'It means they walled the poor sod up alive.'

4

They were screaming outside now. They always did when he came.

He unscrewed the pot of white face paint, dipped two fingers and smeared them across his cheeks. He felt the warmth in his crotch.

Then his eyes hardened in the mirror. There was no time for that. Not now.

They'd found the thing. Everyone was talking about it. He'd seen the news: grainy footage of the body dangling from the wall, head bound in black. He'd known they would find it, sooner or later: like his last bit of work, it was hidden where it could be found.

Another mistake.

Caution and patience.

His cheeks were covered in white now. He began working the red greasepaint around his eyes and mouth, drawing the stick into sharp points either side of his lips. Mistakes were not something he could afford. They would stop him if they could.

But the new thing had done its work well. He'd made a good choice – his first time without the list. He could spot them now. He knew the signs. And he had insurance. Think ahead. He knew where to throw suspicion. It was the reason he'd come to this part of Spain. No one would suspect him. People looked but they never saw him for what he truly was.

Someone knocked at the door. The screaming was louder. He

smiled as he remembered those other screams. Oh, the bastard had wailed, the first in nearly two years. The knocking came again, more insistent.

He opened the door, walked out. The pitch of the screaming rose . Then he clapped his hands together and said what he always did when the show began.

'Hello children. Here's your special friend again: Pogo the Clown!'

5

Monday, March 29th, 2010

A little after midday William Fouldes appeared in the newsroom of *Sureste News* and said to Danny, 'What are you doing?' in a tone that meant he thought his senior reporter should be doing something other than sitting at his desk. Fouldes gestured towards the window. 'Sirens and flashing lights right outside. That means news. Get outside and find out what's going on.'

Danny's week had started badly. First, he'd stayed up half the night searching for a bundle of documents he knew Arthur Cooke had given him last year. He could picture the damn thing – a bulging blue folder held together with elastic bands – but could he find it? His office had been chaotic since Mother had insisted on his removing boxes and other junk from her bedroom.

Secondly, when he'd been halfway to the office, Fouldes had contacted Danny and told him to turn round, drive forty minutes in the opposite direction and cover a ten a.m. press conference. The politician in charge had spent twenty minutes explaining something everyone there already knew: that Almeria was staging a bid to host the 2012 powerboat world championship. The bid had been accepted, judges would be arriving in a fortnight to inspect the province's facilities and he was sure the excellence of Almeria's charms, combined with the sponsorship of some of the province's biggest businesses would blah, blah, blah . . .

The only high spot had been when Danny handed the politician a copy of *The Guardian* opened out to a comment piece, *Spain's Shame* by Daniel Sanchez.

The blood was still wet when Danny got downstairs, a half-yard pool on the pavement outside the commercial centre, glistening in sharp spring sunlight. The victim lay where he'd dropped, surrounded by an orange-suited ambulance crew.

The commotion had drawn crowds from the cafés and bars in the plaza. They were behaving as crowds everywhere behaved in situations like this: stop, stare, chatter, shuffle closer. Smartphones rose above the scattered groups, filming the event for posterity. Danny recognised the elder of the two *Policia Local* officers trying to keep the shuffling crowds from shuffling any closer.

'That's a lot of blood if the guy only tripped and bashed his head,' Danny said.

'Someone hit him from behind with something. But don't quote me on that, OK? The chief will provide all the details later on.'

The victim looked the sort of man you would need to hit from behind. Even with the legs of policemen and ambulance men obscuring the view, Danny could see the man was big but not fat. There was a tattoo on his arm: it wasn't one of the tribal patterns fashionable with youngsters, but one of the old-school lower forearm jobs, blurred now with age. It was the sort of tattoo you'd see on a building site or in an army barracks. The victim's hair – the front part that wasn't covered in blood – was cropped short and grey. Danny flipped open his spiral-bound notebook, wrote the date at the top of a fresh page and walked towards the closest group of onlookers, pen poised.

Another day, another drama.

'Hello everyone,' he said, pitching his voice loud without sounding aggressive or pushy. 'Danny Sanchez, *Sureste News*.

Anyone see what happened?'

They had. Trouble is, they'd all seen something different.

A woman said, yes, the attacker looked Spanish at the same time as her husband told Danny no, the attacker was North African. Up close, the crowd smelt of holidaymaker: twelve a.m. beers, cigarettes and sun-cream. Danny's pen kept time with the words, jotting them down in shorthand.

'Did the victim come out of one of the shops? Or was he just walking along?'

'From the building society over there,' a middle-aged woman said, pointing.

'What happened exactly?' Danny said.

'The bloke come at him from behind, sort of running like,' a young man said, 'then twatted him round the back of the head with something.' He lifted his arm and demonstrated a sharp, swinging motion. 'Hit him again when he was down.'

'Twice,' someone else said.

'Anyone see what the weapon was?'

Everyone began speaking at once. Some claimed to have seen a hammer, others a chisel, one a knife.

'So he hit him twice when he was down,' Danny said. 'Then what?'

'He run off.'

Danny looked up. 'Straight away? He didn't go through the bloke's pockets or anything?'

'Absolutely not. It was all over in five seconds. I only noticed 'cos I was waiting at the cash point and saw the bloke running. Bang. Bloke goes down. Bang, bang, then the attacker was up and running again.'

The rest of the crowd, so divided over the issue of the weapon, nodded agreement.

'Anyone recognise the victim?'

The man shrugged. 'I only got here yesterday.'

Danny turned to the rest of the crowd, intrigued. His question had caused heads to lower.

Rapidly.

'It's Charlie Hacker,' a middle-aged man said, after much prodding from the woman beside him. 'But I don't want my name going in the article.'

'Seeing as I don't know it, there's little chance of that, is there?' Danny said, his tone unconcerned, chummy. 'Who is this Hacker bloke then? Trouble, is he?'

The man drew closer, lowering his voice. 'The whole family is. Call themselves builders. Cowboys more like.'

'Where are they from?'

'Londoners, to judge by the accent.'

'I mean where are they from here in Almeria? Where do they live?'

No one knew. They wouldn't admit to knowing, anyway. Another police car arrived. Danny took a couple of the best witnesses over to the policemen, translated their statements. 'Doesn't look like a robbery, does it?' Danny said when they'd finished. 'His wallet still on him?'

'In his back pocket. And stuffed with money.'

'I'm not surprised. He doesn't look the type you'd pick to mug, does he?'

The ambulance crew grunted as they raised the stretcher into the back of the ambulance. Hacker's eyes flickered faintly as they lifted him. It was a nasty wound. Blood covered his face; his hair was matted with it. Danny took a photo of the pool of blood before a shopkeeper came with a bucket of water and began to wash it away. The ambulance departed; the crowds dispersed.

The walkway from which the attacker had emerged linked the street with the shopping centre's interior plaza. Danny stood at the corner looking down along the road. The shop fronts followed the convex curve of the building. Even if he leant forward he couldn't see more than ten yards.

Interesting: the attacker must have known Hacker, been waiting for him. It was either that or he'd been some nutcase lurking in the shadows, desperate to test his combat skills on the first really hard bastard to walk past.

Hacker: it wasn't the sort of surname you easily forgot. It was ringing bells now, though Danny couldn't place where or why he'd heard it before.

He threaded his way between metal tables belonging to bars and ice cream parlours and walked back upstairs to the office of *Sureste News*. The sun was now high in the cloudless blue sky. Its intense light was reflected from the white walls of the buildings.

The commercial centre formed the hub between the Mojacar Playa area, the long urbanised strip that followed the southern sweep of the coastline, and the hilltop village of Mojacar itself. When Danny had started work at the weekly newspaper eight years before, every square inch of office space on the third floor had been let. Less than half the offices were occupied now; the sun had long since bleached the colour from the orange SE ALQUILA signs in the windows of the vacant lots. The economic crisis hadn't so much bitten in Almería as torn a chunk out and chewed it up. Unemployment was currently running at 30% and had still not peaked.

As Danny passed the door to William Fouldes's office, the editor clicked his fingers at him, indicating that he should wait. Then Fouldes resumed his conversation, phone pressed between ear and shoulder, picking at his nails as he swung in his padded chair. 'Yes, the food there is simply divine. Jeanine and I went there last week.'

Danny leant against the doorframe. As always, the office stank of eau de cologne. Jeanine's photo stood on the far corner of the desk, a posed studio shot. She looked the sort to have one done, pouting vampishly at the camera, heavily made up, the sort who would want to know about your car and salary before accepting an invitation home. By Danny's count, Jeanine was the third woman to occupy the frame since Fouldes took over at the paper the previous year.

Fouldes's smile disappeared in the time that it took the receiver to click. He angled Jeanine's photo back toward himself. 'Scrape your jaw off the tiles, Sanchez, she's spoken for. Did you find out what all the fuss with the sirens downstairs was for?'

Danny explained. Fouldes brightened on hearing that the victim was British. 'Lots of blood you say? Great. That's one for you to cover then.'

'*Another* one for me to cover, you mean.'

Fouldes mimicked the irony in Danny's tone. 'I'm perfectly aware your time off begins on Friday – don't worry.'

'So you're going to squeeze me for every drop you can before I go?'

Fouldes ignored the comment. 'Have you interviewed Peggy Cooke yet?'

'No.'

'Get it done, please. Also on the subject of work, your feature article needs rewriting.'

'Why?'

'When I ask for a *definitive* piece on the number of Brits living in Almería, I expect it to be that: definitive. I've read your piece twice, and as regards precise figures I'm still none the wiser.'

'Perhaps not, but almost certainly better informed.'

Fouldes's mouth became pert with displeasure. 'If I tell you to redraft an article, I expect you to do so. Phone round some councils, get them to make estimates.'

'I did. They don't know how many British people live here. No one does.'

'Get them to make guesstimates then.'

'So you want a definitive article based on guesstimates? You know the majority of Brits here don't register their presence with councils. It's like an iceberg: most of the population is below the surface.'

'Well, there's your new headline: The English Iceberg. Go plant your flag atop it.' Fouldes pretended to busy himself with paperwork. 'Have the new draft ready by tomorrow, first thing. You're not the only –'

Fouldes's telephone rang. He answered and swung his

chair round. Danny headed into the newsroom.

There was no point in arguing: no one knew how many people of *any* nationality lived in the province. Humanity flowed through southern Spain like water through a storm drain: tourists, migrant workers, expats, backpackers, campers, runaways, drifters, tramps. The extent of the problem was evident to anyone who bothered to look at the webpages of official data for some municipalities in Almeria; the number of houses often exceeded the number of inhabitants by a third. The only official evidence of foreigners' presence was when they bothered to register on the *padrón*, the municipal electoral roll. The laborious bureaucratic process that this involved did little to encourage them to do so.

Danny phoned the *Guardia Civil's* press office: no, they *still* didn't have any information on the body found in the walls of the Cookes' house, nor would they have any that day. Danny said what he'd said twice already that morning: 'I'll try again in an hour then, just to be sure.'

The silence from officialdom was no surprise. It was frustrating, though. He couldn't do any more digging on the Cooke demolition story until he had at least some clue as to who the victim was. The press officer had clammed up when Danny asked whether the victim was immured alive. At least he seemed on the right track with that one.

Christ, what a way to go. Why do that to someone? The sex-game-gone-wrong idea was out of the window. Was it a punishment? That sounded more likely, the sort of horror criminal gangs used to punish and intimidate. And Lord knows there were enough criminal gangs in Almeria: Brits, gypsies, Russians, Moroccans, south Americans.

Danny made enquiries about the Henley Consortium, the development company that had built the Cookes' house, but it wasn't easy; like so many others, it had gone bust and the owners had disappeared off the face of the earth. Now that Danny thought about it, he was certain that Arthur Cooke had mentioned something about the actual building work being subcontracted. That wretched folder of documents he couldn't find probably held the answer.

Feeling frustration mounting, he began work on the Hacker assault story. He phoned a contact at the *La Inmaculada* hospital. Charles Hacker had been admitted to intensive care, his skull fractured with some sort of heavy, blunt object.

It was a hammer after all, then.

Danny asked if he would survive and was told the first twenty-four hours would be touch-and-go.

Danny hung up, reached for a packet of crisps. Fouldes was *still* on the phone. He seemed to spend a lot of his day doing that now. Danny knew why. Fouldes was big news on the local expat social scene, rubbing shoulders with the movers and shakers, the moneyed second or third home set. *Sureste News's* entertainment correspondent, Leonard Wexby, had attended one of Fouldes's monthly barbecues and taken great delight in bitching about it later. 'He seemed to have invited people based on the type of car they drove; I was the only person with a vehicle worth less than eighty grand. And his house! What a monstrosity! It had ramparts on the roof. And a bloody clock tower! He might as well have had *parvenu* written above the gates.'

The sound of the editor's voice echoed down the corridor. 'That's right, darling, I'm away next Wednesday night. I'm going to Bordeaux.'

Who's Deaux? Danny thought, ramming a handful of crisps into his mouth.

6

It was a short drive up the E-15 *autovia* to the *La Inmaculada* hospital in Huercal Overa. Arthur Cooke was out of intensive care but still hospitalised. Peggy had agreed to an interview, but said that she preferred to do it in person. No skin off Danny's nose; he would look in on Charlie Hacker at the same time, see if he could speak to any of the family.

Peggy Cooke was handling the situation as well as could be expected, which wasn't well at all. She looked drawn and pale and... *overwhelmed* was the word, really; trying to deal with so many traumas at once: the demolition, Arthur's collapse and the realisation that she'd been showering next to a corpse for the last two years seemed to have numbed her mind. She was slow to answer Danny's questions and when she did she rambled. Danny didn't push her. He got enough quotes to satisfy Fouldes and asked again if there was anything he could do to help.

'Will they still knock our house down?' she said in a distraught voice.

'I don't know, Peggy. But I'll do my damndest to find out, that's a promise. Do you remember who built the house?'

'The Henley something or other.'

'I think they subcontracted the work out. Do you remember who the actual builders were?'

'No. We were in England the whole ... Arthur might know ... but he's ...'

She looked to be on the verge of tears. Danny daren't push anymore. He chatted for a while, calming her. When Peggy revealed that she couldn't remember the last time she'd eaten, Danny went downstairs and bought her a *bocadillo* of cheese and *jamon* and a bottle of water. He left her staring at the wall in the corridor outside Arthur's hospital room.

Danny had to ask directions to the UCI, the hospital's intensive care unit; everything had changed since his last visit. The nurse on desk duty said that Señor Hacker's wife was with him. On his way to the UCI he decided how best to approach Mrs Hacker: go in softly, express his condolences, see if he could help, perhaps assist in translating the doctor's prognosis. Gaining her gratitude and trust would follow. *Poor dear's probably scared witless*, he thought.

Then he saw Mrs Hacker.

It had to be her. In her leopard skin leggings, white fur coat and high heels, she stuck out like a sore thumb beside the other people waiting outside the UCI ward's swing doors, a Moroccan family clad in thawbs and an elderly Spanish couple. As Danny entered the corridor, she was clattering back and forth on the tiled floor, hissing into a bright pink mobile. She was in her early sixties, but her peroxide hair had been piled high above a face painted to look thirty years younger.

Danny lingered near the coffee machine, trying to hear what she was saying, noting that there was no smell of hospital near Mrs Hacker; nothing could penetrate that miasma of perfume.

'... give a shit, Dean. Find him. Do what you have to, but find the bastard, right? For your dad. For me.'

Danny had no idea whom she wanted found, but was damned glad it wasn't him. Mrs Hacker's eyes shone with a cold, hard light beneath the matchstick-thick mascara.

She finished her call. Danny approached.

'Mrs Hacker. Any news on your – ?'

'Who are you? What do you want?' The hostility was immediate.

'My name's Danny Sanchez, I work for a local newspaper and I was –'

'No comment.'

'But I only –'

'*No. Comment*. Keep hassling me and I'll get my boys down here.'

'After they find whoever it is they're searching for, surely?'

Ruby-red lips parted, revealing small, sharp teeth. 'Been earwigging, have you? Careful where you stick that nose of yours – you might end up getting it cut off.' She pressed a button on her smartphone. 'One more word and I phone my boys. They'll give you something to write about, I fucking promise you that.'

Danny backed away, hands raised. She held his gaze, brandished the phone. Danny turned, headed for the stairs.

So much for the fairer sex, he thought, taking the steps two at a time.

7

'Charlie Hacker,' Danny said into his phone, outside in the hospital car park now, pen poised. 'What's the low-down, Leonard?'

Leonard was having lunch. Danny heard glasses chinking and the sound of Leonard extricating himself from a conversation.

'Why on earth would you want to know anything about such an awful bully boy?' he said.

'Someone cracked his head open with a hammer this morning.'

Leonard sounded impressed. 'Well, whoever is responsible is either exceptionally brave or exceptionally stupid.'

'Hacker trouble, is he?'

'Oh, just your typical small town thug. The problem is, so are all three of his sons. Together they're a force to be reckoned with, if rumour is to be believed. The family moved here from Shoreditch just after the millennium, if memory serves. Anyway, it was somewhere like that: there's a definite touch of the barrow-boy in him when he speaks.'

'How do you know him?'

'You don't think I'd waste time consorting with tat like that, do you? I don't *know* him. I know *of* him. I did meet the mother once at a charity do. She's your typical east-end matriarch, terrible woman, all hairspray, heels and quick tan. Rumour has it she rules the family with an iron fist – albeit one with highly-lacquered nails.'

'Any reason someone would want to attack him? Hacker wasn't robbed. And I overheard the wife talking on the phone. Seems she's got her boys looking for someone.'

'Well, he's a builder by trade, so I expect he's made his fair share of enemies. Apache Construction is his company.'

'Apache?'

'The company motto is *"Forget the cowboys and let the Indians have a go . . . "* – a witticism I suspect is wasted on Spaniards, but his clientele mostly comprises expats.'

'And is he a cowboy?'

'I don't think Hacker actually sullies his hands any more. His boys take care of the work now. They use a lot of cheap immigrant labour, cash-in-hand, that sort of thing.'

'Names?'

'Of the boys? Dean, Adam and something-or-other. Irish-sounding.'

'Could there be a link between the Hackers and the Henley Consortium?'

'What a sly one you are, Daniel Sanchez. Do you think this business with Hacker is connected with the dead body they found?'

'Not especially. But a corpse turns up in the walls of a house. Next day a builder loaded with cash is cracked over the head with a hammer but not robbed. I've learned coincidences like that always warrant closer inspection.'

'Far be it from me to place ideas in that fervid little mind of yours, but why not go ask the Hackers yourself? Their builder's yard is on the edge of the industrial estate at Albox.'

'I thought you said they were dangerous?'

'I said they were small town thugs, but I doubt they'll set about you, especially if you go on the pretext of enquiring after their dear old dad's health.'

Danny wasn't convinced; not if Mother Hacker was anything to go by. Nevertheless, forty minutes later he had drawn up outside Apache Construction's building yard.

It was an open area of dun-coloured earth surrounded by a chain-link fence. The company's logo – an Indian chief's head complete with feathers and tomahawk – hung above the gate. Take away the cacti and the deep blue sky and it could be a builder's yard in the UK; there were the same chipped tea mugs, the transistor radio, the discarded tabloid pages.

Danny still wasn't sure that cold calling on potentially aggressive interviewees was a good idea, but he took a deep breath and fought his nerves. A journalist who shied from confrontation was like a surgeon with an aversion to blood: useless.

Rolls of razor wire topped the fence, punctuated at intervals by pictures of a snarling mastiff and messages in English and Spanish warning that guard dogs roamed free on the premises at night. The pictures did little justice to the dogs themselves. As Danny walked through the gates, the heads of two enormous rottweilers smashed against the bars of the cage door that kept them within a fenced-off corner of the yard.

The two-storey building served as both office and showroom. It looked as if a bomb had gone off inside:. filing cabinets hung open; papers and files covered every table and chair. An obviously flustered man wearing glasses was swearing in Spanish as he scratched his head and rushed back and forth between the piles of paperwork. The armpits of his shirt were stained with sweat. Danny knocked at the door. A heavily made-up secretary, blouse open one button too low, greeted Danny with a smile as fake as her orangey tan. Danny smiled back, introduced himself. 'I was looking for the Hacker boys.'

She frowned when Danny said that he was a journalist. 'Dean's over in the warehouse.' She pointed at a large building of unpainted breezeblocks that had been roofed with sheets of corrugated metal. 'Callum's around somewhere, too. Just got back.' Danny wondered whether they'd found whomever it was Ma Hacker wanted.

'Warehouse' was a generous way of describing it. The tangled mess inside was more in keeping with a garden shed writ large. Building materials and knackered tools were scattered everywhere, seemingly dumped at random. Bags of cement leaked their contents onto the floor. Stacks of wooden pallets lined the wall between fencing panels, roof beams, window frames and planks. Two brand-new dry-powder fire extinguishers were screwed to the walls, one near the entrance and another halfway down the building. They looked out of place among the clutter and junk.

Dean Hacker was a Ronnie Kray lookalike: big nose, big eyes, big mouth, everything big. Or perhaps it was the suit he wore that made Danny think about the Krays; it was tailored and he wore a handkerchief folded in the jacket pocket. Whatever it was, he had a Sixties gangster look that worked.

'Some nonce from the council made us have them installed,' he said when he saw Danny looking at the fire extinguishers. 'Anyway, who are you and what do you want?' Dean Hacker's hostility was less obvious than his mother's, but still palpable.

Danny explained who he was, watched the man's face harden. 'I just wanted to enquire how your father's getting along. He was attacked right outside the newspaper offices, you see.' Danny deemed the moment inopportune to mention that dry powder extinguishers were not meant for indoor use.

'He'll live. Unlike the bastard who cracked him.' Hacker picked his way through the clutter. He was light on his feet for such a slab of a man, nifty like a boxer. Danny found himself shuffling backwards toward the door.

'Who do you think attacked him?'

Hacker's eyes narrowed. 'Are you the bloke bothered my ma at the hospital?'

'Nope.' The menacing look in Hacker's eyes meant the lie came to Danny's lips easily, as did changing the subject. 'I was hoping to kill two birds with one stone. I need some information on local builders. Do you remember a company called the Henley Consortium?'

'You ask a lot of questions, don't you?'

'I'm a journalist. It's my jo –'

Danny stopped as a dull thud sounded at the back of the warehouse. Something rattled like a cat flap banging. Then the dog's head rounded the corner. Rheumy eyes turned in Danny's direction. The snout puckered as the massive rottweiler sniffed the air.

It charged, accelerating from 0 to 60 mph in a split second, transforming itself simultaneously into a slavering, gnashing hell hound, its paws thudding heavily on the concrete floor. Instinct took over. Danny leapt at the nearest pile of wooden pallets, desert boots scrabbling at the edges of the wood as he sought to pull himself up. He felt the dog's breath on his ankle as he pulled it clear in the nick of time.

The dog threw itself at the stack of pallets, barking furiously. Dean Hacker's head was thrown back, his big mouth open in silent hysterics. A second Hacker – there was no mistaking those granite features – appeared in the doorway to the warehouse, smiling. 'I heard you had a journalist in here with you, Dean. Thought I'd let Ripper answer his questions for him.'

Callum Hacker was big like his brother but gone to flab. His neck and hands – the only skin visible beneath the filthy shell suit he wore – were covered in tattoos. He turned towards Danny. 'I'd like to say she doesn't bite but she fucking does.'

'Very funny,' Danny said, trying to steady his wobbling sanctuary. 'Get that thing out of here.'

Dean Hacker took hold of the dog by its spiked collar and dragged it across the floor toward the back of the warehouse. He disappeared behind a pile of wood. The rattling sounded again. When he returned, the dog had gone.

'How d'you like our little surprise for burglars?' Dean

Hacker said. 'I had the flap put in when some cunt got in here and stole a load of tools.' He motioned for Danny to come down. Danny stayed where he was.

'Block the flap off with something.'

Dean Hacker laughed again. 'Real tough guy, aren't you, journo?' He shifted a fence panel across to the door.

Danny climbed down. His shin was scraped; he had splinters in the edge of his palm.

Callum Hacker spat at the floor by Danny's feet. 'Interview's over, dickhead.'

8

That night Danny put on a DVD of *The Empire Strikes Back* and curled up beneath a blanket on the sofa. There was no sign of his mother. That was probably a good thing; his visit to the Hackers had unsettled him and the last thing he needed was Adriana Sanchez clucking around. Although most often the epitome of irresponsibility, she was also capable of bursts of cloying, fussy attentiveness, the sort generations of Spanish mothers had honed to a perfect art.

Danny closed his eyes as he listened to the film's opening fanfare. He'd found himself increasingly drawn to films like that recently. Perhaps it was the memories of childhood they stirred. Or perhaps it was because laser blasts and light-sabers made violence look so antiseptic ...

Danny. I need to talk.

It seemed that he had no sooner shut his eyes than he was awake again. He sat up on the sofa, chest heaving, heart pounding. The blue-white glow of the television screen shone on his bare chest. He reached for the remote, trying to remember details of the nightmare. There was nothing, only a vague sensation of disquiet accelerating through fear into blind terror. Random scraps of memory often fluttered into his dreams: snapshots of his childhood and adolescence, people he'd known, worked with. People he'd loved. But when he had a nightmare it was always that, the awkward intrusion of memory into dream, the voice, fuzzed by poor reception, speaking those same words into the mobile.

Danny. I need to talk.

Christ, hadn't he done enough to expiate his guilt?

He gulped air, drank water. The kitchen clock said 04:17. Lucky raised a sleepy head from her basket then settled back down with a slow exhalation. Too early for dogs, obviously, but Danny knew from experience there was no point in his trying to get back to sleep.

First he rewrote the article on the Brit population in Almeria. Then he spent another hour working through the dozen or so briefs – hundred-word articles covering minor news items – he had to produce each week. Then he checked his diary. He had an interview booked at nine o'clock with the manager of a local charity, Shelter All. He looked at the charity's amateurish webpage, made some notes on Shelter All: non-profit, non-religious, telephone helplines offered to immigrants in six different languages. He couldn't really concentrate, though. That bloody bundle of documents Arthur Cooke had given him was somewhere in the house, he was sure. It was like having a hair stuck at the back of his throat.

There was no way he'd thrown them away. Christ, the amount of junk he'd accumulated and stored over the years: press packs, hand outs, reports, pamphlets. He must be borderline OCD. That had been his mother's assessment when she saw the state of his bungalow, anyway. He ate breakfast, drank coffee, checked through the boxes in his office again. This was where they'd been stored, he was sure; among the boxes he'd taken out of his mother's room.

He went in and sat on his mother's bed, trying to picture how the boxes had been stacked. He was sure now; he could see the bloody thing on top of the largest of the boxes, its blue cover poking out. He went back to his office and found the box.

Nothing.

Where the bloody hell had they gone? Fallen on the floor? Slipped down somewh –

Danny stopped, teeth gritted, as he realised where they were.

Danny had rarely entertained overnight guests. Consequently, the bed in mother's room was a rickety old thing. Not today it wasn't, though. In fact, it hadn't wobbled a millimetre when he'd sat down on it. He lifted the edge of the dangling duvet and saw the blue file wedged under the far leg.

He pulled the blue bundle clear, cursing loudly and profusely in Spanish, as he always did when he really needed to vent his anger. There was no language like Spanish for swearing in.

He flicked through the documents. Arthur Cooke hadn't exaggerated when he'd said that he'd included every one; there were hundreds of sheets of paper here, in both Spanish and English. Danny looked at his watch: 08:13. He needed to hit the road.

He put the documents in a drawer in his office, locked it, left food and water for Lucky.

Then he walked to his car, trying to decide how to tell mother that she was going to have to live somewhere else.

9

Tuesday, March 30th, 2010

Around 670,000 people lived in the province of Almeria. Only 80% of them were Spanish.

The other fifth consisted of a vast, polyglot population that coexisted with their Spanish neighbours with varying degrees of success. Unlike other areas of Andalusia, where the foreign presence consisted mainly of retired Britons, in Almeria the majority of immigrants had come in search of work. They were Moroccans and Rumanians for the most part, but if you looked hard enough you would find people from every corner of the world – Senegalese, Bolivians, Estonians, Chinese, Russians.

Bar a few unfortunate occurrences when racial tensions had boiled over into serious riots, relations were generally harmonious. Like many peoples for whom genuine poverty lurked only a generation or two in the past, Spaniards tended to be tolerant of others trying to make their way in the world. This was especially so in Andalusia, where most families had seen one or more relative forced to emigrate in search of work.

Even so, the culture clash could be difficult. Alcohol and pork were inherent parts of Spanish culture; women wore short skirts, went topless on the beach. Some immigrants needed help to adjust. Others just needed to know someone cared.

That was the way Toby Ibañez, Shelter All's chief co-ordinator, explained it.

'Moroccans, Algerians, Senegalese, Nigerians; not only do these people face the occasional intransigence of the native population, they are also adrift within a culture that is totally alien to them. These people are vulnerable. They normally arrive unable to speak Spanish. Criminal gangs within their own communities prey upon them. An organisation such as Shelter All is often the only lifeline they have. That's why we have our motto: "Shelter All – *for* the people of Almeria *by* the people of Almeria."'

Danny nodded, trying not to let his frustration show: it was the third time Ibañez had told him the motto.

Like Danny, Ibañez was totally bilingual. There was a slight South American lilt to his Spanish; however, the two men had agreed to use English, which Ibañez spoke with a Home Counties accent. Danny wanted to like him. Hell, Ibañez was one of the good guys, right? Helping people. Concerned. Selfless. But there was something . . . indefinable that put him off. Perhaps it was the unctuous way in which Ibañez spoke or the smugness that dripped from every word, his eyes moist behind Lennon glasses. He seemed a tad too keen to be liked.

Shelter All was run out of a commercial property in a row of shops in the town of Campo Hermoso; it was flanked by a baker's and an ironmonger's. It consisted of four rooms: a reception area with posters of happy African women in colourful clothing, a second large room with children's playthings, and a third with table and chairs for the language classes the charity organised; the door to the back room was closed. A sign on the door said "Knock before entering". That was where the telephone helpline operated from, Ibañez explained. 'Anyone, no matter their race, creed or colour, can find shelter here.'

'Hence the name.'

'Hence the name. I did think about changing the name

to "Gimme Shelter" when I took over, but I'm afraid I'm more of a Beatles fan,' Ibañez said, as Danny scanned a pamphlet. The joke was clearly Ibañez's party piece. Danny forced a smile.

'How is it funded?'

Ibañez became serious. 'Well, that's a constant struggle, obviously. But luckily the property actually belongs to the organisation, so there's no rent to find. Most of our workers volunteer their time, though we do try to find a little something each month to help the regulars get by. We also get a small subsidy from the provincial delegation.'

'Tell me about the telephone lines.'

'Well, they're manned twenty-four hours a day now. We have a team of ten volunteers who man the phones. Between them they speak six languages.'

'And those languages are available twenty-four hours a day?'

Ibañez's face creased. 'Unfortunately not. That's why polyglots such as Allison – she's on duty at the moment – are so important. But we try to have someone offering English, Spanish and French available at all times.'

'Can I see one of your workers in action?'

Ibañez knocked at the closed door and showed Danny through to the small room at the back of the building. Here, a dark-haired woman sat speaking in French on the telephone. She regarded Danny with intense brown eyes. Danny raised his camera to take a picture. The woman turned her chair toward the wall, shaking her index finger. Ibañez took Danny's arm, guided him out of the room. 'Allison's an absolute workhorse, but very shy. She's not often here in the afternoons. She mans the telephones – or should that be "womans the telephones"? – at night as a rule. She's an absolute angel. So sympathetic. And hard-working; she teaches English to children at local nurseries by day, as well.'

'Where's she from?'

'She's British, but she speaks good French and perfect Spanish. As I say, she's the backbone of our organisation.'

'What about problems?'

'Problems?'

'A place like this, it must attract drunks, druggies.'

Ibañez nodded. 'Of course. And we do our level best to get them the help they need. But we operate a strict policy. Anyone showing signs of intoxication – from whatever cause – is escorted from the premises.' He ran a hand through his neatly trimmed beard. 'Listen, I'd be lying if I said we could wave a magic wand and solve people's problems in a moment. Very often we do find ourselves with problems that stretch our facilities. But anyone who comes here is guaranteed some form of aid as soon as we can manage it, even if it is only a sympathetic ear or a shoulder to cry on.'

Danny prepared to leave. Ibañez asked if he could read the article before it was printed. Danny shook his head.

'I'm writing an article, Mr Ibañez, not a press release. I'll write what I've seen and been told, but the only person that gets to see it before it goes to press is my editor. Don't worry,' he added, when Ibañez's face fell, 'I wouldn't do a hatchet job on a charity. I've been very impressed by what I've seen.'

Danny took a walk around the block. Upon his return, he went to speak to the Spanish shopkeepers either side of Shelter All. The young man in the ironmonger's frowned at mention of the NGO, but obviously did not want to speak to a journalist. The old woman in the baker's shop had no such qualms.

'It's a disgrace – all those people, hanging around there all day. There was one the other day with no shoes on. His feet looked like a goat's hooves, they were so calloused.'

Danny was about to ask more when Leonard phoned. His voice fizzed with excitement.

'Guess what I've just found out?'

'Why would I guess when you're so obviously dying to tell me?'

'You're no fun sometimes, Danny. You don't deserve me. But I'm in a generous mood, so get your pen and paper ready . . .'

10

One o'clock and Danny was on the road, heading back to the Almanzora Valley. Leonard had come good with info on Charlie Hacker. 'There's an expat pub in the village of El Pulpillo where Hacker used to drink. The landlady's name is Irene Sparks. Rumour has it Hacker had *words* – of the Anglo Saxon variety, if you catch my drift – with another patron there recently. Perhaps he could be your hammer-man. Anyway, if anyone has the lowdown on what's happened, it will be this Sparks woman. I hear she's a terrible gossip.'

Takes one to know one, Danny thought, as he hung up.

The village of El Pulpillo was halfway along the Almanzora Valley. El Pulpillo's high street – if it could be called that – was a hundred yards long. There was no pavement, just a white line painted on the cracked asphalt to separate car from pedestrian. Rubber speed bumps had been placed at regular intervals, screwed down with steel bolts. Holes had been ripped in them that were wide enough to let a car pass; few nations tolerated government interference in their lives less than the Spanish.

The expat influence was immediately apparent. The hairdresser's had a large handwritten sign in the window: WE SPEAK ENGLISH. Further along the street was a fish and chip shop and a UK "supermarket", shelves stacked with British imports: Marmite, packets of Bisto, pots of curry sauce. Next door to that was the pub Danny sought.

The sign of the Rose and Crown hung above the main door, its paint blistered and faded by the sun. It looked as if it might have been imported from England. Danny paused to read a sheet of A4 tacked to the glass of the front door: *Pub-watch – out of one, out of them all*. He'd seen a similar poster in the window of the fish and chip shop. Another triumphant British import.

The "pub" had been converted from a Spanish bar. The glass door opened on to a single large room, its floor tiled, its bar made of metal. A pool table stood in the centre of the room. A group of English youths with northern accents was engaged in a foul-mouthed game, supping pints at the same time. One of them stared as Danny entered and sneered as he noticed the bag over Danny's shoulder.

The girl behind the bar looked far too young to be serving in a pub. She said, 'Mum's asleep' when Danny asked to speak to Irene Sparks.

Danny insisted. Minutes passed until high heels could be heard clattering on the stairs. Mum had indeed been sleeping – sleeping it off by the look of her.

'Who the bloody hell are you? I didn't arrange to –'

'Danny Sanchez, journalist, *Sureste News*. I've heard you're the right person to speak to about the local expat community, Irene.'

Danny had been banking on flattery working. It did. Irene's chest puffed out. Curiosity shone in bloodshot eyes as she accepted Danny's card. 'Journalist, eh?' She made a sign to her daughter, who began mixing a Bloody Mary.

'That's right.' Danny roughened the edges of his own accent. He was one of them now. 'Know a bloke called Charlie Hacker?'

Irene Sparks smiled. 'I know why you're here. Hacker got smashed over the head with a hammer yesterday, didn't he? I read that on the local forum.'

'That's right. Any idea who might have done it? Who might Hacker have argued with?'

'Anyone he ever did work for.'

Danny feigned amusement, ordered a mineral water. 'What about recently?'

The daughter plonked the Bloody Mary on the bar. 'Alan Reade,' she said. Irene Sparks clicked her fingers. 'Yep, Reade was always arguing with Hacker.'

'Who is he?'

'Reade? A plumber by trade. Typical Scouser. Rowdy when he's had a few. He is always going on about what a hard nut he is. He's got dates tattooed all up his forearm. Claims they're all the times he was in prison.'

'Do you believe him?'

'Who knows? He certainly has a dodgy reputation. Bit light-fingered, if you catch my drift.'

She gave Danny a wink, just in case he hadn't.

'What did Reade and Hacker argue about?'

'Everything and anything. The work wasn't on schedule, the walls weren't in the right place, he didn't like the workers Hacker sent.'

'What was the problem with the workers?'

'Hacker used a lot of cheap labour. Immigrants.'

Danny had his notebook out, jotting the comments down. He circled the last part. Cash-in-hand immigrant labour was one of the reasons it was difficult to put a definite figure on how many people lived in the province. Tens of thousands of migrant workers flowed through the province each year: north Africans, eastern Europeans, South Americans. It was ironic how some Brits could spend a decade in Spain without acquiring more than a dozen words of the language, but managed to learn the best ways of exploiting the system within a couple of weeks.

'What does Reade look like?'

'Tallish, scrawny, got a scar on his lip.'

'Hair?'

'Long and blonde. Thinning on top but still wears a ponytail.'

'Age?'

'I'd guess early forties, though he might be younger.'

'Is he tanned?'

Irene Sparks laughed. 'Tanned? Alan Reade? He's like a bloody ghost.'

So he didn't sound like the bloke witnesses saw attacking Hacker outside the commercial centre. Still, Reade might have paid someone else to do it. It was worth following up.

'Anything else they might have argued about?'

'His house,' a man further along the bar said. Danny turned slightly, angling himself to include the man.

'House?'

'Hacker's company built Reade's house for him. They were always arguing about it.'

The landlady nodded vigorous agreement, leaning her arms on the bar, enjoying herself now half the Bloody Mary was gone. 'That's right. The bloody thing's only just finished. We thought that would be an end to it, but it only made matters worse. Reade says the Hackers cheated him.'

'How?'

'Oh, first, they stopped work on it for a year. Then he said it wasn't as big as it was supposed to be. And the place stank.'

The man at the bar snorted. 'That's rich coming from Alan Reade.'

'Stank how?'

The landlady shrugged. 'He never described it. Just said it stank. Anyway, I wouldn't set too much store on why they argued. Most of it was too much drink and a lot of that.' She made a yapping bird's beak with her fingers and thumb.

'Any idea where Mr Reade might be?'

'He won't be at his house, if he's got any sense.'

'Why's that?'

'Hacker's sons. There's three of them and together they weigh the same as a bulldozer.'

Danny shook his head. 'Witnesses say it was a dark-haired guy attacked Charlie Hacker.'

'Won't cut no mustard with Charlie's boys. Not when their blood's up. And to be honest, Reade's been mouthing off so long about Hacker, he's got it coming.'

'Like a red rag to a bulldozer, eh?'

Irene Sparks was still shrieking laughter into her Bloody Mary as Danny left the bar and headed to his car.

11

Irene Sparks had given Danny directions to Reade's house. They didn't help much. One set of grey brown hills looked very much like another. Asphalt strips barely wide enough to admit two cars snaked across open plains stippled with tussocks of esparto grass and spiky cacti. At least the almond trees were in bloom, although the delicate pale pink flowers looked out of place among the Almanzora's spaghetti western landscape.

It was a while since Danny had visited the backwaters of the Almanzora. He could see why so many Britons had chosen to retire here. Everywhere there was open, untrammelled space, the horizon ringed by mile-high mountains, the landscape painted in broad swathes of colour, green and ochre for the foothills, red-brown for the cliffs, and above it all the sky, crisp, clear and cloudless like a polished sapphire. This was how it looked for roughly three hundred days of each year. Film makers and photographers loved the light in Almeria.

But evidence of new building was everywhere. Some villages had grown so fast that properties were built on roads that had no name. Properties like Alan Reade's.

Danny drove slowly, trying to spot things considered to be local landmarks; a broken palm tree, a ruined wall, an electrical substation. What really grabbed his attention, though, were the dozens of half-built houses that lined the roads:

some were brick boxes near to completion, others little more than grey concrete skeletons.

The walls of Reade's bungalow were painted a deep burgundy, the windows edged with white. Iron bars covered the glass.

Danny rang the bell and knew straight away that Reade wasn't there. Danny had spent half a lifetime knocking on strangers' doors; he knew when a doorbell rang to an empty house. As he turned, he noticed a woman peering at him through the window of the house opposite. He walked back to his car, waited twenty minutes. Irene Sparks had supplied Danny with Reade's mobile number. Danny tried it; it went straight to answer phone.

Then he took a quick look up and down the road before he walked round the back of the house.

Water in the kidney-shaped swimming pool rippled as a filter hummed . He shielded his eyes with his hands and peered through the patio doors. The house was meticulously clean inside. A bookcase held box files and documents.

Danny reached the far corner of the house and his nose wrinkled. Reade was right about one thing: the place did stink. It was not noticeable at the front of the property, but the closer Danny came to the rear of the house the more tainted the air seemed to be. The window in the wall was frosted. There must be some problem with the sewerage, Danny thought, a blockage in the –

He froze as a vehicle screeched to a halt outside. A door slammed. Rapid footsteps sounded on the gravel, followed by thunderous knocks on the front door; the whole house seemed to shudder with them. 'Come out, Reade, you cunt!' a man bellowed. 'I know you're in there.'

Fear froze Danny as the man ran round the side of the house and glared at him. Not that Danny noticed the glare; he was too busy watching the baseball bat in the man's hand.

This must be Adam, Hacker number three; he had his brothers' pug-face and piggy eyes. And their bulk plus one.

Adam Hacker was a weightlifter and wanted people to know it. That was why he wore a vest, so people could see the steroid bulges of his biceps. Danny thought of his red-rag to a bulldozer quip – it didn't seem so funny now.

'Who the fuck are you?' Adam Hacker said, pointing the baseball bat at Danny. Instinct told Danny to run, but he knew that if he bolted, Hacker would pounce.

Experience took over. If journalism had taught him one thing, it was how to bullshit convincingly at the drop of a hat.

'Alan Reade, I assume,' Danny said, adopting an official-looking swagger. 'We've been looking for you.'

'You trying to mug me off? *I'm* looking for Reade.'

'Lucky for you. I'm from the UK consulate. Reade's in trouble,' Danny said. He opened his wallet, police-style, allowing Adam Hacker to glimpse the purloined UK consulate card he carried inside. It looked impressive enough, with its purple lettering and gilt unicorn, if you only saw it for a second – which was all Danny allowed him.

'Fucking right he's in trouble.'

'Then we're on the same side,' Danny said, striding toward him, hand outstretched.

Adam Hacker stared at Danny's hand. None of the Hacker brothers seemed particularly intelligent. This one, though, was smart enough to realise it; Danny could almost hear the cogs grinding as he assessed the situation. 'Adam Hacker,' he said after what seemed like an age, wrapping a huge paw round Danny's, squeezing hard enough to let him know that was about a quarter of what he was capable. 'What's Reade been up to, then?'

'That's consulate business,' Danny said, taking out his mobile and speaking into it as he strolled away. *I'm a busy man*, his body language was saying, *with things to do*. 'Tell the police Reade's not here,' he said into the phone after pretending it was ringing. He made sure the word "police" rang loud and clear. 'Yes, I'll wait for them.'

A white transit van with a faded Apache logo was parked

outside. Adam Hacker walked towards it andthen turned round. 'When you see Reade, tell him Adam Hacker says "hi".'

'What do you think I am,, your messenger?'

'You think I'm pissing about?'

No, Danny didn't. Not now Adam Hacker had him pinned against the wall, his big ugly face inches from Danny's. 'Consulate, police, I don't give a shit. Get between us and Reade and you'll regret it.'

Danny Sanchez waited for the van to rumble away. Then he ran to his car and drove in the opposite direction.

Fast.

~

Danny worked late at the office that evening. Deadline day was Thursday and he wanted as much of his work to be finished beforehand as possible: once they'd put the paper to bed, he was free, a whole week off, his first in five months.

Danny phoned the *Guardia Civil's* press office numerous times during the afternoon. There was *still* no news on the body found at the Cookes' house.

'How can that be?' Danny said, careful not to sound too pushy; pissing off the *Guardia Civil* was not a good idea. 'It's been two days now.'

The press officer sighed. 'Listen, I just tell the Press what I'm told to tell them. And if no one tells *me* anything, then what can I do? And that's the honest truth. The examining magistrate went to the scene of crime the day of the demolition. He was there all day; then the corpse was taken to the *Instituto de Medicina Legal*. And before you ask, no, I don't know the results of the autopsy. In fact, I don't even know if they've done one yet.'

'What about the house? Will the demolition still go ahead?'

'Not my place to say. But I don't think the fact the place is a crime scene will change anything in the eyes of the courts.'

That was the opinion of everyone Danny had contacted. He wouldn't bother Peggy Cooke with that now, though.

Danny checked his email, saw Fouldes had sent the Brit population article back for further fiddling. 'Final two paragraphs are flabby. Amend.'

Danny typed a one word answer: no.

Enough was enough. If Fouldes wanted more changes, he could do them himself. It wouldn't be the first time. The editor had developed a habit of that recently, making nit-picking "corrections" to Danny's articles that always seemed to involve his removing the best bits. Even worse, he might add twenty words of his own and attribute the piece to "William Fouldes and Danny Sanchez".

Danny poured himself a glass of wine, downed it and poured himself another. Then he phoned his mother.

'Hello, my darling son. How are you?' She sounded out of breath.

'I'm fine. What about you?'

'Couldn't be better.'

'I was just wondering when you're coming home.'

'Lord, Danny, I'm not sixteen years old.' Danny heard the rumble of a man's voice speaking in the background.

'It's just . . . look, a dead body turned up the other day and I wanted to make sure you were safe.'

'Oh, that's so *sweet.*' She said something Danny couldn't hear; the man laughed. 'Rest assured, I'm being *very* well looked after.' A slap sounded on naked flesh. More laughter. Danny hung up.

He no longer wished his mother were home.

12

That night Danny drove to Paco Pino's flat.

'Remind me what we're doing again,' Paco said from the kitchen, chewing an olive.

Danny plonked the huge blue folder of photocopied documents Arthur Cooke had given him on the dinner table. 'Somewhere in here are the details of who built that house. I want to speak to them. Bodies don't end up inside walls by accident. This is how we steal a lead on the opposition. This could be the biggest Alan Smithee exclusive yet. I've been up to my eyeballs all day and I can't look through them all by myself.'

'I thought you said the builder *wasn't* involved?'

'I said I doubted anyone would be dense enough to commit murder and wall the corpse up inside a house directly linked with themselves; but the builder's probably a good place to start, no? Someone on site might have noticed there was a wall that shouldn't have been there. And even if they didn't, they must know who had access to the building site. Walls don't appear like magic. You need time.'

'And bricks,' Paco said, popping another olive into his mouth.

They began sifting through the documents, those in Spanish by Paco, the English ones by Danny. There were hundreds of pieces of paper. Together they represented a guided tour of the dangers of building your own home in

Spain. Translations of nearly every document from one language to the other only served to add to the reams of bumph.

The Cookes had paid their money to the Henley Consortium SL. Judging by the paperwork, this company had actually owned little more than an attractive web-page promising the earth, and a sales office. The consortium had taken deposits from dozens of people, then subcontracted the work out to a tangled web of local businesses; they in turn had subcontracted specific tasks to other companies. The Cookes were among the "lucky" ones; their house had actually been close to completion when the consortium went bust and disappeared off the face of the earth.

After an hour of sifting documents, Danny's head was spinning. Paco's infant daughters didn't help by haring around the living room in their pyjamas. Then Paco's wife, Lourdes, returned and turned the television on. It was an irritating gossip programme, consisting of Z-list Spanish "celebrities" screaming accusations of infidelity and plastic surgery at each other.

Danny finished working through his pile and took some from Paco's. Progress on the Spanish documentation had all but ground to a halt as domestic duties impinged: Paco had forgotten to bathe the girls; then they needed putting to bed, which required kisses and a story and Paco lingering in the girls' bedroom doorway with a dumb look on his face as he watched them sleep.

'I can only stick another half-hour of this,' the photographer said, when he had returned to the table.

Danny needed twenty-two minutes.

'You found something?' Paco said, as Danny jerked forward on his chair. He handed Paco the invoice he was examining It was an invoice from Apache Construction, giving a detailed breakdown of the work carried out, rendered in both Spanish and English. The total sum charged was 123,417 Euros.

The Hackers. The Hackers built the Cookes' house.

Paco looked at the invoice, shrugged. 'What does it mean?'

'I don't know. But the owner of that company had his head cracked open with a hammer a couple of days ago.'

Paco asked something else, but it was blocked out by the questions forming in Danny's own mind. Were the Hackers capable of murder? Danny was sure the Hackers would like people to *think* that they were capable of killing a man. But if they had killed, why hide the body in a house with a paper trail leading back to them? Were they really that stupid? Surely they must have had better chances to hide a body during the house's construction? Somewhere amid the foundations or in a nice deep ditch, for example. Not behind a false interior wall.

But Danny wasn't thinking of that now. He was thinking of another house where a room was too small.

A house that the Hackers built.

A house that stank.

Danny sat bolt upright. Concern spread across Paco's face. 'What is it, Danny?'

'There's another body. Christ, Paco, I think there's another body buried in a wall.'

13

Wednesday, March 31st

'I'm not happy about this,' Paco said, staring around him at the early morning mist. 'What if these Hacker blokes turn up again? I've got kids, remember.'

Danny was wearing his best confident smile as he unloaded tools from the back of his car. 'That's why we we're going to do it nice and fast. We drill a hole, remove a brick, take a peek inside.'

Paco shook his head, blowing air as he looked at the burgundy walls of Alan Reade's bungalow. 'If you're right about there being a body here, the police aren't going to be happy if we tamper with it.'

'And if it's a dead rat, Paco? We're saving them time and effort. Plus giving ourselves a shot at an exclusive.'

'And what if the owner comes back to find us knocking his house to bits?'

'If Alan Reade turns up, unlicensed exterior modifications to his property are going to be the least of his worries. Believe me, I've seen the Hackers. That old cow over the road is keeping watch for them. That's why I let her get a good long look at us, so she won't get confused like she did last time.'

Paco didn't look convinced.

'What about this?' Danny said. 'We say Reade phoned the paper, complained about the smell, criticised the builder and gave us permission to get to the bottom of it.'

'The police will never believe that.'

Danny had already put up with ninety minutes of Paco's bellyaching and it wasn't even eight in the morning. He had wanted to do this the previous night,but Paco had used the excuse of needing to recharge his hammer drill first.

'Look,' Danny said, slamming the boot, 'we'll worry about getting our story straight *if* we find anything. And once we've got photos. Remember, Paco: who dares scoops. Better to ask forgiveness than permission.'

'Can you write that down? I'll have my lawyer read it in court.'

First they knocked at the front door, checked windows for any sign of recent habitation. Everything seemed as it had been on Danny's last visit. Alan Reade was clearly terrified of the Hackers. Danny tried to put thoughts of whether he should also be scared from his mind.

The early morning air at the back of the house was foul with the foetid smell.

'See what I mean?' Danny said.

Paco nodded.

Danny took a hammer and broke away a patch of rendering from the exterior wall, enough to reveal the edges of one of the foot-long hollow grey breeze blocks used in Spanish construction. They both looked around. Reade's nearest neighbour was twenty yards down the road; even so, the hammer blows would sound loud in the early morning quiet.

'If they're not awake yet, they soon will be,' Paco said, hefting the cordless hammer drill.

He drilled a hole in the mortar at the edge of the brick. Both men recoiled as the drill broke through; the stench that leaked from the perforation was nauseating.

Paco pointed at the hole. 'Danny, let's call the police now. Whatever's in there is definitely dead and definitely *not* rat-sized.'

Danny took the pot of vapour rub he'd brought with him,

wiped a generous dollop beneath his nose, gave it to Paco. 'We've come this far, mate. Let's not bottle it now.'

Danny finished drilling and broke away the rest of the mortar holding the brick in place with a hammer and bolster. Twenty minutes later he was able to ease the brick out. A dark hole a foot long and six inches high had been made in the exterior wall. The stench was stronger, now; overpowering, in fact.

Danny clicked on his torch and shone it at the hole. 'It shouldn't be like that,' he said when the torchlight revealed more bricks. ' Spanish construction firms don't build cavities. Someone's created an extra wall inside the house.'

'Just like at the Cookes.'

'Precisely.'

Paco took photos of the cavity. 'Right, who's going to look inside?'

Danny swallowed. 'I will.' He took a deep breath, pinched his nostrils then pressed his face close to the hole, resting the torch against the side of his head.

He looked left, gagging; then he looked right.

And screamed.

Danny jerked backwards and fell, landing arse first in the gravel, numb arms making no effort to break his fall. His hands shook as panic and shock swept through him.

Paco knelt at his shoulder. 'What is it? What's in there?' Danny tried to speak. His mouth jabbered but no sound emerged. Paco used his mobile to peer inside. 'Sweet Jesus,' he whispered, jerking backwards. 'Danny, we've got to phone the police. Now.'

14

The *Guardia Civil* cordoned off the end of the road and wrapped scene-of-crime tape around the gates of Reade's property. It was a blustery, chill day, but groups of people had formed all along the street, chatting in the way that people did when a drama was unfolding on their doorsteps. Forensic officers in white all-in-ones and rubber boots walked back and forth. The first members of the press pack were arriving. One was remonstrating with a Guardia officer, pointing towards Danny and Paco as they sat together on the wall at the front of property. He was probably asking why "those two" had been allowed access to the crime scene. The irony was that Danny wanted to be anywhere else but there.

They'd had no time to work out a story; they'd both sat in numbed silence waiting for the authorities to arrive after Paco had phoned through details of what they had discovered. When asked what they were doing there and how they'd found the body, Danny had opened his mouth and found himself unable to tell anything but the truth. The *Guardia Civil* officer's scowl grew as he listened. 'If you've fucked up any evidence, your editor isn't going to be best pleased with you. I'll see to that personally.'

But Danny's editor was already less than pleased. Fouldes had been on the phone at nine with a stream of instructions. He hadn't taken the news well that Danny was being held for questioning. 'You are aware it's deadline day tomorrow, aren't you? *And* that you're going on holiday on Friday. How long will you be there?'

Danny wished he knew.

Paco stared at the digital screen of his camera, reviewing the images he'd taken through the cavity. He shook his head. 'There's no way we can use these, Danny. They're too graphic. This is the only one we might stand a chance of using. Look.'

Danny pushed the camera away. He was trembling. It had nothing to do with the sharp wind that had started up. Paco placed a hand on his arm. 'That really shook you up, eh? Don't worry, I feel the same.'

Danny's voice quavered when he spoke. It had taken him this long to find the words to explain; it was something that he hadn't wanted to admit even to himself.

'Paco, I've seen a corpse like that before.'

'You mean a dead body in a wall?'

'No. One covered in make-up.'

Paco looked at him. 'Are you sure?'

Danny snorted. Christ, what a question. It wasn't something you forgot in a hurry; a decomposing face smeared with make up, a grotesque parody of a woman, half-whore, half-clown, pig-tailed wig dangling lopsidedly.

'Where did you see it?'

'In England. There was a series of murders I helped cover in 1995.'

'And they were the same?'

'Five young men were killed. Four of them were . . .' Danny waved a hand toward the rear of the house where *Guardia Civil* officers were working to remove the rest of the bricks. 'He did that to them.'

'Did they get the killer?'

'Yes.'

'Is he still inside?'

'Last I heard, he was in a psychiatric hospital.'

'Find out if he's still there. Either way, it's a runner. If he is still inside, we go with the copycat angle.'

Danny nodded. He was struggling to concentrate. He could feel the tic forming around his eye, the tic that came only when something had really, deeply upset him. Nothing had prepared him for this stench of death up close. It was beyond description: tongue, nostrils, throat, all seemed coated in a foetor no amount of coughing, nose-blowing or mint-sucking could rid him of. And that face, a snatched glimpse of horror, made all the worse for its brevity; imagination sometimes painted blank spaces with a horror worse than reality.

But what he saw was really a composite image. He was sure of that now. Christ, they were the same. How could that be? Fifteen years later and here was another body, *exactly* the same.

More police officers were arriving now. A man Danny recognised as the *Juez de Guardia*, the examining magistrate, arrived to oversee the gathering of evidence before the body was moved. There was a brief commotion when the *juez* peered inside the cavity.

'He's new to the job,' Paco whispered. 'I doubt he's seen one that bad before.'

The leader of the homicide detectives, a small Spaniard with a greying beard, rolled his eyes when he saw Danny. 'I should have guessed it was you when they said a journalist found the body.'

Danny nodded at *Inspector Jefe* Andrés Bosquet, a man he'd crossed swords with in the past. The policeman didn't return the greeting.

Danny retold his story: he'd visited the house a few days before when investigating an assault, noticed the stench, decided to investigate. Paco glanced nervously when Danny skirted round the subject of the Hackers. Bosquet made Danny and Paco tell and retell the story, a sure sign he wasn't swallowing it.

'So, you just decided to drill a hole in a stranger's house, then?' Bosquet crossed his arms. 'Where's this Alan Reade?'

'No idea.'

Danny was glad he didn't have to lie. Bosquet looked at Danny, watching him carefully. 'I hope for your sake that's true. As it is, if Mr Reade decides to prosecute for criminal damage, I think he's got a pretty good case.'

The final bricks were out and the body was being removed. Cries and exclamations filled the air. Danny pulled Bosquet close, lowered his voice.

'*Inspector Jefe*, I've seen a body like that before. I think –'

'You'll be running with the copycat angle. Yes, one of the officers overheard you.' Bosquet stared coldly at the hand upon his arm. 'Leave police work to the professionals. And I don't expect to see a word about the state of the dead man in print until we've decided how to handle the investigation.' He held Danny's gaze, then walked away.

The police kept Danny and Paco there for another hour, then let them go.

Danny drove into town, stopped at a bar, ordered a glass of *aguardiente*, drained the fiery liquid in a single gulp. He lit a cigarette. He was getting hold of himself again.

'That was dumb,' Paco said, sipping his coffee.

'What was?'

'Not mentioning those English builders, the Hackers.' Paco pronounced it *HAH-kers*.

Danny shrugged. 'As soon as the police get wind of the Hackers' involvement, they'll be all over them. I want to hear what they have to say first.'

'Meaning we're going there now?'

'Yep.'

Paco groaned.

'Don't worry. You're not coming in. I want you to stay by the car with a camera and a phone. When I give you the nod, wave them in the air so they know I've got back up.'

Paco didn't look convinced.

'Don't worry,' Danny said, draining his second glass of *aguardiente*. 'I'm going to enjoy this.'

15

The gates to the builder's yard were padlocked shut. Thick black smoke rose from behind the office. Danny cupped his hands, shouted. The two caged Rottweilers went berserk as soon as he did so.

Callum Hacker emerged from behind the office, wearing the same shell suit, now stained with soot. He sneered when he saw Danny.

'Didn't you learn your fucking lesson last time? Want me to set Ripper free again?'

'I've come to do you a favour.'

'The only favour you can do me is by fucking off away from my yard.'

Dean Hacker appeared in the doorway, too, looking just as big and ugly as his brother. At least he'd changed his clothes.

'Don't worry, I'm not coming in. Not until you invite me in, anyway.'

Callum Hacker sneered. 'What are you, a fucking vampire?'

Dean laughed.

Danny let them enjoy their witticism. Then he said, 'I'd love to stand here and banter with you, but I'm a busy man and I need to speak to you before the police get here.'

The Hackers exchanged glances. Danny had the bastards' attention now.

'Hear about that house they started demolishing in Los Membrillos?' Danny said. 'Arthur and Peggy Cooke? The one with a dead body in the wall? Seems your construction company was involved. And I've got proof of it in black and white.' Danny waved a photocopy of the invoice. The cocky sneer wilted from Dean Hacker's face. 'And guess what? The police have just found another body at Alan Reade's house.'

He spoke the words clearly, watching both brothers for their response. If either of them had already known anything about the body at Reade's house, their goldfish impressions were Oscar-worthy. Dean Hacker stopped gaping first. 'You're bullshitting.'

Danny shrugged. 'I know you've got someone watching Reade's house. Give the old girl a bell, ask her what's going on outside *right* this minute. And then let me inside, because we're running out of time.'

Danny lit a cigarette while a hurried phone call was made. Two minutes later Callum Hacker returned, ashen-faced, walking towards the chain fence, key in hand.

Danny allowed the faintest smile to curl the edge of his lip. 'Fancy that interview now, do you, Callum?'

As they crossed the yard Danny saw the secretary he'd met on his previous visit heading toward the rottweiler cage with pouches of dog food. To Danny's amazement, the dogs quietened down as soon as she opened the cage. They ran towards her, let her pat their heads.

'Bloody hell, she's brave.'

Callum Hacker spat. 'We got them trained. They're all right with people they recognise.'

'And with people they don't?'

'Let's just say we've only had one attempted break-in since we got them. Bastard left a shoe behind with half his fucking ankle in it. Yorkie and Ripper are the best investment we've made.'

'Yorkie. I'm guessing that's nothing to do with the chocolate bar, right?'

'No, from Yorkshire.'

Yorkshire and Ripper. Very droll.

Callum Hacker motioned for him to step inside the Portakabin. Danny paused on the steps and waved to Paco Pino. Paco waved back, camera in one hand, mobile in the other. 'Just so you know I'm not stupid enough to come here alone.'

Dean Hacker sneered. 'You really think we've been killing people and walling the bastards up?'

'Believe me, I learned the value of caution the hard way. And I'll talk from the doorway here, where my friend can see me, if you don't mind.' The fact that the Hackers had named their dogs after a serial killer had given Danny pause for thought. 'Where's Adam?' he said, spinning on his heel.

'He's not here,' Dean Hacker said. 'He's got stuff to take care of.'

It seemed that Apache Construction had a lot of stuff to take care of. The chaos was even worse than last time. Files and paperwork were everywhere. Through the window Danny could see where Callum Hacker had been at work; flames flickered from a metal bin with holes in. It looked like he'd been burning paper. The bespectacled Spaniard Danny had seen on his previous visit emerged from a rear room, looking even more flustered as he examined a bundle of what seemed to be architect's plans leaking from a red box file. Callum Hacker's eyes flickered toward Danny then he snatched the box file from the man's hands and stuffed it into a drawer.

'I didn't work on either of those houses, I swear,' Dean Hacker said, chewing his nails.

'You don't have to swear anything to me, mate, I'm not the police. But if that's true you're going to need friends to help get that message across. Someone in the media, for example.'

'What do you want to know?'

'When I came the other day, I didn't twig.' Danny whirled his pen at the paperwork spread out around the office. 'All this. It was because of the body they'd found at the Cookes's house, wasn't it?'

Neither Hacker said a word; both stared at the floor.

'I'll take that silence as a yes. What is it you're so worried about? What the police are going to find; or what they're *not* going to find?'

'What do you mean?'

'Word is you use a lot of cash-in-hand labour. Immigrants, day workers, that sort of thing.'

Dean Hacker's face became sullen. 'Yeah, so what?'

'None of whom go through the books?' Sullen silence: another yes. 'Where do these workers come from?'

Dean licked his lips. 'There's a place you can go. Behind a bar, early morning. You just choose as many as you want, load them in the van and off you go.'

'What about Alan Reade? He do any work at the Cookes's house?'

'Yeah. Yeah, he did now I think about it.' Enthusiasm gripped Dean Hacker's voice. 'That's it. It was Reade. He must have buried both bodies. He's always going on about what a gnarly bastard he is.'

Danny shook his head. 'The only reason I'm here is because I don't believe you would be stupid enough to immure a dead body in a house your own company built. But Reade walling up ' – Danny realised "immure" was the wrong type of word to use with the Hackers – 'a dead body in his *own* house? And then complaining to everyone about the stench? Come off it.'

'He tried to kill my dad.'

'As a matter of fact, he didn't. I spoke to a number of witnesses who swear the attacker had dark hair and a tan.'

The information didn't seem to interest either brother. One way or another, Reade was going to pay.

'Who had access to the building site at the Cookes's? And Reade's? How was it false walls got built and no one noticed?'

Dean Hacker shrugged. 'There were dozens of people used on both jobs. Work on the Cookes's house was stopped for two years. The same happened with Reade's project: we stopped work for eight months because the bastard owed us so much money. Anyone could have got in there and built a new wall.'

'Without anyone realising?'

'Sure, if they used exterior bricks. You got a room with nine metres square of floor space. You come back after six months and it's only got seven-and-a-half, no one's going to notice.'

'Did anyone notice a stink?'

'Yes. Alan Reade. And he spent months fucking giving it that – ' he made the bird's beak with his hand – 'to everyone he bloody met, slagging us off. Bastard's got it –'

The nervous-looking Spaniard was back. Danny decided that he had to be the Hackers' *gestor*, an outside administrator hired to steer companies through the Byzantine intricacies of Spain's legal and tax systems.

Or not, as the case seemed here.

The *gestor* squeezed past Danny, held a whispered conversation. When he finished, Dean Hacker sank his head in his hands. Callum booted a wastepaper basket across the room. Then he turned. His eyes had the same ugly look that his brother Adam's had had when Danny met him at Alan Reade's.

'This is your fault, you cunt. Fucking snooping around when you should be minding your own –'

Danny didn't wait to hear anymore. He'd met dozens of Callum Hackers in his time; he knew the signs of a man winding himself up prior to violence. He ran.

Luckily for Danny, Callum Hacker was as ill-equipped for a running race as Danny was for fist fights. By the time Danny reached the gate Callum Hacker was still only halfway across the yard; he looked as if he might be on the verge of a coronary.

'Come here, you bastard!' he screamed with what was left of his breath.

Danny headed for the car. As he did so, two Guardia Civil cars pulled up outside the Hackers' yard. One of the officers noticed Danny hurrying across the road. Recognition flashed on his face, but Danny was already climbing into the moving car, Paco behind the wheel.

16

It was after 3 p.m. when Danny arrived at the office. He stayed until eight that evening. He wanted to finish his work so that he could dedicate every hour of the following day to the story about the dead bodies.

If the *Guardia Civil* had been close-mouthed about the first body, the discovery of a second had induced a case of lockjaw. Something fishy was going on, Danny was sure. Minutes spent exerting gentle pressure had won Danny confirmation that the corpse that had been found at Reade's house was male, but that was all the press officer would say. The man stonewalled Danny so resolutely that it was clear he was acting on orders. He refused to say when a press release would be forthcoming.

The important question was whether the two crimes were linked. They had to be, surely? It was too much of a coincidence: two bodies hidden in precisely the same way a half-hour's distance from each other.

He was sure the Hackers weren't involved. They'd been nervous when Danny went there, panicked even, but in a very obvious, explicable way. They seemed far more preoccupied with the potential financial disaster that was looming over them; fines for companies using illegal workers were astronomical. Leonard's assessment of the Hackers was correct: they were small town thugs, the type that would jump you in a pub car park after ten pints. But murder? No. Real villains were quieter, more cautious. That was how they progressed to *become* real villains. Acting the hard man in public only got you put inside.

Danny tried to put thoughts of the dead bodies from his mind as he went home.

It didn't work.

Every detail of that night in 1995 when he'd seen the first body resurfaced in his mind as he drove. He remembered Ray Taylor's nicotine wheeze, the wet bracken brushing their trouser legs, police floodlights casting ghostly shadows through the pines. Danny had been twenty yards away when the police photographer's camera clicked inside the pill box and the flash revealed a momentary image of the dead man within, strung up like a butcher's shop carcass, face covered in grotesque make-up that was clown-like in its crudity. And now, fifteen years later, here was a carbon copy.

Could there be a link between the two cases? Impossible. The killer had been caught, locked up. Danny had gone to the trial.

Danny jogged through the darkened olive grove that surrounded his house; it was only forty yards from car to front door, but the shadows seemed laced with menace. Spain was never a quiet country, even in rural areas like Danny's. He tried to eat, but the smell of death was still strong in his mouth. After picking at his food, he opened his laptop and typed the name Ishmael Vertanness into the search engine.

The serial killer had his own Wikipedia entry, a whole page of it.

Ishmael Vertanness, or the 'Scarecrow', as the newspapers had dubbed him during the eight months his reign of terror had lasted. Danny read through the account of his background, though he knew it already. Vertanness ticked every box on the serial killer's psychological profile: sexually abused by his father, shunted from one foster family to the next, incidences of cruelty to animals, a childhood fixation with knives. Adolescence had brought minor problems with the police: shoplifting, flashing, a suspended sentence after being caught naked in the grounds of an all-boys' public school. Unable to hold down a job. Sexually impotent.

A quiet man, a loner; that was how his workmates at the factory described him.

A ticking time bomb was what he'd really been.

THE FACE OF EVIL one headline of the time screamed. It was accompanied by one of the few shots anyone had ever managed to get of Vertanness. He stared into the camera from the back of a meat wagon, expressionless. Seen from that angle, you saw how thin the veneer of humanity was painted. His eyes were lifeless, like a doll's.

Danny shuddered as he remembered his own experience of the man. He'd spent a day in the public gallery at Winchester Crown Court and watched Vertanness as a full account of the Scarecrow's horrors were read out. Vertannes had killed five times, all of his victims young, attractive men. Four of them were humiliated in the worst ways possible; strung up, sodomised and emasculated. He'd then spent hours toying with them, smothering them with make-up, placing pig-tailed wigs upon their heads. At some unknown point during the process they were strangled. Vertanness hadn't thrown any light on the matter; in the whole day that Danny had spent in the court-room he hadn't uttered a single word. He had hardly seemed to be aware of where he was. Even when led to the witness stand and threatened with the charge of contempt of court, he said nothing. It was as if he were in a trance. His defence claimed that tests had proved their client to be at the highest extreme of the autism spectrum.

There had been an outcry when the full horror of Vertanness's sexual deviancy became public knowledge. The victims' families had complained about the defence's plea of insanity; they wanted to see Vertanness exposed to the hardships of an ordinary prison. But there was never any doubt in Danny's mind that Vertanness was not all there. One court appearance had to be stopped when Vertanness was found to be masturbating in the dock.

Danny went to the webpage of his former employer, *The Fleet Bugle*. None of the coverage that either he or Ray Taylor had provided could be found there. Apart from the Wikipedia entry, there was little published information about the Scarecrow Enquiry, as the investigation became known. Ishmael Vertanness was one of a long list of serial killers. Danny now had none of his notebooks from that period to help him. He'd burned them all in 2002 when he'd decided to make the move to Spain.

Not that they would have helped much; it was impossible that the body at Alan Reade's house could be linked to Vertanness. According to the Wikipedia entry, Vertanness was still a patient at the Deepmere high-security psychiatric hospital in Berkshire. Danny had phoned the mental health trust that ran the hospital to check. Vertanness was one of their highest-risk patients and had not been allowed off site since being sent there in 1995.

What was the link, then? A copycat? Coincidence? Some sick joke? Whatever the explanation, as he called Lucky inside and bolted the front door shut, Danny was sure of one thing: there was still a seriously-disturbed individual roaming free.

17

Thursday, April 1st, 2010

At 11 a.m. next morning Danny followed dozens of other media correspondents up the steps of the government sub-delegation building in Almeria city, a huge nineteenth century edifice with a colonnaded front and high ceilings. It was rare for the police to hold a press conference relating to a crime; authorities in Spain liked to maintain their distance.

They were all here: reporters from radio, television, local and national newspapers; even some representing the online freebies. Danny heard journalists talking in French and German as he queued to pass through the metal detector. The discovery of the two bodies was turning into a big story.

A line of television cameras on tripods had been set up at the back of the conference room, cords coiling across the floor. Then came the journalists. Those who couldn't find space on chairs crowded the aisles, getting in the way of the photographers scooting back and forth, seeking the best angle for shots. A door at the back of the room opened and the policeman, Bosquet, emerged and sat behind the microphones. The man who followed him was familiar, but it took Danny a moment to place him; it was the politician who had hosted the press conference about the powerboat event. Danny wondered what the hell a politician was doing there as he flicked through his notebook in search of the man's name. It was Jesus Gutierrez.

Considering that they served a nation whose people hadsuch a propensity for talking simultaneously, Spanish press conferences were oddly sedate affairs. There was none of the rugby scrum atmosphere that a pack of UK journalists created. Bosquet went first. His ten-minute discourse reiterated in a truly staggering number of nuances and variations one single fact: that the magistrate in charge of investigating the "cases" – not deaths or murders or killings, *cases* – had declared a *secreto de sumario,* meaning that the evidence would be gathered in secret and not released to the press until the trial.

There were groans. What the bloody hell were they all doing there, then?

Gutierrez then took his turn and spent another ten minutes explaining that the two "cases" (that word again) were in no conceivable way the fault of either the socialist government in Andalusia or Spain's socialist national government.

More groans, Danny's loudest among them. He was cutting it fine as it was. As soon as the press conference finished he would have to charge to the nearest café and get writing on his laptop in order to send his work to the newspaper before the two o'clock deadline. Now it looked as if he'd wasted his time.

Some details did emerge. The body found at the Cookes's house was male, Caucasian, probably aged between forty and sixty. The man had been dead more than two years. No, Bosquet couldn't give any details as to the black substance on the corpse's head. The second corpse was also male, but younger and North African, aged between the late teens and thirty. The state of decomposition was consistent with his having been dead for around four months. That was all he was permitted to say; the hows, wherefores and whys of each case were to be kept secret.

The Q&A session began. A young Spanish journalist was the first to be passed the microphone: 'I would like to ask, given the similarity of the circumstances in which the two bodies were discovered, whether the police consider the two killings connected?'

Bosquet made to answer and stopped when Gutierrez touched his arm; microphones picked up the low murmur of their conversation. No distinct words could be heard, but Danny got the impression that the two men were disagreeing. Finally, Jesus Gutierrez answered the question.

'We can state unequivocally that the cases are not connected.'

Whispered conversation swept the room. Some of the older reporters exchanged looks. Words like "unequivocally" rarely appeared on the lips of politicians without good reason. What was the angle here? Bosquet scratched his beard. He looked unhappy.

Danny put his hand up and waited for the microphone to be passed to him; doing this slowly was an old trick the authorities used to slow the pace of a difficult press conference. He stood to speak. Gutierrez's lip curled momentarily as he recognised Danny.

'I'd like to ask how you can state "unequivocally" that the two murders are unconnected. Isn't it rather early to say? The initial autopsy reports are barely –'

'The *cases* are not connected.'

A hand was extended to take back the microphone.

'I wanted to ask about that word "cases". It's rather vague. Surely we're talking about murders here?'

'I'm afraid I can't answer that.'

The hand reached for the microphone again. Danny leant away. 'So the police aren't considering the possibility that a serial killer might be on the loose?'

Politicians' smiles had a certain way of freezing when they fought to hide displeasure. 'I would say it is far too early to form *any* type of conclusion – and that use of incendiary phrases such as "serial killer" would be deeply irresponsible. Now kindly pass the microphone on.'

A forest of hands shot up. Nothing more was revealed. The police chief and Gutierrez stonewalled everything almost until the conference was at an end.

Gutierrez looked at his watch, gathered his things, stood up and bent to the microphone. 'One last thing. Dental records and DNA of the first case to be discovered were sent to various European police forces and compared with existing records. I'm pleased to be able to reveal that this has resulted in the positive identification of a British man in his early fifties who was resident in Spain, but that is all I'm able to say at this juncture.'

Another old trick: save the real news until last then get the hell out. Jesus Gutierrez pushed through the journalists crowding round him. Danny had sensed something was up and was perfectly poised to catch the politician as he stepped from the rostrum. 'A police source told me the second corpse – sorry, case – suffered mutilation in the area of the genitals,' Danny said in a low but clear voice. 'Care to confirm or deny that?'

Danny had fired the question speculatively, but it was obvious that he'd hit his target. Gutierrez's eyes blazed. He took hold of Danny's arm, steered him towards Bosquet, whispered something in the man's ear. The policeman's eyes opened wide. 'Source? What source? Who told you that?'

'Then it's true?'

'I don't want to see a word about that in print, do you hear?' Bosquet said. 'Not one word. I warned you yesterday. Who was this source? I want a name.'

Other members of the press were beginning to take an interest. Danny nodded towards a nearby door. 'Why don't we go somewhere private where we can discuss this?'

The other journalists howled as Danny was led into an office. Straight into the wolf's lair; out of the public eye, Bosquet dropped any pretence of civility.

'Name. Now!'

Danny held his hands up. 'I'll come clean. There is no source. I was making an educated guess to see how you reacted. Looks like I hit the nail on the head.'

'I don't believe you,' Bosquet said. 'How did you know enough to make such a guess in the first place? Someone must have talked.'

'As I tried to tell you yesterday, in 1995 a series of murders occurred in England with the same M.O.: young male victims, make-up, the wig, everything. And with their cocks and balls cut off.'

Bosquet began to say something and stopped when Jesus Gutierrez laid a clammy hand on Danny's shoulder. Gutierrez had turned his smile full beams on. 'You know as well as I do that the incidence of serial killers is very low in Spain. Now, let's do a deal. We'll give you some exclusive information about the police operation; you keep any copycat serial killer theories under your hat for the time being.'

'Impress me.'

'Police are currently working on the assumption that the young man in the second case died as the result of a sexual game gone wrong.'

Danny made no effort to hide his scorn. 'A sex game that involved him having his *cojones* cut off?'

'Has anyone told you categorically that they were?'

'No, but I could see –'

'Then it's pure supposition on your part, isn't it?'

Danny could see where this was going. 'Right, so the whole "tell me who the source was" thing a minute ago was just a bit of horseplay?'

'As regards official confirmation or denial, I'm afraid so.'

'What's the angle here? Why are you so desperate to make out these two *killings*' – Danny stressed the word – 'are unconnected?'

'My only interest is to see this matter reported accurately. There are details from the autopsies that you don't know.'

'Enlighten me then.'

Gutierrez continued to smile, said nothing.

'I tell you what,' Danny said, 'give me the name of the British man you found at the Cookes's house and I promise not to mention the possibility of a serial killer being on the loose.'

Gutierrez looked at Bosquet. The policeman's face was difficult to read; he seemed permanently angry.

'OK,' Gutierrez said, 'we'll give you the name, but I don't want it published.' He pointed beyond the door, where the hubbub of angry voices could still be heard. 'That lot will tear me to pieces if they know I've given you something exclusive.'

Danny could live with that.

Gutierrez read from a sheet of paper. 'Phillip Samuel Cohen.'

'I take it this guy had a criminal record?'

'You've got your name.'

'How else would the police have had his dental records?'

Gutierrez's patience was fraying. 'All right, yes, he had a criminal record. Now that is all. Remember our deal: not a mention of serial killers or anything else incendiary.'

Danny snuck out via a back door, avoiding the press pack. He wanted to keep his private chat a secret. He went to a café, got his laptop out. He'd been working for fifteen minutes when he remembered that his mobile was still turned off.

He had thirteen missed calls from Fouldes.

Unlucky for some, Danny thought, dialling the number.

'Danny, you'll have to come to the office,' Fouldes said without any preamble.

'But I haven't finished –'

'Send what you've got and get up to Mojacar. Now.'

The phone went dead. Danny finished the article in ten minutes, paused, then added a final paragraph. He included a detailed description of what he and Paco had found at Alan Reade's house. He made a point of highlighting the similarities between the discoveries of the two bodies before quoting

Gutierrez's "unequivocal" statement.

He paused, then added a final paragraph.

Spanish police refused to comment on the possibility of a link between the recent killings and a spate of 1995 UK murders known collectively as the Scarecrow Enquiry,which investigated the deaths of five young men. Four of them had had their faces daubed with make-up in a manner similar to that used on the victim at the second Almeria property. The killer, Ishmael Vertanness, also emasculated his victims.

Danny finished the final sentence with a flourish. There. At no point had he specifically mentioned the possibility of a serial killer being on the loose.

Gutierrez could go screw himself.

18

It was a forty-five minute drive to Mojacar. Danny took an hour. No sense rushing. If Fouldes didn't want him to write any more, technically he was on holiday. The closer he arrived to the two o'clock deadline, the less time Fouldes would have to piss him about with last-minute orders. Because that's what this was, a farewell 'fuck you' from editor to reporter, Danny was sure.

One thing confused him, though; normally nothing pleased Fouldes more than imposing long drives on his reporters, but this time the editor's voice had been laced with barely-restrained fury. Perhaps there was some justice in the world after all, Danny decided.

When Danny finally arrived, Leonard Wexby was sitting in the plaza outside, gossiping in Spanish with a lawyer and a member of the council. As entertainment correspondent, his deadline was a day earlier than Danny's and he loved to rub it in, by sunning himself outside the offices when others were working. He waved as Danny crossed the plaza.

'Not now,' Danny said. 'I know I'm still working.'

'No, I just wanted to warn you,' Leonard said. 'Fouldes is hopping mad.'

'Why?'

'There's a married couple up there. Husband's the sort of bigwig Fouldes loves sucking up to, but they won't have anything to do with him. They want to speak to you.'

'With me?'

'Only, specifically and exclusively.'

'How do you know he's a bigwig?'

'Oh, you can always tell. The way he dresses, carries himself. Plus they arrived in that.' Leonard pointed his walking stick toward a cherry-red BMW parked opposite. Danny couldn't tell the model; it was a top-end one, though. The personalised number plate read MIKE T.

Danny made his way upstairs. Leonard was right. Fouldes was *really* pissed off.

'Danny, I'd like you to meet –'

'Michael Thorndyke.' The man pushed past Fouldes, hand extended. The grip was strong, despite the softness of the palm. 'My wife, Jocelyn. We want to speak to you.' Fouldes's face flushed a slightly deeper shade of carmine as Thorndyke turned his back on him. Danny allowed himself a shrug of helplessness as Thorndyke led him toward the door.

They went downstairs, took a table at one of the bars.

Thorndyke had self-made man written all over him, Danny decided; there was an unmistakeable *no-bullshit* dynamism about him. And he was rich. Even without having seen the car, Danny would have known. One look at Thorndyke and you could tell he had it all: the berth at the marina, the cliff-top property with security gates and cameras. His face was hard and humourless, the way rich men's were when they set their sights on becoming even richer.

'I want you to know I was opposed to this idea, but my wife brought me round,' Thorndyke said when the coffees came. It was obvious that she hadn't managed to bring Thorndyke round very far; his mouth remained a straight line, jaw set. The thought of having to ask for help was obviously distasteful to him.

The silence lengthened until the wife said, 'We want to ask for your help regarding our son, Craig. We can't get in contact with him and we –'

'Your boss recommended we speak to you,' Thorndyke said, interrupting.

'Fouldes?'

'No, Ms Pelham-Kerr. We are personal friends of hers.'

Right. Danny's *boss's* boss, the owner of the newspaper.

So, they were friends of the White Witch. That was what had rattled Fouldes's cage. The Thorndykes were stars twinkling in the jet-set constellation Fouldes so desperately wanted to form part of. He would have given his eye teeth to be down here with them now, ingratiating himself.

Danny sipped coffee while he considered how to deal with the situation. 'It's very flattering, but contrary to what Ms Pelham-Kerr might think, I'm not an expert in finding missing people. The last was –'

'Craig *isn't* missing.'

'Then why . . . ? I'm sorry, you've lost me.'

Thorndyke was losing patience. 'As my wife already stated, Craig is un-contactable. But we know where he is. At least we do at the beginning of every ruddy month.' This last said as an exasperated aside.

'What happens at the beginning of each month?'

Mrs Thorndyke said, 'We put . . .' at the same time as Thorndyke said, 'She puts . . .' They both stopped and looked at each other. '900 Euros gets put into Craig's account on the first of each month,' Thorndyke said. 'And withdrawn on the first, second and third, 300 Euros each time. That's how we know where he is: the bank statements all indicate he uses a cash point in this area.'

'Mojacar?'

Thorndyke nodded. 'Seven-thirty sharp. And that's the only time that bone-idle good-for-nothing has ever dragged himself out of bed at that time.'

'This might be a dumb question, but if you know where he's *going* to be, why don't you speak to him yourselves?'

Mother and father looked at each other. After a moment's silence, Jocelyn Thorndyke fielded the question. 'We've tried that already. In fact, our last attempt at effecting a reconciliation was what prompted Craig to disappear. We think it might be better coming from a stranger. We only want to talk to him. Especially now these dead bodies have turned up.' She shuddered. 'We saw it on the news yesterday. We drove straight down from our house in Valencia as soon as we heard.'

'When was the last time you heard from Craig?'

'Last week. He sends us text messages.'

'Saying what?'

'Leave me alone. That's if he's in a good mood.'

'When was the last time you saw him? Or spoke to him on the phone?'

Mrs Thorndyke looked at the floor. 'Three months ago,' Michael Thorndyke said. Danny breathed a sigh of relief. It wasn't Craig stuffed in the wall of Alan Reade's house, then.

Michael Thorndyke continued talking. 'The building society we use for Craig's account is a small regional one; it only has a handful of outlets. We wanted it that way, didn't want him having easy access to the money. They still charge in Spain for using cash cards at other banks,' Thorndyke said when Danny raised his eyebrows. 'I knew Craig would be too stingy to pay the bank charges.'

'What happened then?'

'We waited for him outside the building society, here in Mojacar.' The Thorndykes became quiet. It was clear that memories of the family reunion were not pleasant ones.

'There was a . . . bit of a scene,' Jocelyn Thorndyke said.

'He was supposed to be off travelling.' Thorndyke's voice rose irritably. 'We divide our time between the UK and Spain, so we didn't realise he'd only travelled as far as Almeria until then.'

Danny finished his coffee, wiped his fingers on a serviette. 'Well, I'd love to help, but unfortunately I'm going on holiday this afternoon; I won't be able to look into this for a week or so.'

Thorndyke held his gaze. 'We're *personal* friends of –'

' – Ms Pelham-Kerr. I know. You said.' Danny folded his arms. 'I get it now. You're not asking, you're telling. Is that right?'

'If you want to put it so crudely, then yes.'

'We'll see to it you're reimbursed for any trouble you might be put to,' Mrs Thorndyke said, when Danny rolled his eyes.

'And what is it, precisely, that you want me to say to Craig?'

Mrs Thorndyke began to say something, but Thorndyke spoke over her. 'Tell him that if he keeps worrying his poor mother we're going to declare him a missing person and the first thing we'll do is have you write a nice long article about what a naughty boy he's been, complete with the most embarrassing photos of him we can dig out.'

Danny flipped open his notebook. 'OK, I'll do it. And keep your cash. But tell Ms Pelham-Kerr I want an extra day's holiday in lieu of the day I'll be missing tomorrow.'

Danny wrote down details of the building society's address and the time: 07:30. 'I'll need a photo of Craig, too.'

Mrs Thorndyke fished in her bag, handed Danny a Polaroid. The happy, healthy boy in the photo couldn't have been more than thirteen.

'A recent photo.'

'That's the last proper photo we took of him, all the others are digital so we –'

'Just give it to him, Jocelyn.'

She looked at her husband, flustered. Then she handed Danny a computer print out.

The ravaged face that stared from the paper was unrecognisable; it didn't look like the same person. Angry-looking cold sores provided the only colour on the bone white skin. If his cheeks had been any more sunken, the outline of his teeth would have shown. Craig's hair was dyed jet black, the fringe swept down across one half of his face. The only eye on display was sunken and bloodshot. His ear was covered in piercings, his t-shirt tight and trendy.

'He fell in with a bad crowd,' Jocelyn Thorndyke said when she saw Danny's reaction. Danny wasn't sure whether her calm, persuasive tone was for his benefit or her own. 'He got into all sorts of bother back home.'

'The sort of bother you can tell me about?'

Jocelyn opened her mouth to speak, but her husband interrupted. 'Drug bother. Cocaine and ecstasy, mostly, though from his arrest record he seemed to operate an open-doors policy when push came to shove. That's why we thought he'd be better off out here in Spain.'

The one place in Europe that rivals the UK for cocaine consumption, Danny thought. *Brilliant.*

'Well, I'll see what I can do tomorrow,' Danny said, asking for the bill, eager to conclude the meeting. 'Let's hope Craig is in a receptive mood.'

Thorndyke looked at the bill, fished in his pocket for change. They agreed that Danny would phone tomorrow after he'd contacted Craig.

Mrs Thorndyke was profuse in her thanks, Thorndyke less so. *This is a business contract*, his firm handshake seemed to say. *Make sure you keep your end of it.*

Danny watched them drive away and finished his cigarette. Then he counted the money Michael Thorndyke had left; it was the precise cost of the two drinks that he and his wife had consumed. Danny fished in his pocket to pay for his own coffee, shaking his head. Christ, but you could tell Thorndyke was rich.

William Fouldes sat in his office staring at that week's front page story. Sanchez's article on the discovery of the two bodies was a good one.

Again.

But then how it could it not be with a subject matter as juicy as that? Bloody Danny Sanchez always seemed to have the luck. Life just dropped things into his lap. Like being bilingual.

William Fouldes had studied long and hard to get his Spanish as good as it was. Brits marvelled at the fluidity with which he spoke it, Spaniards always complimented him. It was perfect. Everyone said so.

Almost perfect.

Jesus, but that irked him. "Almost" was not a word William Fouldes liked.

He mopped his brow. He was getting flustered. He knew why. What the bloody hell did friends of Ms Pelham-Kerr want with a loser like Sanchez? Surely they realised *he*, William Fouldes, was the editor? Christ, only three months ago Sanchez had been driving a car that looked like a reject from a demolition derby. William Fouldes belonged to their world. He was one of them. Surely the Thorndykes could see that?

The phone rang. They were waiting for him to send through the front page story. Fouldes didn't answer. First, he cut and pasted an extra fifty words and added them to the end of the article. Then he highlighted the words "by Danny Sanchez" and removed them, then wrote something different in their place.

The phone rang again. He answered it this time.

'Front page is on its way.'

19

After leaving the Thorndykes, Danny drove straight to the premises of Shelter All.

Winter in Almeria is still cold, but on the coast it is as close to warm as anywhere north of Africa. With the help of some warming wine (a litre costs sixty pence), it is easy to keep out the chill on the odd days when the rain and wind pick up. Around November each year, Europe's vagabond dropouts begin to arrive, some obviously too drugged or drunk to participate in normal society, others lacking the wish to do so. Most head for the provincial capital; others live a semi-nomadic life, tramping from one place to another, sleeping on beaches. Craig Thorndyke sounded as if he was one of them. If so, there was a slim chance he might have passed by Toby Ibañez's charity.

Ibañez was in the reception, speaking French with a large African woman who was holding a baby and looking nervous. She listened intently to Ibañez; her expression slowly calmed. Seeing Ibañez in action, Danny felt a twinge of guilt at having previously judged the man so harshly; it was obvious from Ibañez's tone of voice and his mannerisms that he genuinely cared about the woman's plight. The conversation ended with Ibañez slipping a hand into his pocket and passing the woman a bank-note.

'Danny,' Ibañez said as the woman waddled out, baby

bouncing on her hip, 'I didn't expect to see you again so soon.'

'Toby.' For the first time, the name didn't sound forced on Danny's lips. 'I was wondering if you could help me. Do you recognise this young man?'

Danny showed him the photo of Craig Thorndyke. Ibañez looked slowly and carefully, then began nodding.

'Do you know, I think I *do* recognise him. Is he English? Posh accent but tries to hide it?'

'That sounds about right. When was the last time you saw him?'

'Months ago rather than weeks.'

'Any idea where he might be now?'

'Your guess is as good as mine. I got the feeling he was sleeping rough. He certainly smelt that way. To be perfectly honest, I found him a little creepy.'

'Creepy? How?'

'Oh, just a feeling. He had that thousand-yard-stare people get when they've taken one too many LSD trips. Cold sores round his mouth. He's obviously a very troubled young man.'

'Any idea where he might be now?'

Toby looked genuinely distressed at not being able to help.

'What about whats-her-name?' Danny said, motioning toward the telephone room. 'Might she know?'

'Allison? She's not here today. I'll ask the chap on duty, though.'

A neatly-dressed young Moroccan sat by the telephone. Yes, he recognised Craig Thorndyke; no, he didn't know where he was. His expression betrayed a faint glimpse of disgust as he looked at Craig Thorndyke's ravaged features.

Danny walked back to his car, thinking. If Craig Thorndyke was going to withdraw money from a cash-point in Mojacar at 07:30 next morning, logic dictated that he had to be somewhere close by. He paused, his key already inserted in the door of the Golf.

Balls, he'd give it another half-hour. He fancied a bottle or two of wine tonight to celebrate the beginning of his holiday. Then he would sleep late.

Danny took a walk along Mojacar's beach front. The two Germans were easy to find. Klaus and Justus worked the same stretch of beach every year, building elaborate sand sculptures, living off the coins that were tossed to them. They had real talent. One year they'd built a replica of the Alcazaba, the province's famous castle, a mini-Alhambra. This year they'd constructed a huge dragon, large enough for them to light candle stubs in its snout and eyes.

Sleeping rough anywhere was a risky business, but Klaus and Justus were well equipped for it. If the sight of Klaus's amphetamine eyes and gap-toothed grin didn't put you off, there was Justus: six-three, twenty-stone plus, most of it covered in biker tattoos. Klaus was the artist; Justus did the donkey work, carrying buckets of water up from the sea to wet the sand which Klaus sculpted. Danny had written an article on them a few years ago. He remembered Klaus speaking pidgin English with an accent somewhere between Arnold Schwarzenegger and Herr Flick. He obviously hadn't taken any language classes in the interim period.

'Ja, I am remembering you,' he said when Danny introduced himself. Danny sat on the edge of the wall and cracked the top from the ice cold litre bottle of San Miguel he'd bought on the way there. He drank in the Spanish way, holding the bottle an inch from his mouth, careful not to let his lips touch the bottle neck; Spaniards were always disgusted by the way foreigners shared spittle covered cans and bottles. He offered the bottle to Klaus, who accepted gratefully.

Justus sauntered up with two brimming buckets of sea water. The big man might as well have been carrying egg cups for all the strain that he showed. The bottle was passed to Justus, who, for all his years in Spain, had never seemed to have mastered the Spanish technique of drinking from shared bottles. He rammed the neck into his mouth and sucked greedily at it. Danny refused politely when the

German offered him the bottle back. There was little point in taking it anyway; Justus had drained most of the contents in a single mighty gulp. The big man smiled at Danny, slapped his enormous belly.

Right, he'd won their gratitude. Time for work. He unfolded Craig Thorndyke's photo.

'You ever see this guy?'

Klaus looked at it and smiled. He showed it to Justus. He smiled, too, then began to laugh, a huge Teutonic belly-rumbling of a sound. '*Der Schwul!*' he said, pointing at the picture.

'What's so funny?' Danny said.

'He is . . . how you say?' Klaus pursed his lips, began bobbing his head up and down. It took Danny a moment to realise he was miming a blow-job.

'You know him?'

'Ja.'

'And Craig is gay?'

'For money, ja. He tell me he will' – the blowjob motion again – 'for 20 Euros. Justus tell him "nein".' Klaus laughed, pointed at one of the buckets, mimed the action of tossing it at someone.

They spoke a while longer, but the conversation was hard going. Danny finally established that the bucket-flinging incident had happened the previous year, in (probably) December. Neither of them had seen the young man again.

Danny walked back to his car, staring at Craig Thorndyke's photo. A rich dad, a doting mother and he ends up turning 20-Euro tricks on a bloody Spanish beach.

Danny shook his head. 'You dumb bastard, Craig.'

20

Friday, April 2nd, 2010

His first day of holiday and Danny had to get up an hour-and-a-half earlier than normal. The irony was not lost on him. His decision the night before to implement the celebratory wine-drinking plan and to hell with the consequences did little to improve his mood.

He got to Mojacar for 07:00, reached the building society at 07:15. It was halfway along the Mojacar Playa strip. Danny parked outside and wiped condensation from the window. The buildings glowed white as the sun rose from the silver-blue waters of the sea. The first customer came at 07:23. He was obviously Spanish. Two more people came during the next ten minutes: a young Spanish woman and a blonde man with a ponytail. He could have been British,but when he turned Danny saw that it definitely wasn't Craig Thorndyke. This man was way too old.

The next person came at 07:46: an elderly woman, German from the looks of her, on her way to the beach for an early morning dip.

Danny looked at his watch, checked the time.

So much for 07:30 sharp.

More people came; none of them was Craig Thorndyke.

At 08:03 Michael Thorndyke phoned. 'Well?'

The imperious tone of that single word decided Danny: he

really didn't like this bloke.

'Well what? I've been sat here right outside waiting since 07:15 and he's not come.'

Thorndyke harrumphed. 'You must have missed him.'

'Which bit of "right outside" do you not understand? I'm telling you I've been watching the cash point from a distance of roughly eight yards with a totally unobstructed view. Your son didn't come.'

'You'll have to go back –'

'I don't *have to* do anything, Mr Thorndyke. You asked me for a favour and I've done it. Just so there's no hard feelings, I'll stay here until nine to make sure, but if you don't hear from me again it's because Craig hasn't come. Goodbye.'

Danny hung up, switched the phone off.

Craig didn't come. Danny picked up a copy of *Sureste News* on the way home. It did nothing to improve his mood. The front page story – his front page story – was credited to "Staff Reporter". And Fouldes had tacked on a pointless two-paragraph coda.

There was no point in arguing; the bloody thing was printed now. All the shouting in the world couldn't change that.

I'm on holiday, he repeated. *I just want to relax*.

He stopped beside the beach, tossed rocks into the sea. There was no point in going home yet. He couldn't concentrate. Questions kept turning in his mind: questions about the bodies. He sat in his car, checked a post he'd made on the local expat forum late the night before which asked if anyone remembered a man named Phillip Samuel Cohen. Cohen obviously hadn't been part of the province's movers and shakers; otherwise, Leonard would have known him.

There were already seven replies; some of the Brits out here seemed to spend their life on forums, bickering, gossiping, moaning. Five were facetious nonsense. The other two both said a man by that name used to live in the town of Zurgena.

Back to the Almanzora Valley. Danny wasted most of the morning asking around bars, knocking on doors, trying to locate the house Cohen had rented. He found it in the end, a modest little flat. Danny spoke to the neighbours. Yes, they remembered Cohen; a tall, blonde man, early forties, one said, typically British, kept himself to himself. 'He had a girlfriend. She used to come around sometimes.' Then Danny spoke to the young Spanish couple now renting the property. They knew nothing about Phillip Cohen, but suggested Danny contact the landlord. As was often the way in Spain, the landlord owned two other properties in the street.

Danny rang the bell. The door was answered by an elderly Spaniard. He greeted Danny with a neutral expression.

'How can I help?'

'Do you remember a man named Phillip Samuel Cohen? He used to rent the property back there.'

'Why?'

Saying he was an old friend would be the wrong thing to say; the man's face had clouded at mention of Cohen's name. Danny told the truth; that he was a journalist carrying out research about the man.

The man's expression darkened even more. 'Journalist? What's he been doing?'

'Why should he have been doing anything? I just want to know a bit about him. How long did he rent the property from you?'

The old man invited him in, looked for his records. Cohen began renting the property in January 2001. He stopped in November 2007.

'Did he cancel the rent?'

'Nope. He just disappeared one night. It didn't bother me, I had his deposit.'

It was likely that was when Cohen had been killed, then: November 2007.Something was bothering the old man, though. Danny asked him what it was.

The old man chewed his lip, debating what to say.

'He left in a real hurry,' he said eventually. 'He left a lot of things behind. My son and I had to clear them out. We found . . . magazines. I burnt them.'

'What type of magazines?'

'Filthy ones. Men. With other men.' His eyes were angry now. 'And not just any men. He'd taken photos of people from here, in the village. My neighbours. My friends. My family. He'd cut the heads out, stuck them over the faces of the men in the magazine.'

Danny drove home wishing that he hadn't bothered following up on Phillip Samuel Cohen.

He spent the rest of the day cleaning his house, with his stereo on full blast: *Powerage*, *Sabotage*, *Toys in the Attic*. It was early evening by the time he had finished. He went outside and sat on the patio with his guitar. It was still cold; when the wind blew from the north it carried with it the chill of the Sierra Nevada. He supped wine and strummed flamenco. His fingers fluttered over the strings, sending soft, liquid notes of *tarantas* into the night sky as he gazed up at the stars.

The shadow on the wall made him jump. Adriana Sanchez stood there, accompanying him with soft, cup-palmed handclaps.

'Don't stop on my account, Danny,' she said, looking disappointed.

'I don't like being watched.'

'I can't imagine why. You're quite good.' She pulled up a chair and sat at the table opposite him, lighting a cigarette. 'Well, if you're not going to play, we'll have to chat.' He could tell from her easy smile and lidded eyes that she was tipsy.

Adriana Sanchez looked good for her age, in the sense that she actually *looked* her age. Unlike many women approaching sixty, she used make-up sparingly, choosing combinations that highlighted and complemented the strong points of her features, rather than try to paint herself a face two decades past its sell-by date. It helped that she possessed the classic combination of Spanish beauty: olive skin, dark hair and large, brown almond-shaped eyes.

'Say something, then,' she said, reaching over to sip from his glass.

He knew from her expression what it was she wanted him to ask, so he made of point of not doing so.

'I like those trousers you're wearing. Very colourful.'

Her shoulders drooped and she puffed.

'Aren't you going to ask where I've been? I was supposed to be back *days* ago.'

'You've met someone.'

'Oh, he's wonderful, Danny. Jacques. French. I've spent the last Lord-knows-how-many nights at his house in Sorbas, right up in the mountains.'

Nights. Not days. The choice was deliberate, the implication clear. Danny was a journalist. He noticed things.

One look at her and you knew romance for Adriana Sanchez had been more about lovers than love, although Danny saw none of the unhappiness in her face that was supposed to be the punishment for such a shallow approach. But then, Adriana Sanchez had always been good at avoiding unhappiness. She was like a ratchet. If anything caused her distress, she simply clicked forward a notch and locked the past away, never looking back.

During his childhood, she'd behaved more like an unruly elder sister, disappearing for months at a time before sweeping in unannounced to turn Danny's life upside down once again, lavishing him with sugar-sweet attention. And then, just as suddenly, she would be gone. Danny could still taste the tears of those mornings when he had rushed into her room to find the bed empty and realised she was gone.

Again.

The *abuela* would greet him, grim-faced, whispering the words she always did: *Estamos condenados a quererla*. We are condemned to love her. That *was* how it felt sometimes, like a punishment.

'I'm very happy you've met someone, mother, but I don't need to know the ins and outs of it.'

For a moment, the mask of simpering excitement slipped and her eyes narrowed. 'An unfortunate choice of phrase, Danny, given how scandalously wicked we were the whole time.'

That was always her tactic when she felt she wasn't given the attention she deserved: to scandalise, to shock. Danny had a perfect image of her doing the same to the *abuela* one evening when she'd come in. That had ended in a full-blown screaming match, the sort of banshee exchange that was the result when Spanish women locked horns.

Adriana Sanchez laughed. 'Don't be such a prude, Danny. You remind me of my mother when you look like that.' The amiable tipsiness returned. 'That's what you could do with. A girlfriend, I mean. I was chatting with your friend, Paco, on the phone. He says it's been ages since you had a girlfriend. How long's it been?'

'That's none of your business.'

'Do you know what? I think you're having a mid-life crisis,' she said as he picked up his guitar and walked inside. She spoke to his back, safe in the knowledge that Danny would be unable to let her have the last word. He got as far as the kitchen before turning back.

'Why do you think that?'

'It happens when men get to your age, get overweight and unfit. Take that car, for example.'

'What about the car?'

'It's ridiculous for a man of your age to be driving around in a car like that. A stripe over the bonnet, spoilers on the back.'

'I bought it like that.'

'*Precisamente*. You see how you were drawn to it subconsciously? That's proof of the inner turmoil you're experiencing, darling. And that stupid Star Wars poster in the living room. You're a bit old for that rubbish, aren't you? If I'd known I was planting the seeds of a lifelong obsession, I'd never have taken you to see that damned film.'

'You didn't take me to see it. The *abuela* did.'

'Are you sure?'

Yes, Danny was sure: the experience was indelibly stamped on his psyche. Not only was the *abuela* unable to understand a word of what was going on, she had taken him to the cinema dressed head to toe in black, mourning for her husband's recent death. Her resemblance to Darth Vader had not gone unnoticed by Danny's schoolmates.

Danny counted to five, determined to avoid an argument. 'Listen, I'm dead on my feet. I'm just going to unwind by playing some guitar, then I'll hit the hay.'

His mother was not to be cheated. 'You're very good on that guitar, aren't you? Which *palo* of flamenco was that? I expect you get it from your father. He was very musical. From what I remember of him, anyway.'

Danny turned, too quickly – the edge of the guitar knocked against the table, the wine glass toppled. The subject of Danny's father was the red, raw hook always guaranteed to get a rise from him, the splinter embedded so deep he could never cut it free.

Then they argued, and, as their tempers frayed, the conversation slipped inevitably into Spanish. The argument ended the way all Spanish arguments do: lots of exaggerated hand gestures, each side retiring in opposite directions muttering to ensure that the other could not be thought to have had the last word. Mother went inside; Danny headed into the garden. Then his phone rang.

It was Michael Thorndyke.

Again.

He'd phoned three times already during the course of the day, but Danny had ignored the calls.

'Mr Thorndyke. I'm really sorry but I can't help –'

'You missed him.'

'Missed who?

'My son. We contacted the bank. Three hundred euros was withdrawn from the account Craig uses this morning at 07:36.'

'Then he sent someone else. I was watching –'

'You missed him, Mr Sanchez. You'll have to go again tomorrow and keep your eyes open. It's as simple as that.'

Danny had never liked being interrupted. He felt his knuckles whiten around the phone, counting to five. This was a personal friend of The White Witch after all. Danny got as far as three when Thorndyke said, 'Now listen, you messed things –'

'No, *you* listen, Thorndyke. I don't know what sort of lick-spittles you're used to bullying around, but I'm not one of them. I did you a favour this morning, but you just burned up any reserves of goodwill I had left. Hire a private eye to find your son, Mr Thorndyke. Good night.'

Danny hung up, then turned his phone off. He went to his office, switched the computer on. He'd made a decision. He was going away on holiday.

And he knew where he wanted to go.

PART II – LA MATANZA

May 5th, 2000

The three hunters had been walking all day. The road was edged with small rectangular sheets of metal divided into black and white triangles; they were nearing the edge of the hunting preserve now.

The eldest, Cipriano, stopped to look at his watch. There were two hours of daylight left, two-and-a-half maybe. Vaya mierda de día, *he thought, hawking a gobbet of spit onto a boulder. What a shit day. They'd found nothing of any worth.*

His son, Carlos, walked fifty metres behind, carrying the day's catch: two hares and a pheasant. It was hardly worth the petrol they'd spent driving out here.

Cipriano shook his head. It was his fault: he was old enough to know better than to listen to a young fool like Nacho Morales. He could hear Morales now, voice thick with brandy: I know a place, a place where no one ever goes. *Morales had been right about that; why would anyone bother coming all the way out here? The hunting was terrible.*

Cipriano's feet ached from traipsing uphill for hours. He swung the wineskin from his hip, rested a booted foot on a rock as he aimed a jet of rough wine at his mouth. Away to his left, buzzards circled against the vast blue of the sky. He raised the wineskin in silent salute. I wish you better hunting than I.

The wineskin was nearly empty now. He'd drunk too much. That was why he'd missed the only decent shot of the day, a huge boar. Another reason this had been a day to forget.

'Let's head this way,' Nacho said, shotgun cocked over his arm. He pointed toward a copse of pine trees. 'There's a path over there will lead us back down to the road. We can walk to the car from there.'

Cipriano shouldered his rifle, threaded his way through the gorse-covered hillside. That was it. A day wasted. They weren't going to find anything by going this way.

They walked in silence for ten, twenty minutes. They were nearing the area where the buzzards had been. Ragged wings thrashed the air at the sound of their footsteps; the birds had been on the ground, feeding.

Then came another sound, metallic, like the rattle of chains.

Nacho was the first to scream. Cipriano unslung his rifle, rushed forward then stopped as he, too, saw what was dangling from the tree in the centre of the clearing.. The rifle fell from his hands.

They'd found something now.

1

Saturday, April 3rd, 2010

The plane shuddered as it dipped into cloud; the seat-belt light pinged above Danny's head. They were beginning the descent into Gatwick.

Here he was.

Home.

Danny mouthed the word, seeing if it caused any sensation. He'd lived the first thirty years of his life in England, but was it still home? He had no friends here now, no relatives. This was the first time he'd returned since he'd departed eight years ago. All he could see from his window seat was a grey, cloudy mass. That was pretty much what he felt inside, too.

He'd grown up imbibing a mishmash of Spanish and British ways. Children had teased him for his exaggerated hand gestures, his Andalusian lisp. *Dago Danny* they called him at school. Now Spaniards called him *el inglés*, The Englishman. Fate had decreed he would never really be allowed to call anywhere home.

He collected his hire car, headed for the M3 and hit stationary traffic five minutes after turning onto the M25.

Some things were still the same, then.

Home or not, southern England was certainly familiar: the neat lines of red brick houses, the hedgerows, the anaemic sky. How different it looked from the massive desolate spaces of Spain's interior. Rain glistened on the bare-branched trees at the edge of the motorway. Here was another difference: seasons. It hadn't occurred to him before; on the Andalusian coast the evergreen foliage and cloudless azure sky held no clue as to which month of the year it was.

It was a ninety-minute drive from Gatwick to Fleet, the commuter town on the north-eastern tip of Hampshire where Danny had grown up. Distances in England seemed so small. You could happily drive for ninety minutes in Almería without even leaving the province.

He booked into a room above a local pub. The irony of it was not lost on him. Seventeen million Britons travelled from the UK to Spain each year in search of rest and relaxation; Danny was probably one of a handful forced to make the reverse journey. He'd decided on his destination the previous night, a decision spurred both by anger and by wine; between his mother and Michael Thorndyke there was precious little chance of anything remotely resembling R&R in Spain. So, he would head back to Fleet, revisit his past.

The cobwebs of memories had been lurking in his mind for too long now; he was uneasily aware that his run-to-the-sun had actually been running away. It was time to face up to things. Plus, if he was going to explore links between the Scarecrow Enquiry and the body found at Alan Reade's house, Fleet was the only place from which to do it.

He'd no idea what he would do with the rest of his time, though. Visit a castle? Spend a day in London? Anyway, such decisions could wait until tomorrow. Today, he wanted to relax. And visit Denise. He'd not spoken to her since Ray's funeral, eight years ago.

That was wrong.

It was strange to be back on his old beat. He'd spent a decade reporting on the lives of the people in the town, yet he recognised no one he saw on the street. It was amazing how time could fold in upon itself, smother the past; there seemed no trace left of his version of Fleet. Shops remembered from childhood were now vacant lots. Pubs had changed names. And coffee shops had sprung up all over the place.

He walked to the town's library and asked for microfiche copies of the *Fleet Bugle* from March to November 1995. Checking up on the coverage he'd written of the Scarecrow enquiry was a good way of killing time while he decided what to do with his holiday. Besides, he was curious to see how much his prose had improved in eighteen years.

'I'll have to go downstairs to the archives,' the librarian said. 'Are you sure that's all you want?'

Danny nodded. He was sure; the dates were indelibly etched on his mind. It was the first big story he had ever covered, a cub reporter's dream come true. A full-blown serial killer had begun stalking the streets of southern England just six months after Danny had started work.

It was a long time since he'd used a microfiche reader. It would have been simpler to go to the newspaper office and go through their files, but he wanted to avoid the premises of *The Bugle* if he could; too many memories.

He started at the beginning with the article he and Ray Taylor had written about the discovery of the first body: *CHILDREN FIND PILLBOX HORROR.*

The discovery of the mutilated corpse was the biggest news event to have happened to Fleet in living memory; a body found in the water catchment area, the huge tract of hill, heath and forest between Fleet, Aldershot and Farnham. Danny remembered Ray Taylor hadn't wanted to take him along; it was a story that would likely hit the nationals and by rights it belonged to *The Bugle's* senior reporters. But police had cordoned off the only official access route. There was no other way in,unless you knew the path through the woods. Danny did; he'd spent his childhood messing around in the forest on his BMX bike.

There was a footpath on the far side which led straight up the steep slope of a hill. Paratroopers from the nearby barracks in Aldershot used the place for training. Danny led Ray Taylor up there, the veteran reporter trying to conceal how out of breath he'd become. They came at the crime scene from the other side, where the police had not set up surveillance.

The red-brick pill box – part of a hastily-erected line built to defend against Nazi invasion – was lit by floodlights which silhouetted the branchless trunks of pine trees, hundreds of them growing close together. Police officers were setting up a white tent beside the pill box. Danny offered to sneak forward with Ray's old camera to see if he could get a photo of the pill box's interior.

A scene-of-crime officer emerged when Danny was still twenty yards away. The SOCO was shaking. From within the pillbox the police photographer's camera clicked. For a split second, the flash lit the interior and the doorless opening of the pill box filled with an image that remained fresh and crisp within Danny's mind fifteen years later: a naked body was dangling from hooks and chains embedded in the ceiling. And that face. The same face he'd seen wedged in the wall of Alan Reade's house; the pig-tailed wig, the make-up, horribly smeared and distorted. In that split second glimpse it had seemed that the victim's features were melting.

Danny – barely twenty-one – cried out. Police officers spun round, hurried him away with angry words. A senior officer remonstrated furiously with Ray Taylor. 'If that little prick's trodden through any footprints there'll be hell to pay.' Ray Taylor stood his ground and defended his young colleague; it had been the first time Danny realised he actually liked the man. Taylor was a grumpy old git even on his best days.

Danny moved the microfiche. The true horror of the crime had begun to leak out over the course of the next forty-eight hours. The police stationed officers outside the houses of the three boys who'd found the body. The families were given counselling. *The Fleet Bugle* ran a special four-page pull-out detailing everything that was known about the murder and made an appeal for witnesses to come forward. Owners of white vans in the area were traced and interviewed, more than 7,000 of them. And then a second body was found outside Andover and the public's worst fears were realised; the crime at Fleet was only the beginning. Public horror turned to anger as the body count mounted, the killer evidently targeting young, attractive men. Most often they were middle-class, with girlfriends. When a witness described seeing a thin, scruffy man with wild hair, the killer's nickname was born: the Scarecrow.

Danny scanned the rest of *The Bugle's* coverage. Ray Taylor had written the majority of it, but Danny – having got his foot in on the story's first rung – was his unofficial number two. That had caused a lot of bad blood; some of the paper's other reporters had worked twenty years without getting a shot at anything half as juicy. But that was Ray; a little bad blood would never deflect him from doing exactly what he wanted to, exactly the way he wanted to.

It was the first time that Danny had experienced the buzz of being a journalist, of being well-informed on a subject of interest. Back in 1995, people in Fleet talked of nothing else and no one talked more than Danny Sanchez, twenty-one going on forty, holding forth in pub beer gardens on the minutiae of the police investigation, masking the yawning gaps in his knowledge with a sly wink and a tap of the nose – *can't tell you that, mate*. He smiled at the memory of it; Christ, what a repellent little shit he must have been. Popularity had gone to his head; it was the first time in his life that anyone had listened to him.

Danny worked through all the coverage of the murder. Once Ishmael Vertanness had been arrested interest in the case waned and new stories emerged to take its place. After an hour, Danny had seen enough. His memory refreshed, he drove to Ray Taylor's house.

If Danny had to point to one person and say 'He taught me all I know,' it would be Ray Taylor. Except Taylor had never actually *taught* him anything. 'Write me out a list of everything you've learned so far,' Taylor said at the end of Danny's first week with *The Bugle*.

Danny gaped. 'But you haven't taught me anything.'

'Shouldn't have to. All a good reporter needs is eyes, ears and a pinch of common sense. If you haven't learnt anything this week, stay home Monday.'

Danny's "training" had lasted a month, stumbling around after Taylor, running errands, fetching cups of tea, looking for telephone boxes. Then came his "big break"; Taylor promised to let Danny write some words. Danny smiled at memory of the story, a pigeon-fanciers' convention held at a local church hall; the type of mundane event editors gave to trainees and reporters in the doghouse, a story so dull you would have to sweat blood to get 250 words of copy.

But Danny had walked eagerly from table to table, collecting quotes. And then chaos; shouts, screams, commotion as a ginger tomcat sped across the floor, pursued by stewards. Pigeons were thrust into cages and held above heads as the moggy was chased from one end of the room to the other, leaping on tables, hissing and spitting.

Sitting in the pub afterwards, Ray Taylor sipped his orange juice and said, 'What's the angle on the story, then?', asking the way people did when they already knew the answer. Danny wracked his brains, desperate to please.

Lots of Pigeons.

A Cat.

He blurted the words when they finally came: 'Cat among the pigeons.'

Taylor nodded, the faintest curl of satisfaction on his lip. 'Do 300 words for tomorrow. If I don't have to mangle it too much, your name can go on.' He stood, lit a cigarette from the stub of another, pulled on his long sheepskin jacket.

'Did you see how the cat got in there?'

Taylor spoke without turning. 'Under my coat. Best leave that bit out though, eh?'

Danny wrote the article and Taylor stayed true to his word; it was the first to bear the legend "by Danny Sanchez". The *abuela* had cried when she saw it and shown it to all the neighbours even though she couldn't understand a single word of the text.

Danny's smile faded as he parked outside the modest three-bedroom Victorian semi-detached the Taylor family had lived in. Ray's daughter, Denise, had inherited the house. Danny hoped she still lived there.

He pushed the gate open, noticing it no longer squeaked, and knocked at the door. It took Denise a moment to place him. 'Danny? Danny Sanchez? Is that you? I wish you'd told me you were coming, I'd have put my face on.'

Denise extinguished her cigarette, began hurriedly cleaning mess from surfaces, shuffling her slippers along the plastic covering in the hallway. There were photos of Denise on the wall when she did have her face on, about an eighth of an inch of it, whilst wearing a ridiculously short skirt.

'My hen-do,' she said.

'Congratulations.'

She invited Danny through to the living room. A chubby toddler stared at him for a moment and resumed banging plastic building bricks. A photo of Ray Taylor stood above the mantelpiece. It was a good shot: that long, cadaverous face, the slight fleck of grey in the fringe with its yellow nicotine stain. He was smiling for the camera, but the creases round his eyes held a glimpse of his usual stern expression.

Ray Taylor wasn't like the other journalists at *The Bugle* ; Danny had realised that from day one. For starters, Taylor didn't drink – anymore; he was too relaxed around drunkenness to have been teetotal his whole life. And there was a definite touch of the horsehair shirt to the way he approached reporting. Ray Taylor was never a hack. He was driven by the need for accuracy, for the truth. When Ray Taylor reported something, he nurtured facts like a mother with a newborn. Ray Taylor cared.

'You were the only one Dad had a good word for at *The Bugle*, you know,' Denise said, bringing tea things, settling them on the table. 'All the rest were a load of . . . well, you worked with Dad,' she said, glancing towards the baby. 'You can fill the blanks.'

Danny could indeed.

They made small talk – never Danny's strong point – and he told her about his life, realising how little he'd done in the last eight years. She made the usual comments: so lucky to live in Spain, you're not very tanned. Denise got up to make more tea. Danny stopped her.

'Do you still have your dad's notebooks, Dee? The notebooks he kept from *The Bugle*?'

Her nostrils flared momentarily. She took two deep breaths then nodded. 'I thought about throwing them out. But his whole life was contained in them. There's a box full of them up in the loft. You're probably the only one can make any sense of them.'

It wasn't so much a loft, more a triangular crawl space formed by the property's peaked roof. It was stuffed full of junk; a plastic Christmas tree, a doll's house, tinsel, abandoned toys. Mercifully, the box was near the front.

As Danny removed the lid, Ray Taylor's spirit rose to greet him: stale cigarette smoke, cheap, pungent aftershave.

There were dozens of notebooks inside, all of the same type: A5, spiral bound, blue cover, and all methodically labelled and dated. The dates were the only things legible to the untrained eye; the rest was filled with Ray's shorthand. Taylor was old school on that count; he'd been dismissive of dictaphones – they were bulky things back in the day – and contemptuous of any journalist unable to keep pace with 120 words a minute.

Taylor had tossed Danny one of those same blue spiral notebooks on his very first day. 'Date. Top of the page. Every day. Without fail. You get called to testify in a court case, those'll be evidence. There's enough think journos scum without you go in with messy notebooks.'

It remained a constant source of fascination to Danny how someone who wrote such accomplished prose could mangle spoken English to such an extent. Perhaps it was the Capstan full strength permanently clamped between his lips; words came in breaths between puffs, Ray's head constantly weaving to keep the smoke from his eyes.

Danny was glad of those dates now. He looked through the notebooks until he found the one relating to the first Scarecrow murder. The notebook was packed with information, a master class in how to cover a major murder story in five or six pages of A5 notepad. There were details of interviews with police officers and eyewitnesses, a complete breakdown of the victim's last known movements, contact details for the dead man's family; every scrap of information Taylor had been able to beg, borrow or steal, all neatly written down.

There was one other notebook at the bottom of the box, one with a yellow cover. This had no dates. Or rather, it was filled with dates, but wasn't dated at the top of each page. As Danny read the shorthand transcriptions, he realised that the notebook related exclusively to the Scarecrow enquiry.

'How are you getting on, Danny?'

The voice made him jump. Denise was below, cradling her child. Did he want more tea?

'I'm fine, thanks. Actually, I wanted to ask a favour.'

Denise smiled the way women do when they second guess a man. 'Take as many of the notebooks as you want, Danny. You're the only one can make sense of them. Also, I think Dad would have wanted you to have them.'

Danny took all the blue notebooks relating to the period of the Scarecrow enquiry and the one with the yellow cover. He climbed down from the loft. Denise was waiting for him, her face serious now. 'You don't blame yourself, do you, Danny?'

'Of course not. Why would I?' Danny felt his face freeze into the awkward neutral non-expression unprepared lies always provoke.

'It's just . . . well, after all that stuff you said at the funeral. About Dad's phone call. And then two weeks later you were gone. You dropped the job at the paper and disappeared to Spain.' They were at the front door now. 'It wasn't your fault, Danny. You were like a son to him. Dad would never have blamed you.'

Danny smiled at her, then turned quickly to hide the tears welling in his eyes.

He wished he could believe her.

2

He spent the rest of the day buried in Ray Taylor's notebooks.

Danny remembered Taylor being preoccupied with the Scarecrow enquiry, but hadn't realised the extent of his obsession. Judging by the yellow notebook, Taylor had gone on investigating the matter long after Ishmael Vertanness was caught and sentenced. There were numerous references in the notebook to the killer's incarceration, attempts to contact the psychiatric team in charge of his care, attempts to delve into Vertanness's background.

On the later pages, Taylor's attention had turned to another set of murders that were committed between 1998 and 1999. These were the Cross-Border Killings, so named because they were perpetrated in the Scottish / English border country. Danny remembered them vaguely. They exhibited striking similarities to the Vertanness case. Male prostitutes had been the targets, their bodies mutilated by the killer, their faces daubed with make-up. The killer had struck three times but disappeared after a witness spotted him at the scene of his last crime. The witness had provided a detailed photofit. Police never caught him. With Ishmael Vertanness incarcerated, the murders were attributed to a copycat killer.

Two words were repeated on a number of different pages throughout the yellow notebook, always written together in long hand, always circled.

DOROTHY????

ORSON????

Danny flicked through the blue notebooks. There was no mention of the two words in the reports of the investigation. It was obviously some connection Taylor had made afterwards. Why would he have continued delving? Vertanness had never admitted to the Scarecrow killings, but the evidence against him was watertight. Serologists could place him at all five killings through blood, saliva and semen. Three witnesses had picked Vertanness out of a line-up and identified him as the driver of the white van seen at two of the crimes. Had Taylor thought Vertanness was somehow implicated in the Cross-Border Killings?

Dorothy.

Orson.

Danny pondered the two words. The mother of the second victim was named Dorothy Knowles, but Taylor had not highlighted her name in any way. As for Orson, only one name came to mind: Orson Welles. The notes contained no clue as to what relevance the words had to the rest of the text. Were they some sort of codename? On one page, arrows came away from the names leading to a shorthand message: contact statement reader/Scarecrow.

So, Taylor had wanted to contact the statement reader from the Scarecrow enquiry. The words stirred a memory; Danny and Taylor sitting in a car opposite Fleet police station, watching the entrance hall taken over by the chaos that only a media pack from the nationals could cause.

'All them wankers will be pestering the SIO and getting nowhere. Why's that, do you think?' Taylor said.

'Because a senior investigating officer directs a murder enquiry and will therefore be up to his or her eyeballs.'

Taylor blew a smoke ring by way of commendation; Danny had remembered what the initials meant. 'Exactly. The SIO chooses the direction of an investigation, decides which bits are worth following, decides where the teams of detectives will start knocking on doors. But all the information that comes in flows through one person: the statement reader.'

'Sort of like a drain in a sewer?'

It was the first time Danny heard Taylor laugh; it was a dry, hoarse sound somewhere between a wheeze and a cough. 'Yeah, something like that. That's who we're going to speak to. His name's –'

And that was where Danny's memory hit a brick wall. He could remember all the trivia – the time of day, the cold wind, the beeps and shouts as television vans tried to park; he could even hear the soft patter of rain falling on the car roof. He just couldn't hear the man's name. He flicked back through the notebooks. The name would be there somewhere. Only the once though: Taylor prided himself on the accuracy and power of his memory. That was another thing that intrigued Danny about DOROTHY/ORSON; it must have been something significant for Taylor to have written it down three times.

He flicked through the pages that recorded the beginning of the investigation. Here it was. SIO: Detective Chief Superintendent Phillip France. Statement Reader: DS Harry O'Byrne. Harry O'Byrne wouldn't have been stationed in Fleet. The incident room had been set up in Fleet, but the actual team was drawn in from all over the place. Someone must know where he was, though.

If Ray Taylor had wanted to speak to O'Byrne, so did Danny now.

First, he tried the obvious. He Googled the name, did a Facebook search. There were dozens of Harry O'Byrnes, but none whose profile Danny recognised. This Harry O'Byrne was obviously one of the few humans left on the planet without a Facebook account. He and Danny already had something in common.

Fleet police station was a hundred yards from the pub where Danny was staying. Eight years ago he'd known by name every cop's face that haunted the place. How many would still be working there now? An unfamiliar desk sergeant looked up as Danny walked in out of the rain. 'Help you, sir?'

'DC Wickes around?'

He shook his head.

'DS Ronald Walton?'

Another shake of the head, this time accompanied by a frown. 'Neither of them work here anymore. Can I ask who you are?'

Danny showed his press card. 'I'm trying to find a DS O'Byrne.'

'Never heard of him.'

Danny explained he needed to contact O'Byrne. The desk sergeant wrote the details down but Danny left the station convinced that the note was already in the bin. He phoned Hampshire police's press department, said he wanted to know where DS O'Byrne was currently stationed.

'That's not information we can give you.'

'Can you pass a message on to DS O'Byrne, then?'

'He no longer serves on the force.'

'Do you have a contact number then?'

'That's not information we can give you.'

He went back to the pub, ordered a pint. He was on holiday, he reminded himself.

Except that he wasn't. Journalists never were. Not good ones, anyway. There was always one more question to be answered, one more doubt to be removed. It was the price you paid for making disbelief a primary professional quality. Ray Taylor had been on to something. Danny had never known the man's instinct to fail him. Danny would find out what. He owed the poor sod that much.

Not yet, though. Danny enjoyed the pint in a way made him want at least another four, then perhaps a few double Jamesons to round off the day. He rose with the full intention of putting his plan into action, but found himself instead placing the empty glass on the bar and leaving the pub.

He'd go for a walk, he decided.

Must be an age thing, Danny thought, heading out into the drizzle.

3

He walked without any real aim. This was a Fleet he recognised; wet but not cold, the cars hissing by, shop lights glistening on the pavement as evening fell. He sheltered beneath a tree to send an SMS to his mother saying he'd arrived safely.

Adriana Sanchez had caught him twenty minutes before he was due to leave in his taxi for the airport. That was typical of her. Under normal circumstances, she wouldn't have surfaced before midday, but the one time Danny wanted her to be soundly asleep she was up with the larks.

'But where are you going?' she said, noticing the luggage. 'Oh, please don't say it was because of last night. Don't say I've forced you out of your own house.'

That was precisely the reason Danny had wanted to avoid her; hangover-induced contrition was the last thing he needed.

It was exactly what he got though.

It took his mother a heartbeat to transform into a fussy, flustered Spanish matriarch, insisting on making him coffee and would he be able to get something to eat on the plane and when would he be back and please don't leave on my account . . .

And then the tears.

Danny had ended up apologising to *her* while the taxi driver beeped his horn outside.

The rain was stopping now. Danny walked along Fleet high street, noting the number of vacant lots there. It wasn't quite the commercial apocalypse he'd read about, but you could see that shops were struggling. The crisis didn't seem to have hit as hard in England, though. Christ, in Almeria the queues outside the unemployment offices started two hours before they opened.

Danny stopped on a bench and phoned Sureste News's office. Two days away and Danny was already getting antsy about what information he was missing.

Niall, the newspaper's cub reporter, answered. 'Aren't you supposed to be on holiday, Danny?'

'I am. I'm in England.'

'In England?' Niall scoffed. 'I'll ask again: aren't you supposed to be on holiday?'

'Listen, Niall, what's the score with the Hackers? Any news?'

'The police arrested all three of them, held them all night for questioning. And they've got an APB out on Alan Reade. His photo's all over the local Spanish press today. The Spanish media are pushing the angle that he's the killer. At least of the body found at his house.'

'Can you email the mugshot to me?'

'Sure. The police are also going round checking on other houses built by Apache Construction. Fouldes added a piece to the website inviting people to phone in if they were clients of Apache Construction. We've had half-a-dozen phone calls already. People are scared witless they might be living with corpses stuck in their walls.'

'Make sure you forward the info to the police. You can use it as a bargaining – '

'Way ahead of you, Danny. And, yes, that's precisely what Fouldes has been doing. Seems the bit with the immigrant workers was the least of the Hackers' worries. Word on the street is loads of their actual building work wasn't going through the books. They were charging people in pounds, getting stuff paid into English bank accounts – all sorts of fiddles playing both sides off against the middle. They're in deep *caca*, financially speaking. It's just a question of who gets to them first: the UK tax office or the Spanish one.'

'Have the police arrested the *gestor*?'

'No idea.'

'Find out. Have a sniff round at the Hackers' yard. The *gestor* might be there. A word of warning, though. Don't go near the bloody dogs. They're worse than the owners.'

As a rule, Niall shied from tough assignments. His voice became nervous. 'Dogs?'

'I think my signal's going, mate. You're really break . . . up. Niall? Niall?'

Danny hissed into the phone for good measure, then hung up. After that, he walked, revisiting childhood haunts, pubs he'd drunk in. Without realising it, he found himself approaching the street he'd grown up in. He stood a while outside the red brick house the family had rented for more than four decades. Hands in pockets, Danny tried to calculate how much the three-bedroom semi-detached was worth. His grandparents had come to England in 1937. Danny had handed the keys over in 2002, when he left for Spain. Forty-five years of rent. Christ, they must have paid for the property ten times over.

His grandparents had lost everything – business, house, family – when they fled Spain, the victims of Republican repression in the city of Malaga during the early part of the civil war. The *abuela* had insisted on paying for rented accommodation for the rest of her life. 'You never know when disaster may strike,' she'd said. 'It comes like lightning from a clear sky. Never put down roots, Daniel. Never.'

Danny's moving out at nineteen had been the greatest trauma of her life. It was every Spanish woman's nature to fuss and fret about her relations, but women of the *abuela's* generation saw worrying as their principal role in life. Where would he eat? What would he eat? How would he clean his clothes? Who were these people he was going to share a house with? Would they rob him?

She tried everything to bring him back; bribery, coercion, emotional blackmail, badgering, often all at the same time. She cooked all his favourite meals. That was a tough one to resist. Food-wise, Danny enjoyed his roasts and bacon butties as much as the next man, but British cuisine couldn't compare with the Spanish. The *abuela* had spoiled him for months: empanada, paella, huge salads, fried fish, thick, strong coffee.

The downside to Spanish cuisine was that it took so bloody long to eat; lunch was the cornerstone of Spanish family life, something of vital importance, something requiring time and tranquillity. The notion of a midday sandwich on the run was anathema to the Spanish, especially for ones of the *abuela's* generation. 'Why is everybody always in so much of a rush in this country?' she used to say.

In the end, the mild stroke she had suffered brought Danny back. Friends had teased him when, now in his early twenties, he began living with his grandmother again. But in that respect, too, he was solidly Spanish. The *abuela* had cared for him as a child; when old age crippled her, it was his turn to care for her, cooking, cleaning, keeping her company. And then she was gone. Twenty-one years old, two months into his new journalistic career and he found himself alone. Adriana Sanchez, already based in New York, sent a wreath and left the rest to Danny.

It was the first time he realised what a fragile thing his family life was, had always been; a father he'd never met, an itinerant mother flitting back and forth and a barely-remembered grandfather. The *abuela* was the only constant. And she was gone. He had no one. The solitude had seemed too immense to bear.

He looked at his reflection in the living-room window of his former house.. He'd been sitting there the day after the *abuela's* death, fighting back tears, thinking bleak thoughts, when the knock sounded at the door: Ray Taylor. And a bottle of whisky.

'I thought you might need someone to talk to.'

It was the only time that Danny ever saw the man drink. They sat in the living room and drank the whole bottle neat, chain-smoking, Taylor silent but attentive. They hardly said a word, but Danny remembered it as one of the few times he'd ever felt he'd really communicated with someone.

'How did you know?' Danny said, when the bottle was empty and he was wobbling towards the door to show Taylor out.

'We're reporters, Danny. It's our job to know.'

And with that he was gone, back to work, the collar of his leather jacket pulled up against the wind. It was only as Taylor turned the corner that Danny realised the significance of what he'd just said: *we're; our*.

Tears had come then. Danny wasn't alone, after all.

And how did you repay him?

The thought came with sudden, spiteful force. The day seemed to darken in a moment. He'd known that this would happen if he came back. The guilt had always been there, lurking at the edges of his mind. In Spain it had been dissipated; here, it was focused. It had something to feed on.

Danny. I need to talk.

Those were Ray Taylor's last words. Danny knew. He'd checked. Checked with the diligence only a professional reporter driven wild by grief and desperation could muster. Danny had spoken to everyone, every fucking member of staff, every contact, every person he could think of that Taylor might have phoned.

Nothing.

Taylor had phoned him and him alone. He'd reached out and what had Danny said? Sorry, Ray, bit busy. Can I call you back, Ray? Speak tomorrow, Ray.

Except that, at that precise moment, there hadn't been any more tomorrows in Ray Taylor's life.

Denise was wrong. It *was* his fault. It had always been his fault.

Bollocks, he decided. He was going to get pissed. English pissed; eight pints then on to a curry house. Anything to numb the pain.

He crossed the road without looking. Or rather, he looked but in the wrong direction, a tough habit to break after eight years in Spain. A car screeched to a halt, beeped. Danny waved his hand by way of apology, turned when he heard the window lowering. Part of him was glad; he was spoiling for an argument.

Angry words died on his lips when he saw the driver was a woman. She brushed dark hair away from her glasses, stared at him.

Then she said, 'That *is* you, isn't it? Danny Sanchez from Form VIII?'

4

He spread the first of the newspapers wide.

So, it was true. They'd found his last piece of work, the one at Reade's house. He made sure his face betrayed nothing as he read. Faces were easy to control. You could paint faces, paint them anyway you wanted. No one knew that better than he did. He'd made his life's work from painting people's faces, painting them the fucking faces they deserved.

*He fought sudden anger. His face would crack. They'd learn his secret. Caution and patience. And change. Adapt. No one must ever suspect who he really was inside, w*hat *he really was. People looked at him but they never saw a man. That was why he did his work. Those pricks soon learned who he was.*

Shoe's on the other foot, now. Shoe's on the other foot, Mamá, you cunt.

CUNT.

He stood, screamed in rage, kicked at the hollow bedroom door: once, twice, three times; kicked until a hole appeared in the flimsy surface.

No. This was no good.

He breathed deeply, smoothed ripples of emotion from his face, swallowed the ball of anger. He was nervous. First the body of the old thing; now evidence of his work with the new. He hadn't done this work for years and now after one single job they'd already found the body. It had taken him so long to find a suitable replacement, to bend it into shape. Would they know?

Would they realise?

He read the Spanish newspapers first. They hadn't seen. Good. They hadn't seen the signs. Blood throbbed in his crotch. Nobody knew to read the writing. He wrote his message so clearly and the dumb bastards never got it. Because the writing wasn't always there.

That was good. It had always been a risk since both damned houses had been finished. That was bad luck. He'd covered his tracks well. He always did. That was why he'd disposed of the old thing, found a new one. Caution and patience.

He turned to the English newspapers. They were all the same. They hadn't made the connection, either.

Except one.

His hands shook as he read the front page story; it mentioned his work in the old country. He could have howled. Instead, he walked to the tailor's dummy, wiped its face clean then began daubing the greasepaint.

Mamá.

Mamá.

Mamá.

He carved the word three times into the dummy's chest with the Stanley knife, then wiped lipstick into the gouges. It looked almost real: sticky smears of red. He was calmer now.

But it was too close. How had that fucking stupid paper got so close to the truth? He walked out on to his balcony, looked down at the unfinished house below, thought about its secrets. Spring sun warmed his skin. Spain had made him lazy. He'd found himself a niche here, a comfortable groove, but forgotten the golden rule: The Work Came Before EVERYTHING.

It was time to move on. Again. His hand quivered as he stared at the article. The paper had ruined everything. A decade of quiet labour, gone in a single sentence.

It was time to move on, yes. But he would leave a reminder to anyone who sought to follow him. He'd make sure they paid. It would be something special. Something sticky, wet and red.

Something like Mamá's cat.

5

Sunday, April 4th, 2010

For the first time in months, Danny Sanchez woke slowly, prising himself from sleep's sticky clutch, blinking and yawning.

He'd drunk too much. That was the first thought as his system came back online. All the signs were there: the numbness around his frontal lobes, the gloopy ache in the back of his head; his mouth was filled with a bitter, sicky taste no amount of swallowing could rid him of. He raised his head, saw an unfamiliar bedroom. A paisley dress hung from the back of a chair.

The next two thoughts occurred simultaneously.

This is not my room; I'm not wearing anything.

Neither was the woman next to him. She shifted her weight, snuggling her head down into the pillow. Danny stared at her long, dark hair, lower jaw dangling stupidly. Vague memories began to stir: a drunken clinch in a pub car park, a taxi ride somewhere, sudden passion as soon as the front door closed. Christ, what was her name? It was a girl he'd gone to school with. He could see her face now, leaning out of the car window in front of the *abuela's* house asking if it really was him, little Danny Sanchez from Form VIII.

The floodgates of memory were opening. They'd chatted in the street after she nearly ran him over, arranged to meet up for a drink. One drink had quickly become two and then four; inhibition-freed admissions of schoolroom crushes followed as reunion became flirtation and then seduction.

Was that true? Had he had a crush on her? If he had, it certainly wasn't helping him recall her name. He could remember other things now, though. Christ, but he'd laid it on thick for her, done his hard-bitten journo act, shown off speaking Spanish, writing shorthand. The picture he'd painted of his professional activities, a Pulitzer nomination would be only a matter of time.

That was the taste he couldn't get rid of; like his nose, the Sanchez palate was extremely sensitive to bullshit, especially when self-produced.

He sat up slowly, swung his legs out of bed, trying not to disturb her. Where were his clothes? His boxer shorts dangled from the dresser. Nothing else was visible.

He went out to the landing and gripped the banister as the pain in his head slopped forward, his brain like an acidic egg yolk, and he nearly stumbled. Clothes, both his and hers, lay strewn across the landing and down the stairs leading into the front room. He followed the trail, wincing as the stairs creaked beneath his weight. He could still taste her lipstick on his mouth, smell her perfume on his skin. He remembered nothing about the sex, though.

He managed to find everything bar his socks. He didn't dress, though. He was unsure what to do. He took the travel toothbrush and toothpaste he carried with him everywhere and brushed his teeth in the kitchen sink, then ran his head under the cold tap. It didn't make him feel any better. He shook his head dry, stared at his two options: kettle or front door.

It had been such a long time since he'd been in this situation. Honour dictated that he shouldn't simply slip away. But he couldn't go upstairs again without knowing her name. He tiptoed through the house, looking for something that might help him.

A laminated pass card on a length of blue ribbon came to his rescue: Marsha Constance. That was it. She'd sat opposite him in Physics, a quiet but friendly girl. He took a good look at the photo on the card. She was pretty in a homely sort of way; big-boned was the polite way to describe her build. Danny favoured no particular type; female companionship had been far too infrequent for a pattern ever to have emerged. Marsha seemed to share one thing in common with previous partners in that she looked good without much make-up.

Make-up was the wrong thing to think about in his condition. An unpleasant image of the Alan Reade corpse popped like a bubble on the surface of his consciousness. He fought nausea, drank a glass of water. Then his eyes were drawn to the logo on the pass card: Surrey constabulary.

Another sluice gate of memory opened.

Marsha worked for the police as a call taker, answering 999 calls, assessing the severity of emergencies, reporting them to the correct police unit. He remembered the early parts of their conversation now; not all of it had been mere flirtation. He could see Marsha's face as she answered his question: 'Yes, a friend of mine works in HR. We've got all the data there on police personnel.'

Including the telephone numbers and addresses of ex-coppers.

Christ, was that why he'd slept with her?

He searched his memory, decided no. The evening remained a blur, but there was a pleasant, roseate edge to the fog, the warmth that only comes from mutual attraction. It had been obvious from the start of the evening. Besides, the idea of his seducing anyone for information was as laughable as it was unlikely.

He made two cups of tea, headed back upstairs. Marsha was sitting upright in the bed, wearing pyjamas now. A joss stick burned in a holder beside the bed.

'When I heard you creeping down the stairs, I thought you were about to run out on me.'

'As if.'

He felt ridiculous, barefoot in his boxer shorts, the cold seeping up from the wooden floorboards. He climbed back into bed. She blew on her tea. Nervousness came off her in waves.

'Just so you know, I don't do this sort of thing on a regular basis.'

It took a moment for Danny to realise what she meant. 'No, neither do I.'

She raised a dubious eyebrow. 'Come off it, after what you told me about all the big stories you cover, you must get to meet loads of women.'

Danny sluiced tea around in his mouth; the foul taste had returned, sudden and strong. They sat, staring at the foot of the bed. She blew on her tea again, sipped it. Her nose wrinkled.

'For future reference, I take sugar in tea.'

'I'll get you some.'

'It doesn't matter.'

Danny swung his feet back into the bed, disappointed at not having another excuse to leave the room. The awkwardness between them was thickening now into something almost tangible. She had mentioned "future reference". The question had been subtly posed; would there be another time? It was obviously what she was thinking. When he said nothing she turned to him.

'Do you regret last night, Danny?'

'Of course not.'

At least he didn't have to lie: how could he regret something he couldn't remember?

'So . . .' – the pause she left seemed endless – 'where do we stand?'

Danny slapped the mattress. 'I'm quite comfy sat right here.'

A weak effort at puncturing the tension, rewarded by the weakest of smiles. A thousand things were going through

Danny's mind. This was why he didn't do relationships. They were so much bloody effort.

She blew on her tea. 'Shall we see each other again?' Her tone was perfectly measured, neither enquiry nor suggestion.

'If you like.'

'Meaning you're not really bothered?'

That was another thing Danny was now remembering about relationships; women were so bloody good at them. He was floundering, out of his depth.

'Meaning that if you would do me the honour of allowing me to take you out for another evening, I would be delighted.' He surprised himself when, after the words were said, he found he actually meant them.

She placed a hand on his, holding his gaze. Her smile was genuine now. 'That's the sweetest thing anyone's said to me in a long while.'

'Let's not drink so much next time, though, eh? I've got a bastard behind the eyes.'

She swung her legs out of bed. 'I'll get you some aspirin.'

He had her on side. It was now or never. He squeezed her hand.

'Listen, Marsha, before you go, I need to ask a favour . . .'

6

'What is it, Niall?'

Sureste News's cub reporter stood in the doorway of William Fouldes's office.

'There's some woman on the phone, wants to speak to Danny.'

'Which is a physical impossibility as, according to you, Sanchez is currently sunning himself in the UK.'

'Yes, I know but –'

'Meaning the only logical response was to give her that information, hang up and not bother me. It's bad enough having to work on a Sunday without being bothered with inane calls.'

'But she's calling from *The Sunday Times*.'

For the first time Fouldes looked up from his computer screen. 'The Sunday Times? Did she ask for Sanchez by name?'

'No. She said she wanted to speak to the journalist who wrote the piece on the two bodies.'

'Put her through. And close the door.'

Fouldes's phone beeped.

'Hello, my name is Gillian Wood, of *The Sunday Times*.'

'Hello, Gillian. William Fouldes, here, editor, *Sureste News*. I believe you wanted to speak to me.'

'Did you write the article that appeared on the murders? It just said "staff reporter" on the article.'

'Yes, we normally do that when I write stuff. Doesn't do to show how short-staffed we are.' Even with the door closed, the lie made Fouldes's voice drop.

'It's a good article. You should be proud. One question, though: how did you make the link with the murders in Britain? That's quite a bold assertion. I take it you're referring to the Scarecrow enquiry? Or the Cross Border Killings?'

Damn it. How had Sanchez made the link? For a moment, Fouldes was stumped. Only for a moment, though; a decade on Fleet Street had made dissimulation second nature to him.

'You know I can't reveal my sources, Gillian.'

Her voice lowered, became playful. 'You have sources, do you, William? And how would I persuade you to share those sources with me?'

Fouldes joined the game. 'Oh, I'm sure we can work something out. The trouble is, you're so far away.'

'Perhaps I'm nearer than you think.'

Fouldes looked at the number on the screen. He felt a flush of blood to his crotch as he noticed the number had the 950 prefix; she was calling from Almería.

'I see you're here already, Gillian.'

'You're good, William. One last question. Are you sending anyone to follow the story up in England? Have a try at speaking to Ishamel Vertanness, perhaps?'

'I might be. But I really think we should meet up, discuss all this over a drink. I'd love to meet – '

'Oh, you'll be meeting me, William, sooner or later. Ciao.'

The phone went dead. *She fancies herself the crafty one, does she*? Fouldes thought. Well, two could play at that. He knew people at *The Sunday Times*. He'd get her mobile number. Perhaps even find out which hotel she was staying at.

Fifteen minutes later William Fouldes sat chewing his lip. He'd phoned every person he could think of at the paper; acquaintances, old colleagues, even people he considered enemies. They'd all said the same thing; there was no Gillian Wood at *The Sunday Times*.

7

Lucky for Danny that Marsha had spent so long blowing on her tea; it would have scalded him otherwise.

Lucky, too, he'd already gathered his clothes, as Marsha gave him precious little time to do so as she chased him from the house. 'You rotten bloody bastard. I knew straight away when you said you were a journalist not to trust you. You think sleeping with me means I'll get you someone's address? Honestly, the crap I've had to put up with from men.' Her tearful cries still rang in his ears.

The cries had obviously rung in the ears of her neighbours as well; an elderly woman peered at Danny from the bay window of her lounge as he stood in Marsha's garden pulling his trousers on and surveying the damage. He was missing his socks, his hair was soaked with tea and he'd no idea where he was. Apart from that, he was fine.

He looked along the street of terraced Victorian houses. It was filled with cars. The houses had small gardens in front of them. Marsha's had a neatly kept row of herbs and flowers. He racked his brain, trying to remember where Marsha had directed the taxi the night before. He could remember tipping the bloke, but the destination remained a mystery.

A family emerged from the house opposite. The father instinctively drew his children closer as he noted the sockless, wild-haired apparition across the road now pulling on his desert boots.

'Excuse me,' Danny said, breaking out his best smile. 'Could you tell me where I am?'

North Camp. That wasn't too bad. He could get the train back to Fleet from Farnborough. Or call a taxi. He patted his pockets, then searched his bag, desperation growing. He couldn't call a taxi.

No mobile.

Bollocks.

He stared at Marsha's front door. Something smashed inside. Now wasn't the time to go back. There was a newsagent at the end of the road. Danny bought Lucozade and sandwiches, ate them sitting on a bench while he decided what to do. There was nothing for it but to brave her wrath again. He needed that mobile; it had years of contact numbers stored in it. He went back to the newsagent and bought a card, a well-wisher's one with flowers on the front; there wasn't anything else appropriate.

Marsha,

Deeply sorry for misunderstanding this morning. Things happened so fast I really didn't have a chance to make myself clear. I'm sure if you reflect on the shortcomings of my physical appearance you'll realise seduction is not a primary weapon in my arsenal of journalistic techniques. Part of the job is to seize opportunities as soon as they arise – this one I mistimed, primarily because my romantic technique is so rusty. Make of this card what you will but please let me buy you lunch by way of an apology. I'll wait for you at The Swan at one-thirty.

Danny

He walked back to her house, heard the sound of a hoover inside. He popped the card through the door, knocked once, then walked away fast. It was nearly midday. He stopped at the end of the road, assessing his options.

Balls to it, he'd go to the pub now, have a hair of the dog.

It couldn't make him feel any worse.

~

Marsha arrived a quarter of an hour early. She tossed his mobile on the table.

'I know this is the only reason you put that card through my door. When I read it I phoned to tell you to bugger off. Then I heard the Star Wars theme tune coming from inside the house and the penny dropped.'

'I gave you my number, then?'

'Don't you remember?' She lowered her voice to a rough approximation of Danny's. '"We must get together again before I leave, Marsha." "Here's my number, Marsha." "Don't forget the international code, Marsha." I was tempted to smash the bloody thing. Lucky for you, I'm a Star Wars fan, too.'

'Where was the phone?'

'Between the cushions on the sofa. It must have fallen out of your pocket when we . . .' Her voice failed and she blushed.

'Take a seat, please. Let me get you a drink.'

She hesitated before sitting down. Her hands remained in her pockets. 'I'll have a lime and soda, please.'

'Want to keep your wits about you?'

'Yes.' A two-beat pause. 'And I have work later.'

Danny got the drinks, steered the conversation away from her professional capacities. He'd seen her frown at mention of work. They made chit chat. Danny felt better now, in control. It wasn't only the beers he'd drunk. They were on his territory now. This he could do – put people at their ease, talk to them. They ordered food. Danny paid. She was beginning to thaw.

'Look me in the eye and say you didn't sleep with me because you want this policeman's address,' she said finally.

'Cross my heart.'

She looked deeply into his eyes as he spoke. He held her gaze.

'I was lying when I said I didn't like your card. It made me laugh, actually. I'm sorry, I think I threw myself at you last night.'

'As long as you don't throw anything else at me, consider yourself forgiven. To be honest, I don't really remember much. I mean, apart from the good bits,' he said, when her frown returned.

'It's been a while for me, too. I'm divorced. I think I mentioned that last night. He ran off with a younger, slimmer model.' Her voice was resonant with anger. 'What's your story?'

They spoke. The thaw continued. They finished lunch. She crossed her knife and fork on her plate, dabbed her mouth with a napkin. 'Right, you've bought me lunch. Apology accepted. Now, tell me about this DS O'Byrne? Why do you want to contact him?'

'Do you remember the Scarecrow enquiry?'

'Are you serious?'

It was a stupid question. The whole area had been in turmoil for months after the murders began, had reached fever pitch as each fresh body appeared. School gates were crowded with cars waiting to pick up pupils, the town streets empty of children well before dark. National newspapers had done their bit, stirring the public into afrenzy. It hadn't taken long for fear to give way to anger; someone set fire to an old man's house because he was rumoured to ogle schoolgirls on their way home. A young man was found beaten half conscious, the word 'pervert' written across his forehead in marker pen.

Danny leant across the table, trying to impress upon her the urgency of his request. 'O'Byrne was the statement reader on the police investigation for the Scarecrow enquiry. He's not on the force any longer, though. I need to speak to him.'

'Why?'

'I worked on the story at the time. And now something similar has occurred in Spain.'

She wasn't convinced. It was time for the heavy guns. Danny slipped out Paco Pino's photo of the body inside the wall at Alan Reade's house. Marsha cried out when she realised what it was. People in the pub turned to look. Danny tucked the photo back inside his bag.

'It's the same, Marsha. Just the way the bodies were left in the Scarecrow murders.'

'But they caught the killer. I remember seeing it on the news. Someone Vertanness. He's in Deepmere. They proved it was him.'

'I know. That's why I need to contact Harry O'Byrne. As statement reader, the whole investigation will have gone through him. I need to pick his brains. But no one is going to give out an ex-copper's address to a member of the public.'

She thought about it. 'It would be totally unprofessional of me. Why don't you just go to the police and tell them what you think is happening?'

'Because this is my story. Believe it or not, some people in the police sell information to newspapers. A word in the wrong ear and it'll be front page of the nationals in a matter of days. Besides, it could be nothing. Perhaps some nut read about the Scarecrow enquiry and decided to emulate it.'

They parted awkwardly. Danny forgot where he was and tried to blow two air kisses as he would have in Spain. Marsha recoiled momentarily, then tried to kiss him on the mouth just as Danny was apologising. He tried to return the kiss but it was too late. 'I've got to get to work in Guildford now. I'll see what I can do.'

Her face was red and flustered as she hurried away.

Danny watched her go, wondering who the hell started the rumour Spaniards were good with women. Must have been the same one persuaded the world the English were punctual and organised, he decided, as he downed the rest of his beer.

8

There was nothing for it but to wait. Marsha would either help him or she wouldn't.

He phoned the mental health trust in charge of Deepmere hospital, spoke to the press officer. No, she said in a way that sounded like she thought Danny was the one in need of mental health care, it would definitely *not* be possible for a member of the press to speak to a patient as severely disturbed as Ishmael Vertanness. Nor would members of his psychiatric team be permitted to discuss his case.

No surprises there. Sometimes you had to risk making a fool of yourself just to cross off the most obvious lines of enquiry. Danny had developed a thick skin over the years.

He walked along the Farnborough road to the station, caught the train back to Fleet, walked round the pond and watched trains rumble past on the nearby tracks. The beers had cured his hangover, but he didn't want to drink more and risk having another one tomorrow. He found himself checking his phone every five minutes, worried that he might have missed a call. He walked back to the pub, checked his email. His inbox was crowded with the usual nonsense: spam adverts for Viagra, emails inviting him to press conferences. He deleted the lot.

That just left the email from Niall.

Here's that mugshot you asked for. I went to check on the Hackers' place. No joy with finding the accountant. No sign of any dogs either – seems the Hackers' former cleaner has taken them in.

N.

Danny opened the attachment, trying to imagine what sort of person would volunteer to take in a pair of eight-stone rottweilers named Yorkshire and Ripper. The mug shot of Alan Reade filled his computer screen.

Danny knew instantly he'd seen the man's face before: gaunt, a faint scar across the upper lip, blonde hair swept back into a ponytail. It took him a moment to realise where, though – the cash point in Mojacar. He thought about the timing.

Christ, Alan Reade had Craig Thorndyke's cash card.

He blew air, reeling as he tried to fathom what the hell it all meant. Two dead bodies walled up in two different houses, one a copycat of a series of 1995 murders, the builder of the house cracked over the head with a hammer and now this: the owner of the house where the second body was hidden withdrawing money from Craig Thorndyke's bank account. He blew air again. Nothing made any sense. One thing was certain, though: Craig's parents needed to know.

Michael Thorndyke sounded less than enthusiastic about the call. 'I thought our business was concluded, Mr Sanchez.'

'What time did you say Craig's cash card was used?'

'07:36.'

'I think you'd better contact the Spanish police, Mr Thorndyke.'

'Why?'

'Because a man the police are seeking in connection with murder has your son's cash card.'

The pause lasted about three seconds. Then Thorndyke went berserk, demanding that Danny return to Spain, offering to pay for his ticket, threatening legal action when he refused. Danny tried to calm him but soon lost patience. 'When you've contacted the police, I'll be happy to make a statement by telephone.'

He hung up. Then he spent the next two hours hanging up. Thorndyke wouldn't stop ringing, but Danny couldn't turn the damn phone off because he was waiting for Marsha to call. In the end, he called the Spanish police himself, told them all he knew. They wanted to know when he'd be back in Spain. He said he didn't know.

Hours passed. Marsha wasn't going to phone. Christ. He'd done his best to impress upon her how important it was. He walked some more, bought dinner from a kebab shop – the final stage in his hangover cure – and went back to his room at the pub. The call caught him drifting off on his bed.

'I've got the details. Harry O'Byrne, lives in Newbury. At least that's the last known location we had for him when he took early retirement from the force in 2004.'

'And the address?'

'You do realise I'm risking my bloody career doing this, don't you?'

She was right. Danny had sounded pushy. 'OK, well, thanks, that's something for me to get started on.'

There were sounds of muffled conversation. When Marsha returned to the phone, she sounded out of breath. 'God, that was my supervisor. My heart's in my mouth here.'

'Thanks, Marsha. I really appreciate the help.'

'Wait, Danny.' A pause; a sigh. 'Osbourne Street. And that's all I can tell you.'

'I owe you a night out.'

'Yes, you bloody well do.'

9

Monday, April 5th, 2010

Next morning, Danny rose early and made the forty-minute drive to Newbury. Osbourne Street was on the town's outskirts. It was a long, winding road close to a school. Danny drove up and down it a couple of times, looking into gardens and front windows, hoping to recognise O'Byrne. He was a thin man with brown hair and a moustache, Danny remembered. At least, he had been fifteen years ago. God knows what he looked like now.

Lady Luck was not with him. He parked up to consider his options. He didn't much fancy knocking on doors at random, asking which house belonged to Harry O'Byrne. That was an easy way of bringing the police down on him. There was a newsagent two roads down from Osbourne Street. It would be worth a try.

A teenage girl stood behind the counter, flicking through a magazine and chewing gum.

'Hello,' Danny said. 'I'd like to settle the paper bill for O'Byrne, Osbourne Street.'

The girl pulled a ledger from beneath the counter and flipped it open, ran a lacquered nail down the page. 'Fourteen pounds fifty.'

Danny sucked air through his teeth. 'He didn't say it would be that much. This is Patrick O'Byrne at number 60, isn't it?'

The girl looked at the ledger. 'No, H. O'Byrne, number 82.' She was flicking through the pages of the ledger now, perplexed. 'We don't have any record of –'

But Danny was already on his way to the door. 'Don't worry, I'll sort it out with my friend and get him to come himself.'

Harry O'Byrne's house was the sort of neat, compact bungalow people bought to retire to – easy to clean, cheap to maintain, but with enough garden to be able to enjoy the sun. Not that the sun had bothered today. Danny pulled his coat tighter as he parked opposite the bungalow and stepped out of the warmth of his car.

Danny barely had to touch the waist-high gate before it swung open. The hinges were spotlessly clean. A sensible hatchback was parked in the car port, a Christian fish symbol stuck to the rear of the car. Danny knocked. He heard sounds of movement behind the door and someone looked through the spyhole. The door opened a fraction, chain on. A man's face appeared.

'How can I help?'

Not overtly unfriendly but far from welcoming. This was O'Byrne. Even if he hadn't recognised the man, Danny would have known him for an ex-copper. He'd spent so much of his life around police, he'd learned how to spot them: the self-assuredness, the firmness behind his words, the way O'Byrne looked at him, assessing who this unknown male on his doorstep was.

'I'd like to speak to you about a case you worked on in 1995.'

The door opened wider. 'The Scarecrow enquiry? Who are you?'

Danny handed him a copy of *Sureste News* and pointed at the front page. 'It's simpler if you read that. I'll take a walk around the block, come back in ten minutes.'

When Danny returned, O'Byrne invited him in. 'Shoes off, please.' The request didn't come as a surprise; not from a man who wore a tie inside his own home. Danny unlaced his desert boots, praying that he hadn't worn a pair of socks with holes in.

As it turned out, he hadn't worn a pair at all. O'Byrne's eyes flickered towards the odd socks – one black, one striped – and his head gave the faintest of nods, as if some previously-formed opinion of Danny had been confirmed.

O'Byrne was more or less as Danny remembered him fifteen years ago. And yet . . . something was missing. He'd seen it in journalists when they retired, too. A spark within them dulled. They missed the buzz, the sensation of being at the centre of things.

A woman appeared on the stairs, buttoning her coat. 'Harry, love, I thought I heard the door a mo . . . oh,' she said, seeing Danny.

Like her husband, Mrs O'Byrne was the picture of lower middle-class respectability. Danny could have picked her out as a policeman's wife even so; it was the eyes, which were prematurely aged, the deep wrinkles at the corners caused by too many late nights lying alone, worrying in the darkness. She did her best to smile. It was obvious that she was wondering who this stranger was whom her husband had invited into her home with such alacrity.

'This is Mr Sanchez, dear. We're just going through to the conservatory.'

O'Byrne's wife noticed Danny's socks, too. She winced. 'Shall I make some tea when I come back from Hilda's?'

'That would be lovely, dear.'

She nodded toward Danny. 'Pleased to meet you, Mr Sanchez.'

The words rang hollow. You learned to notice these things. She wasn't happy about Danny's being there.

O'Byrne took Danny through to a glass conservatory at the back of the house, left him there while he went in search of something. Danny had a couple of minutes alone to marvel at the perfectly symmetrical rows of tomato plants and lettuces in the garden, before O'Byrne returned with a cardboard file filled with documents.

'I knew you were a journalist as soon as I saw you,' he said. His tone of voice indicated it had not been a pleasant deduction . 'First of all, let's get the preliminaries done with. Anything I say is off-the-record unless I specifically give you permission to quote me – and even then I don't want my name mentioned. If I do grant permission to be quoted – something I doubt will happen – I am "a source that formerly served with the UK police". Are we clear on that?'

'Perfectly.'

O'Byrne held up a Dictaphone. 'Just to make sure, I'll be recording the whole conversation. Piss me about and we'll see each other in court.'

Cagey as only an ex-copper could be. Danny hoped the man's memory was as sharp as his savvy in handling the press.

'What did you make of the article?' Danny said.

'It's certainly interesting. But I fail to see what you want with me. I don't work for the police anymore.'

'You were the statement reader for the Scarecrow enquiry, though, correct?'

'I was one of them. It was a huge enquiry.'

'But you were there from the very beginning?'

A nod.

'I only want to ask your opinion.'

'Ask away.'

'Could the crimes be linked? I mean the killings carried out here and the recent murder in Spain.'

'How could they be? Ishmael Vertanness has been in Deepmere since 1995.'

'In relation to the Scarecrow enquiry, who or what was Dorothy?'

O'Byrne shifted in his seat. 'Where did you hear that?' His expression, alert from the start, was now wary.

'I was researching some notes another journalist made

about the case. The name Dorothy was mentioned a few times, always written in capitals – like it was a codename or something.'

O'Byrne's discomfort grew as he considered. 'I'll explain, but first I want you to be aware of the gallows humour that exists in police investigations of this nature. The worse the crime, the blacker the humour. It's a way of . . . letting off steam, I suppose.'

'I know all about it.'

'With cases like this we try to keep precise details of the crime secret. It's not simply a question of stopping panic from spreading; it helps when we come to interview suspects. If they reveal knowledge of the crime scene that hasn't been made public, it helps us pinpoint strong suspects. We only ever allowed the press to mention that Vertanness had emasculated his victims.'

'There was more?'

O'Byrne's eyes went somewhere else momentarily. 'Some bodies you can never get out of your mind.'

Danny nodded. He knew all about that, too. When O'Byrne spoke again, his throat was dry.

'Yes. In each case the mutilation was accompanied by a word carved into the flesh of the crotch, just about here.' He drew an imaginary horizontal line across the fly of his trousers.

'What did it say?'

'Toto.'

'Toto? Like the dog in the Wizard of Oz?'

'Precisely. And so it wasn't long before our killer was nicknamed Dorothy in the incident room.'

Danny had already guessed as much. 'What did it mean? Toto?'

'We never figured it out. We had a team investigating links with the book and film. And the band as well, scouring lyrics and song titles trying to find some hidden meaning. Obviously, when the second victim's mother was called Dorothy, the nickname was changed toute suite.'

'Why didn't this come out at the trial? I mean about the "Toto" word?'

'It did. Mention was made of the fact Vertanness had carved letters into the victim's flesh.'

'But not the specific word? The press would have picked up on it. Hell, the red tops would have had a field day with the Oz connection. Why was it kept secret?'

'That I'm not prepared to tell you.' Danny knew from O'Byrne's stubborn eyes and crossed arms that there was no point in pushing.

'Why call Vertanness the Scarecrow?'

'It was the Press who christened him that. Some reporters had already got wind of the Dorothy nickname – it was the Oz connection, I suppose. Plus a witness mentioned seeing a guy having hair all messed up and ruffled "like a scarecrow". It just stuck.'

'What about Orson? Who or what was he?'

For the first time O'Byrne looked fazed. His eyes bulged. 'How the . . . who told you about that?' he said, sounding angry now.

'Standing on the shoulders of giants, I'm afraid. Ray Taylor was my mentor.'

'Ray Taylor.' O'Byrne said slowly, as if exhaling smoke. 'There's a name I've not heard in a long while. He was a damn good reporter.'

'That's rare praise coming from an ex-policeman.'

'Coming from an ex-policeman, it's not praise at all. Taylor was a royal pain in the arse; always sniffing round where he shouldn't, asking awkward questions.' O'Byrne shifted in his seat. 'So, you worked with Ray, did you? I thought I recognised your face from somewhere. Do you still work locally?'

'I'll be happy to fill you in on my entire work history once you answer my question; who or what was Orson, Mr O'Byrne?' Danny recognised an attempt to change the subject when he heard one.

O'Byrne's hand strayed toward the file while he debated whether or not to open it.

'OK,' he said eventually, 'I'll explain about Orson. But I can't do that without showing you photos of the crime scenes.' O'Byrne paused with his hand on the cardboard folder. 'Have you had breakfast?'

Danny nodded.

'That's good. Because you won't want any lunch, I can assure you of that.'

10

O'Byrne opened the folder and laid a series of black and white photos on the table. 'These are Ishmael Vertanness's first four victims.'

Danny winced, eyes blinking, as if instinctively trying to shut out the images. They were all variations on the same grotesque theme: male bodies were hanging like butchered meat in a series of interior locations, their most intimate areas hacked and rent asunder. And there was always that face, that hideous feminine mask, eyes dark like bruises, lashes thick with mascara, lipstick smeared into sharp points.

Danny could take no more. He looked away.

O'Byrne noted his reaction. 'One of the poor sods who had to photograph this needed a year off to recuperate. A SOCO left the force altogether.'

'I didn't think police were allowed to take anything of an evidential nature away from the incident room?'

'They're not.' O'Byrne's eyes challenged Danny to probe further. 'There's one more I want to show you. Vertanness's fifth victim.'

He placed the final photograph in front of Danny.

The man's body lay face up amid leaves and mud, trousers and underpants clinging to one ankle, sweater pushed up to reveal his bare breast. It looked like he'd been savaged by a wild animal. A dark puddle lay beneath the jagged tear that ran horizontally across his throat; dozens of stab wounds covered his abdomen, ugly, vertical mouths in the white flesh. His penis and testicles were small pale shapes amid the pubic hair.

'Notice the difference?'

'Of course. There's no make-up. And he's not tied up. And the victim still has his genitals.'

O'Byrne was counting on his fingers. 'And the body's outside. And this cut across the throat. And the stab wounds. And this final man was a rent boy; the other four victims were all heterosexual. And there were about twelve other differences in the M.O. If it weren't for the fact Vertanness left body fluids all over him, we'd have thought it had been done by a completely different killer.'

O'Byrne indicated the photo of the first victim, the one Danny himself had seen in the pill box. 'Have a close look at the floor in there. What do you notice?'

Danny forced himself to look, feeling a faint pulse in his gut as he prepared to face his worst memory. Strangely, the reality was far more mundane than the horrors he had imagined. He saw nothing; there was nothing but the body. Nothing on the walls; nothing on the floor. It took him a moment to realise that was precisely what O'Byrne was referring to.

'The floor's been swept.'

'Yes, it has,' O'Byrne said. 'This is a pill box out in the woods. And yet inside there are no leaves, no empty cans, no broken bottles. Vertanness was a serologist's dream. He left body fluids all over the place; saliva, semen, blood. And we had hairs, fibres from his jumper. Forensically speaking, the guy had practically written his name down for us. It was only a matter of time. So why sweep the floor?'

'Perhaps he was trying to be careful.'

O'Byrne pointed to the photograph of the fifth victim. 'Does that look like the work of someone capable of being careful?'

Danny's eyes flickered toward the image. O'Byrne had a point.

'So what are you trying to say?'

'I've not finished yet. Killing number one in the pill box. At some point, Vertanness went outside and spent a considerable period of time sat on a tree stump twenty-two yards from the cabin.'

'How do you know?'

'A fingertip search of the area found seven cigarette butts by a tree stump, all belonging to the brand Vertanness smoked. DNA tests matched them to him.'

'Couldn't he have smoked them inside the cabin, then dumped them there?'

'No. He stubbed some of them out on the stump itself. Others had been extinguished by being twisted into the ground with his foot.' He made a swivelling motion with his slipper.

Danny did mental arithmetic: four to six minutes a cigarette. Say four. Vertanness would have been nervous. Even if he'd chain-smoked them, that was twenty-eight minutes.

'We estimate he was outside for a period of thirty-five minutes to an hour.'

'Couldn't he have gone back and forth during the killing?'

O'Byrne shook his head. 'The ground was wet. The tracks don't match. One set leading there, one set leading back.'

Danny finally understood what O'Byrne was getting at. 'You think Vertanness went outside and left someone else alone in there with the body?'

'Precisely. Someone who swept the floor afterwards to ensure no trace of their presence was left.'

'And this didn't give cause for concern during the investigation?'

'Obviously it was an avenue we pursued. That was why we gave the perp a name: Orson.'

Danny twigged straight away: victim, killer and Orson. 'Like the Orson Welles film, yeah? The Third Man?'

'Yes.'

'Why was this never made public?'

'There was no evidence of Vertanness sloping off to be alone at any of the other crime scenes.'

'Orson got wise to it and warned Vertanness not to do it?'

'That's what some of us thought. The other possible explanation was that Vertanness's behaviour at the pill-box was a one off.'

'Is that likely?'

'With a beast like Ishmael Vertanness, anything is possible.'

'Did you not ask him about Orson?'

'Of course. But the bastard wouldn't even admit to the crimes. Never has. How can there be an accomplice if he won't admit his guilt?'

'What did he say about it during interrogation?'

'Nothing. And when I say nothing, I mean nothing: we threw everything we had at him and he never spoke a single word in dozens of hours of questioning. Actually, that's not true. Sometimes he'd start speaking and do you know what he'd do? Repeat what *we'd* been saying. Not just random sentences; entire stretches of conversation. We played the tapes back; he never made a single mistake. He had everything memorised, word perfect, even the intonation. We set some real hard coppers loose on him and it even put the willies up them. It was like he wasn't even there most of the time. You could slam the table next to him and there was nothing, no reaction. He didn't even flinch.'

'So the defence's autism thing wasn't a get-out clause?'

'Something wasn't right with him.'

'Why wasn't the Orson theory pursued after the arrest?'

O'Byrne sighed. 'Remember, this was only months after the whole Rachel Nickell / Colin Stagg mess blew up in the police's face. Remember that? The police honey trap, the one that kept us looking in totally the wrong direction while the real killer went on to kill again? Orders from on high – and I mean the very highest of the high – were we did everything on the Scarecrow enquiry by the book. There were a lot of us believed in Orson's existence but the SIO didn't want, and I quote, "any hocus-pocus muddying the waters". There was only one thing they wanted and that was a good, solid conviction. We got Vertanness. Witnesses identified him, semen traces matched, fibres matched. It was a cast iron conviction, and once we got it we were all reassigned.'

Danny's mind was racing. 'But there were still doubts, weren't there? That's why you kept the specifics of the "Toto" word out of the court case? So you'd still have something to work with if the Orson theory came alive again.'

O'Byrne hesitated then nodded.

'There were just so many factors that indicated it might. The first four killings showed such a high level of restraint and caution. The murder scenes were carefully chosen for their remoteness, the possibility of getting a vehicle in and out without attracting too much suspicion. The fifth killing shows none of that. Vertanness simply butchered the poor boy in the open.'

'You think Vertanness slipped the leash?'

'Could be. With the first four, the point of the killing seems to have been what happened to the bodies *afterwards*. Autopsies show some of the wounds were inflicted hours after death actually occurred. The fifth was simply a madman slaughtering randomly. Plus Vertanness was an oddball. I mean, not only was he ugly as sin, he was the type of misfit nobody in their right mind would have gone anywhere near, a total loser. And yet four times he managed to get close enough to sensible, intelligent young men to strike them with a clean sap across the back of the head. There were never any signs of a struggle – no scratching, no skin under the fingernails, no bruising. Once I could buy: he got lucky, he got someone dumb or naïve. But four times? In a row? No way.'

'You think he had an accomplice?'

'That's one explanation, isn't it? He worked with someone more trustworthy – his own form of honey trap.'

'And what happened when the bodies began turning up in the north? The Cross Border Killings.'

'Copycat.'

'Christ. You mean no one ever thought to mention the Orson theory?'

O'Byrne's voice rose to match the indignation in Danny's. 'The police force is prone to the same rivalries and bickering as any other organisation. And here it was even more difficult, because you're talking about the complications involved in cross-border crime. The first two victims were snatched in Scotland, their bodies dumped in north England. The third one was snatched in England, dumped in Scotland. That's a monstrous jurisdictional snarl-up right away.

'The Scottish / English rivalry isn't limited to the football field, you know. By the time it had been sorted out who was running which investigation, the last thing anyone wanted was the extra complication of trying to link the new killings to some for which the murderer was already behind bars. Plus the M.O.s weren't entirely the same. The victims in the Cross Border Killings were all rent boys. And the "Toto" word was missing. That was emphasised by those championing the copycat theory; every part of the killer's signature was there bar the one part that hadn't been made public.'

Danny listened, then said: 'Orson could have done it on purpose. He would have been working with a different killer. He'd showed signs of knowing how to throw the police off before. He could have changed the signature on purpose.'

'According to the forensic psychologist we consulted on the Scarecrow enquiry, that doesn't happen.' O'Byrne looked through the file. 'Here we are. I quote: *The modus operandi is the way in which a murderer kills. With a spree killer there can be a great deal of variation, normally due to the fact that the killings are the result of psychotic incidents. They will often use what is closest to hand or simply strangle or beat their victim to death. With the serial killer, there is normally less variation. They tend to use what they know works.*

'The killer's signature, however, refers to specific ritualistic acts carried out during and after the murder. Serial killers are each motivated by a specific, warped fantasy, often masturbatory or sexual in nature. The fantasy dominates them to such a degree that mere fantasy no longer satisfies them. They begin to act out the fantasy. The victim is an unwilling cast member in the theatrics of the fantasy. The ritualistic aspects of the signature do not change. They can become more elaborate over time as the killer refines the aspects of his fantasy that please him most, but it will not deviate, precisely because it is the whole reason for the killing.'

Danny was looking at the cardboard file. There was a sheet of paper at the top of the pile. It looked like a list of names. O'Byrne snatched at it when he saw the direction of Danny's gaze. He folded the paper, tucked it into the pocket of his shirt.

'What was that?'

'A list of suspects in the Cross Border Killings. I'm afraid I can't let you see that.'

Danny motioned toward the photos. 'Can I make a copy of these?'

'Certainly not. As you said, I'm not even supposed to have them myself.'

'Why have you got them, then?'

O'Byrne slumped back in his chair. 'Do you know, I haven't thought about this for a long time. And believe me, it took me a very long time to get beyond worrying about it. It's a cliché, isn't it, the policeman obsessed with the unsolved case? Typical of my luck, I had to obsess over a ruddy *solved* case.'

'How was Vertanness caught?'

'Good, solid police work. And a little luck. It's the only way *to* catch these bastards.'

For the first time, Danny felt O'Byrne wasn't telling him the entire truth. You learned to notice those slight, involuntary pauses that preceded a lie. And then the waffle that followed them.

'I'm sure you know the statistics,' O'Byrne said, his usual measured tone quickening. 'Most murders occur between people that know each other. When there's no link, when a stranger randomly kills someone they've no connection to whatsoever, the police's job is monstrously complex.'

Danny made a mental note to look into the hows, wheres and whys of Vertanness's capture. But there was something else he wanted to pursue. 'What do you think of psychological profiling?'

O'Byrne made a half-shrug. 'It's certainly not the exact science that is presented in books and the cinema. But it's another tool the police can use; one which, in my opinion, can be extremely useful when applied with the correct level of caution.'

'Did you meet the forensic psychologist who worked on the Scarecrow enquiry? The one who wrote that report you just quoted from?'

O'Byrne was too good to be fazed. 'Why?'

'Do you know who the Executive Director of High Secure Services at Deepmere psychiatric hospital is now?'

'The person that runs it.'

'I mean his name: Edward Shelley.'

Again, O'Byrne's face betrayed nothing. 'What of him?'

'According to the notes for the Scarecrow enquiry, he was used as a consultant to help draw up a profile of Vertanness.'

'Where are you going with this?' The sudden hard edge to O'Byrne's voice meant he knew precisely what Danny wanted.

'You must know him or have had contact with him.'

'I'm not phoning asking for favours.'

'Come on. You've seen the evidence. Let me have a shot at

speaking to Vertanness. Perhaps he's softened after all these years. Perhaps he's ready to speak.'

O'Byrne leant his forearms on the edge of the table, steepled his fingers for emphasis. 'Mr Sanchez, Ishmael Vertanness is a monster; the worst I saw in twenty-seven years of policing – and God knows I saw some in my time. But Vertanness was in a league of his own. There'll be no softening. There is nothing *to* soften. I know words like "evil" are outdated concepts now, but if it exists, Vertanness's soul is black with it. He is simply not human.'

'Just give it a shot. That's all I ask.'

O'Byrne rolled his eyes. 'OK. I'll phone Shelley, see what he says. But I don't like asking favours from any –'

The door to the conservatory slid open and Mrs O'Byrne walked through with a tray of tea and biscuits.

'I don't know how you take it, Mr Sanchez, so I've brought . . . oh my *goodness*.'

O'Byrne moved like lightning when the door slid open, but he wasn't quick enough to collect all the photos. Mrs O'Byrne's hands shot to her horrified face. Danny lifted shoeless feet as the tray clattered to the floor. Tea pot, cups and saucers smashed.

'You should have knocked, love.' O'Byrne rose, put a hand on her shoulder. 'I'll get the mop and broom.'

Muriel O'Byrne stood motionless amid the wreckage. Then she turned toward Danny. The hostility he'd sensed on arrival was palpable now.

'Harry's got a weak heart. Not that he'd ever tell you. You men never do when you're ill, do you? Too proud. That's why he left all this behind.' She gestured toward the table. 'He mustn't be excited.' Mrs O'Byrne hurried out of the room.

Danny began soaking up tea with kitchen roll and realised how futile the exercise was. It was amazing how far liquid could spread. The thought made him remember the photos they'd just been looking at.

Danny was out of his chair in a moment, fumbling his

camera out of its case. He wouldn't get another chance. He opened the file, pulled out the photos of the victims. He photographed, one, two, three, then heard footsteps. His camera was back inside his bag when O'Byrne entered the room.

Danny's eyes strayed involuntarily toward the file. The photos were still half out. O'Byrne followed his gaze, frowned.

'I want you to go. Now. I'll phone Shelley for you but that's the end, OK? I don't want you to bother me ever again.'

11

Danny drove back to Fleet. It was well past lunchtime, but O'Byrne had been right; food was the last thing he fancied. He parked in the town centre, smoked a cigarette. It seemed to disappear in a couple of drags; that always happened when he was nervous.

There was no avoiding it now. He needed outside help, larger resources, and there was only one place he still knew anyone. He extinguished the cigarette with a twist of his heel and walked toward the offices of the *Fleet Bugle*.

He pushed the door open, walked upstairs to the office he'd called home for – he did mental arithmetic – ten years. There was no reception area any more. No secretary either; you just pushed the door open and walked straight up to the first floor offices.

The newsroom was how he remembered it, more or less; some of the desks had been shunted around, the posters on the wall were different, but the decor was more or less the same. Shabbily-hidden shabbiness was how they used to joke about it. Piles of paper teetered on the edges of desks. Even the strategically-placed Ficus tree that hid the damp patch on the wall was the same; just much bigger and less healthy-looking.

There was a metaphor in there Danny didn't care to contemplate.

The newsroom was empty. That was good; *the Bugle's*

reporters were where they should be – walking the streets, reporting things, talking to people. Too many newspapers sat back on their arses these days and did the job with press releases and quotes culled from the internet.

He crossed the newsroom towards the editor's office, careful not to look at the two desks in the far right corner; the desks that were once his and Ray's. He knocked at the half-open door and stepped through.

The Bugle's editor gaped. Then she swung in her battered office chair, smiling. 'Now this is precisely why I tell those bastards at head office we still need a secretary; any bit of old scruff can just wander in.' She rose, leant a hand over the desk. 'Daniel Sanchez, how the devil are you?'

Kimberley Swatton was a tall, attractive woman with a homely manner and a booming voice. Her cheeriness contrasted with the Dickensian trappings of her office; nothing had changed in here, either.

'Got any ciggies?' she said, motioning for Danny to close the door. 'Let's be naughty while the kids are away.' She lit one of Danny's Ducados, coughed as she drew on the harsh black tobacco. 'Lord alive, how do you smoke these things?'

'I bet you still finish it.'

She took another puff. 'You know me too well.'

They sat either side of her desk, flicking ash into a metal wastepaper basket, the window open, catching up. Then she sat back and sighed. 'Anyway, Danny, you'd better tell me what it is you want.'

'Am I that transparent?'

'I wasn't always a desk jockey. I did my stint as a reporter. You don't forget your instincts. Much as I enjoy your company, you're not one for social visits. Never were. You and Ray Taylor were like two peas in a pod. No wonder you got on so –' Her hand shot to her mouth. 'Lord, Danny, I'm sorry. That was so crass of me.'

She was right. It was crass. But understandable; Danny and Ray *had* got on. They'd been the backbone of the paper;

in fact, the two workhorses that could be relied on to get the lowdown on anything, no matter how dirty or dangerous the job, covering each other's backs, competing. And then, within two weeks they were both gone; Danny to Spain, Ray to . . . wherever it was fifty-eight-year-old atheist socialists ended up.

It was a complete fluke that Danny had found Ray. Danny rarely visited the office, but that night he had, he'd used his key to sneak inside after drinking at a nearby pub with a girl. He was showing off.

He'd wondered about the light in the newsroom as they climbed the stairs, giggling. And then he saw Ray crumpled over his desk. He knew straight away it was a suicide attempt. The scene was too calm, too prepared for it to be anything else. The girl screamed and ran. Danny pieced together what had happened as he waited for the ambulance.

After the office had closed, Ray had come back in and drunk a 75cl bottle of Jamesons while listening to Shostakovich's Leningrad symphony on a tiny cassette player. Then he swallowed God-knows-how-many tablets, sat at his desk and waited for death, redundancy letter screwed in one hand, a letter to Denise in the other.

Danny held Ray's head, tears clouding his eyes, as he waited for the ambulance crews; the phone call he had received that afternoon came into bitterly sharp context: Ray Taylor's voice, sounding oddly weak. *'Danny. I need to talk.'*

Danny hadn't thought much about it at the time. Hell, he was the hotshot reporter with places to go, people to see. 'Ray, I'm driving,' he'd lied. 'Can't talk right now. I'll call you back.'

That had been a lie, too. He hadn't bothered. Or he'd forgotten. Memory clouded which it was. But the awful fact remained: Ray Taylor had chosen Danny in his lowest moment.

And Danny had failed him.

The ambulance crew pumped Ray's stomach there in the

office, managed to get him conscious enough to feed a tube up through his left nostril. Danny watched the tiny fragments of white tablet as they sucked them out, hoping it would be enough to save him.

Ray was in a coma by the time he reached hospital. He died that night, Danny and Denise receiving the news together. Danny had gone into hysterics. Relatives of the Taylor family had wondered why Denise was having to comfort someone else on the night of her father's suicide.

Danny's life crumbled after that; everything he'd thought solid proved to be made of spit and sand. Continuing at *The Bugle* was impossible. He handed his notice in next day, then phoned in sick. The bastards had killed Ray, snatched from him the foundations of his life for the sake of scrimping a few miserable pennies. But the cushion of anger deflated quickly, punctured by guilt and grief.

It wasn't *The Bugle's* fault. It was Danny's. He waited until after the funeral. Next day, he left for Spain with a suitcase and a guitar. His last glimpse of Fleet was from the rear window of a two a.m. taxi, a drunk trying to read the cardboard sign atop the huge collection of household items piled on the lawn: HELP YOURSELVES. ADIOS.

He was never coming back, he'd decided, so fuck it.

But he had come back. Danny realised that there were tears on his face. Kimberley was pale with contrition. She handed him tissues, hugged him, then brought two coffees. 'It's poor recompense for a faux pas of such gargantuan dimensions,' she said, opening a drawer and withdrawing a hip flask, 'but I hope a tot of this will help you forgive me.' She poured liberal measures into both mugs.

Danny sipped his brandy-laced coffee. 'You're right, Kim. This isn't a social call. I need to ask a favour.'

'Ask away.'

'Does the paper still use a clippings service?'

'Not as much as we used to. The powers-that-be expect everything to be culled from the internet.' She patted the side of the enormous monitor that occupied half her desk. 'But will they invest in flat screen monitors? Will they hell.'

'But you've still got contacts with one?'

'Let's find out, shall we?' she said, lifting the receiver of her phone and putting it on speak. It rang once and a gruff voice said, 'What do you want?'

'Now is that any way to speak to a lady, Nathan?'

The voice laughed, a short, harsh bark of a sound. 'What do you want, M'lady?'

'Access to your data banks. I've got a young man here needs a favour.'

'What does *he* want then?'

Kimberley motioned for Danny to speak. For a moment their eyes met and they exchanged brief smiles. Kimberley had played her hand masterfully; Danny had no option now but to reveal what the source of his interest was. Contrition only went so far; once a reporter, always a reporter.

'I'm looking for details on UK murders work –'

'Nice small subject then.'

'– working backwards from 1995.'

'And not in a digitised format. Even better.' The man's tone was so sour that Danny expected the receiver to pucker.

Kimberly butted in. 'Come on, Nathan, don't tell me there isn't a monthly package of the latest juicy murders gets sent off to some true crime magazine.'

There came a sound of smoke exhaled. 'Maybe.'

'Well then, half your work's done, isn't it?'

'What am I looking for, exactly?'

'Anything before 1995 involving unusual circumstances with the body being tampered with,' Danny said.

'How unusual?'

'Genital mutilation. Or the body being interfered with in some way after death. Particularly with make-up being applied to the face.'

The sound of spluttering. 'You're right, that does help narrow things down. I'll see what I can do.'

'So,' Kimberley said, replacing the receiver. 'You're here because of the Scarecrow enquiry? Is this something to do with Ray? I remember he was always ferreting around on that long after they locked Vertanness away.'

Danny ignored the curiosity sparkling in Kimberley's eyes as he shook her hand once more. 'It's good to see you again, Kim. I'll speak to you tomorrow. Keep the cigarettes, I've got plenty.'

'I hope if you're working on something of interest to the good citizens of Fleet you'll remember your former allegiance?' she shouted after him.

Danny went back to the pub. His phone rang: O'Byrne.

'I spoke with Edward Shelley.'

'What did he say?' Danny knew from O'Byrne's tone it was bad news.

'Absolutely out of the question. He said, and I quote, "Deepmere is the patients' home, not some Victorian bedlam for random strangers to come in and gawk".'

'Thanks for try –'

'I stuck my neck out for you and got an ear-bashing. Our business together is concluded. Goodbye.'

The phone went dead.

12

Danny sat up that night with Ray Taylor's yellow notebook.

Was it possible? Had there been someone else involved? Ray Taylor thought so. From the first mention of Orson in the notebook, Taylor had begun fishing, looking into other crimes, other serial killers. There would be no holiday, now, he realised, no R&R, no more drinking. Here was salvation. He owed it to Ray to track this story down. And he knew how the story's byline would run: by Ray Taylor and Danny Sanchez. Eight years gone but back in black and white.

Ray would have loved that.

Danny decided to start by asking the question, if Orson did exist, what problems would he face? The first was obvious; why run the risk of involving someone else? Serial killers were normally driven by some deep desire to project their twisted fantasies onto the real world, using other human bodies to create their tableaux. It was something intensely personal. There were exceptions – the Moors Murderers, Fred and Rose West – but serial killers usually operated alone.

The second problem was one of practicality. Where did Orson find these people? Supposing Ishmael Vertannes were a mere tool, how had Orson managed to find him?

Here was where the Orson theory foundered. Because, presuming Orson did exist, he was probably behind the Cross-border Killings. How had he managed to strike lucky twice? To find not only someone willing and capable of killing, but someone he could be sure would not buckle, someone who would not go running to the nearest police station?

He looked at the dates. The third and final Cross Border killing had occurred in January 1999. The killer had never been caught. Assuming Orson was real, it was possible he was behind the killing in Spain. That left a gap of roughly a decade. Here was another problem that discredited the Orson theory: where were the other bodies? There were few absolutes when dealing with serial killers, apart from one: once they had the taste, they did not stop. The deviant impulses that forced them to act were so profound that they could no more choose to stop than cease to breathe.

Danny jumped when the phone rang: his mind had been drifting dark waters. He looked at the name on the screen and was surprised when he felt faint butterflies of excitement tickle the pit of his stomach.

'Hello Marsha.'

'How are you doing? I hope you don't mind me phoning you.'

'Of course not.' Danny didn't have to lie: the nerves in her voice had made him smile.

'I was just trying to employ the two fundamental principles of journalism,' she said.

'You've lost me.'

'Don't you remember explaining? "All a good journo needs is tenacity and a love of the truth".'

Danny winced. Had he really said that? Lord, what a wanker.

'Anyway, I'm just phoning to find out if you had any luck finding what's-his-name in Newbury?' Her voice more confident now.

'Yes, I found Harry O'Byrne. And he proved to be very useful.'

'I'm really glad.'

'Which means you and I have a dinner date.'

She said nothing, but Danny got the feeling that *now* Marsha was really glad.

'Is tomorrow night OK, Marsha?'

'That works for me. Where are we going?'

'Pub and then a curry?'

'Sounds good. Even if it is what we did the other night.'

They'd had a curry? Danny had absolutely zero recollection of that. It did explain how he'd managed to spend so much cash, though: he'd assumed he'd lost a wad of notes somewhere along the line.

'I'll phone you tomorrow about five-ish to arrange things, OK?'

'Cool. Night then, Señor Sanchez.'

'Night.'

'Sleep well.'

Danny hung up. Was it his imagination or had she blown him the faintest of kisses before the connection broke? Those damn butterflies were still there. Danny shook his head. Life was never simple. A bloody love affair with a woman a thousand miles from home was the last thing he needed now.

He leant back in bed, set his laptop beside him, searched the internet for videos on serial killers, found an interview that seemed suitably definitive. An American professor of criminal psychology was being interviewed on the subject of humans who kill strangers.

'What we are dealing with here are sociopaths,' the frizzy-haired academic began. 'The sociopath is basically an entirely different species of human being. The key point is the retardation of the development of certain elements in their character that allow them to empathise with others, to project emotion and understand that others also feel. For the sociopath, the world exists only as a series of needs and desires they themselves feel. Beyond that, there is nothing. The concept that others can feel and emote to the same degree as them is an utterly alien concept, one it is impossible for them to grasp: you might as well explain Nietzsche to a toddler. The sociopath simply does not possess the necessary tools to comprehend.

'However, they quickly learn deceit, the ability to hide this fault. They begin to mimic the responses people expect of them. The problem is that the damage is normally done during childhood. It's very rare that one of these individuals doesn't come from an abusive background. The abuse they suffer during childhood – be it violence, sexual or both – causes them to create a fantasy world to which they escape, a private world where they are strong and masterful. The issues this causes don't begin to manifest themselves until adolescence or –'

Danny stifled a yawn as the commentary became increasingly convoluted. The upshot was that no one knew precisely why they did it and no one knew how to spot it.

Or stop it.

That was the problem. Nearly all of them were twisted in infancy. It was like a plague bacillus, grown within the nucleus of the family, passed from each generation to the next – deviance, sadism, perversion – until it exploded into someone like Ishmael Vertanness.

He'd read about Vertanness's background. He'd suffered a childhood of unimaginable brutality: beaten and abused by parents, teased and tortured by elder siblings. One arm was covered with the scars of cigarette burns inflicted by his brothers. Vertanness had been seven at the time, the brothers nine and eleven. What hope was there when childhood was crushed beneath such casual brutality?

And yet what could you feel for Vertanness? Sympathy? Understanding?

Danny yawned again. Answers would have to wait until the morning.

13

Naked, he walked to the window and looked down at his house.

Silver moonlight glinted on bare grey brick; the windowless apertures were empty eye sockets. He always thought of it that way; his house. Because it was *his in all but name. He had made it his. He'd lived elsewhere at first but the thought of people gawking at his house, seeing nothing of the beauty it contained, broke his heart.*

The breeze carried with it the faint rustle of fan palms. Somewhere a dog barked.

Sound carried out here. That was why he could no longer use the old house. Not since they built up here, on the ridge behind it.

They were perfect times, before the new buildings. Sometimes he would leave the thing to work alone and wander the garden, listening to its music, the quavering peaks and troughs, the breathy, ragged pleas. How long had he been doing his work, now?

Back in the old country they'd come close. They'd even given him a name. Dorothy, they'd called him once. He liked that name.

14

Tuesday, April 6th, 2010

The phone woke Danny.

'Sorry,' Marsha said when he answered, 'did I call really early?'

'I don't know. What time is it?'

'I did then.' She sounded flustered. 'I'm really sorry, Danny, it's these odd shifts I work. I just wanted to ask if we can make it about eight o'clock tonight.'

'Fine. I'll phone you at eight.'

Danny was permitted just enough time to touch the edges of sleep again before Kimberley phoned.

'Sorry, Danny. I've just remembered you're on holiday. Do you want me to phone back later?'

Danny swung his legs out of bed. 'No. How can I help you?'

'I've got your press cuttings here. Nathan's very quick, isn't he?'

'I'll be over in fifteen minutes.'

'Not so fast, buster.' Her tone still playful.

Just.

Danny had been expecting this. 'I thought you said you'd get me this info as a favour?'

'And I stand by that. But one good turn deserves another and it's been a dry week news-wise. I've been doing some research of my own. Fascinating article you wrote about those two bodies they found in Spain. I presume it was you. The byline said "Staff Reporter".

Danny's hand tightened on his mobile momentarily, imagining it was somebody's neck.

'Yes, I did write the article.'

'You can tell me all about it when you come to the office, then.'

Danny walked to *The Bugle*. There was more activity in the newsroom today. He didn't recognise anyone. People stared with interest as Kim steered him into her office and closed the door. He answered Kimberley's questions truthfully; he knew better than to try and lie to her. Yes, he was here following up a possible link between the murders. No, he didn't have anything concrete; it was just a suspicion.

He told her nothing about the Orson theory or his visit to O'Byrne, though. That belonged to him. And to Ray Taylor. She regarded him with a wry smile, holding out an envelope. 'I can tell you're hiding something from me. It's your eyes, I think. You stop blinking when you're dissimulating.'

Danny reached across the desk, plucked the envelope from her hands. 'Fascinating.'

The envelope was filled with photocopies of news cuttings. Danny stood up.

'Do you want to make some copies of these, Kim?'

She raised her mug of coffee, patted a pile of papers beside her. 'Way ahead of you, Danny.'

Danny looked at the envelope again, saw it had been steamed open.

'You ought to be ashamed of yourself, going through someone else's mail.'

'You'll notice the letter is actually addressed to me, Danny,' she said, her voice no longer quite so jocular. 'You will bear that in mind, won't you? A circulation-boosting exclusive would really ease the pressure on a lot of necks.'

'I'll keep you in the loop, have no fear.'

Danny walked back to his room and spread the clippings

out on the bed. There were about three dozen altogether, all relating to one sequence of events, the 1994 murder of a Gloucester University employee. The clippings were divided into two sections. The first detailed the murder.

It had not attracted much attention: a few brief notes in some of the nationals, more detailed coverage in regional newspapers. Adrian Kimber, an employee of Gloucester University's Psychology department, had been found dead atop Bredon Hill, a local landmark, on March 28th, 1994. The twenty-seven-year-old had been tied up, sodomised and had his genitals slashed. Death was either from loss of blood or strangulation – reports differed – and, crucially, his face had been covered in make-up. The body had been found by dog walkers. From the brief descriptions provided, the make-up sounded as if it had been applied in a different way from the Vertanness killings; one witness described Kimber's face as having been "painted like a tart's"; another that he looked like "a doll".

The second set of clippings related to the suicide of a Gloucester man, Nicholas Todd, four days after the murder. Todd had a long history of mental illness and had previous arrests for indecent exposure. DNA testing linked Todd to Kimber's killing.

The coverage of this aspect of the story was more extensive – accounts of the police press machine trying to ensure the successful resolution of a crime got maximum coverage. Some articles from a regional newspaper related how Todd and Kimber had known each other through a day centre where Kimber had worked as a volunteer. One hinted at a possible relationship between the two men. This aspect of the crime had finally attracted the attention of the red top press: *Gay love tryst ends in hilltop slaughter and suicide* was the most tasteful of the quarter-page articles included.

Many articles mentioned Adrian's parents, Brian and Beverly Kimber, who lived in the town of Tewkesbury. One even mentioned the street, Sebastopol Avenue. That was in

1994, though. Would they still be there, sixteen years later? If they were, they were ex-directory, as Danny found when he phoned Directory Enquiries. Tewkesbury was a two-hour drive from Fleet. It was a long way to go on the off-chance.

Many of the articles were taken from one local newspaper, *The Gloucestershire Herald*. He found a telephone number for the paper and asked to speak to someone on the news desk.

'Hello. Who's that?' a young man's voice said.

Danny explained who he was. 'I was hoping you might be able to give me a contact number for Brian and Beverly Kimber – their son was murdered early in 1994.'

If the young man had heard this final sentence, he didn't acknowledge it. 'Spain, eh? You're a long way from home, Danny. Anything I should know about?'

For some reason, Danny was certain he was being spoken to from a chair leant back on two legs. 'Look, I'm based in Fleet and I want to establish if the Kimbers are still living in Tewkesbury before I drive up there. It's just background information I'm asking for.'

'That's a long old drive for background information, isn't it?'

'Listen, can you help me or not?'

'I'll speak to the editor, see if he knows anything. Phone back in thirty minutes.'

The phone went dead.

Danny slapped the edge of the table. '¡*Mierda*!' He knew what would happen now. Whomever he'd spoken to would check if the Kimbers were still local all right – and if they were, he'd start poking around, annoying them, trying to sniff out the reason for Danny's interest.

Danny did the Tewkesbury drive in ninety minutes. It didn't take long to find the Kimbers' house. People he asked in the street seemed friendly, eager to help. His enquiries raised none of the suspicion that asking for a stranger's address would have in Hampshire. Tewkesbury still obviously operated as a close-knit community. Brian and Beverley? Yes, they still lived in the same house, the one with the extension, down there where the road sloped toward the river.

Danny identified the house. What should he tell them, though? He'd no right to burden them with half-baked suspicions. For all he knew, their son's murder was completely unrelated to anything else, a one-off tragedy. How to persuade them, then, to allow him to rake the ashes of their grief?

Danny walked up and down Sebastopol Avenue, butterflies in his stomach. It was always the same on death knocks – the trade-name for cold-calls on the bereaved – no matter how many you'd done. They were an unknown quantity. You never knew what reaction ringing the doorbell would elicit: tears, anger, aggression? Death knocks like this, years after the actual events, were sometimes worse than when the bereavement was recent; you ran the risk of reopening old wounds, of derailing lives that had taken years to find some purpose again.

It would be easy to fob the Kimbers off with a lie, but Danny avoided lying whenever possible. Deliberately deceiving people in order to get information carried an illicit buzz that was addictive. Take the short cut one too many times and you found yourself doing it permanently.

Bollocks, he decided, after walking past the garden gate three times: just knock and see what happens.

There was no door bell. Danny swung the knocker, tack-tack, then noticed the sticker with a red STOP sign fixed next to the door: WE SAY NO TO DOORSTEP SALESMEN.

He heard one deadbolt slide open, then another.

The man who answered was in his early sixties. He greeted Danny with the uncertain, suspicious eyes Englishmen reserve for uninvited strangers on doorsteps. 'If you're selling something, we don't want it. Can't you read the sign?'

'It's about Adrian,' Danny said to the rapidly closing door.

It paused, an inch from closing, then swung wide open.

Anger replaced suspicion in the man's eyes. 'What the bloody hell is it with you people? Sixteen years of grief we've had since that bastard did for our son. If you ever do that to my wife again . . .'

He was advancing now, fist raised. Danny took three quick steps back, held a hand up in mollification.

'Whoever that was, it wasn't me, I swear. Ask your wife whether it was a Spanish journalist bothered her.'

'Spanish? You're not bloody Spanish.'

Danny begged a moment, took out his Spanish I.D. card. Brian Kimber looked at it, turning it round and round in his fingers as if trying to find some flaw in it.

'I'm sorry if other members of the press have bothered you. But it's really important I speak to you about –'

'Leave us alone.'

'Please, I think it's –'

'BUGGER OFF!'

Brian Kimber followed Danny to the end of the driveway, made shooing motions over the fence at him. Danny tried one last time to reason with him, to apologise.

No dice.

He walked to the end of the street. Now what? Two hours back to Fleet? Wait and try again in an hour? He needed coffee and a cigarette. He walked towards the high street, stopped when a car beeped and frowned when he realised the driver was beeping at him. The car pulled up beside him, engine idling. 'Hey,' the male driver said, 'you a journalist?'

'Who wants to know?'

The man smiled. 'Kimber told you to piss off, didn't he?'

Danny angled his head to take a better look at the man inside the car. He was around Danny's age, shirt and tie both too grubby and creased to be considered smart. Danny already knew the guy was a journalist from the way he spoke – you didn't approach a stranger so confidently without practice – but the inside of the car confirmed it. The back seat was loaded with crumpled newspapers and files, the floor littered with empty packets and wrappers, all evidence of a life lived on the move. Post-it notes with times, dates and places were stuck across the dashboard and the door to the glove compartment. He wasn't the journalist Danny had spoken to on the phone, though. This bloke's voice was deeper, more assured. The man got out of his car and locked it.

'Jim Durkin, *Gloucestershire Herald*.'

Danny hesitated before shaking the proffered hand. 'News travels fast around here.'

Durkin pointed to a house across the street. 'I know the woman lives in number 65. I've had her keep an eye on the Kimbers' house ever since a Spanish journalist spoke to one of our cub reporters this morning.'

'What did you tell her to look for?'

'Bloke with a shoulder bag and a camera.' Durkin gave a wry smile; they were the same two items that dangled from his own shoulder. 'Can I buy you drink?'

'I take it you're not offering simply out of professional courtesy?'

'I covered the Kimber murder. I know the parents. I can get you in to see them.'

'From what I gather, someone's already poisoned the well.'

Durkin shrugged. 'You know what cub reporters are like, all piss and vinegar. Young Laurence went in two-footed. I can probably sort it with the parents, though . . .' He let the sentence fade, kicked a stone.

'If I tell you what it is I'm working on?'

'Sounds kind of harsh put like that, but, yeah. Perhaps we can help each other.'

'I tell you what. Get them to speak to me and you can sit in on the interview. You can make of it what you will.'

'Internet's a wonderful thing, ain't it? Just tap Danny Sanchez into Google and up pops this.' Durkin withdrew a printout of Danny's *Sureste News* article. 'You think there's a connection between Adrian Kimber's murder and the bodies found in Spain, don't you?'

Danny kept his expression neutral.

'Tell me one thing before I speak to them.' Durkin held Danny's gaze. 'Are you certain about whatever this is? Because I can tell you those people are still hurting about their son's death like it only happened yesterday. The father had a nervous breakdown because of it; the mother went grey in a matter of months.'

'No, I'm not certain. But something strange is going on. That's why I want – need – to speak to them.'

'Wait here a moment, then.'

Durkin swung the garden gate open.

15

It was a long time since Danny had been in a house like this: the sofa with its neatly arranged cushions, lace doilies set out on the coffee table, a valance above the window made to match the fabric of the curtains. Leather-bound volumes of Reader's Digest were arranged in the bookcases that lined the walls. A carriage clock stood on the mantelpiece above a crotched fireguard. The clock ticked conspicuously in the way that Danny had noticed clocks always seemed to do in unhappy houses; it was something to do with being surrounded by silence, he supposed. Two photographs stood on either side of the clock, each depicting a young man wearing a mortarboard.

'That's Adrian there, on the right,' Brian Kimber said.

Danny recognised him from the press cuttings. Adrian had a genuine smile above warm, brown eyes, his skin still red from shaving, the Adam's apple prominent.

'How old was he here?'

'Twenty-five, I think.'

'Twenty-six, Brian.' The woman who entered the room corrected her husband with a fussy tone, as if always having to do so. 'It was taken six weeks after his birthday. Six weeks and four days.'

Two years before his death, then, Danny thought. They sat down. Brian Kimber apologised for speaking rudely to Danny. 'You should have said you were a friend of Jim's.

What is it you want to know?'

That was the question. What did Danny want to know? He saw Durkin's eyes flash toward him as he helped Beverley Kimber with the tea things. Durkin was thinking the same thing; what was it brought this bloke all the way from Spain?

Danny began reviewing details of the case. It was always best to approach painful subjects this way, build up a cushion of mundanity before touching on more sensitive issues. Adrian Kimber still lived with his parents in 1994. They last saw him at nine o'clock on the March night of his murder, when he had received a telephone call and gone out shortly afterwards in his car. No one knew who had made the call; the police had traced it to a public phone in Tewkesbury high street. Next morning Adrian's body was found on Bredon Hill, which was a fifteen minute drive from the town.

The Kimbers responded well to Danny's questions. They spoke clearly and concisely without betraying any obvious signs of distress. Brian Kimber opened a scrapbook filled with newspaper clippings, most of which Danny had already seen.

'Of course, that whole business down the road in Gloucester was happening at the same time. Poor Adrian didn't even warrant mention in some of the national newspapers.'

It took Danny a moment to realise to what Brian Kimber was referring: the Cromwell Street murders. The investigation into the Wests' house of horror had begun in February 1994. Poor Adrian Kimber's death could not compete with a front page atom bomb like that. Kimber seemed about to say more on the subject of newspapers. then thought better of it, perhaps because he remembered that he was sitting down with two journalists.

The scrapbook was filled with clippings, dozens of them. The Kimbers must have collected every possible mention of Adrian Kimber's death that had appeared in the press and carefully pasted them into the book with the dates written beside them.

Correction: not *every* possible mention. Those relating to the allegations that Kimber and Todd were somehow romantically involved were conspicuous by their absence.

Danny asked more questions, ones he could tell the Kimbers were tired of answering: Yes, Adrian had known Nicholas Todd through a day centre he worked at as a volunteer. No, they weren't friends. No, it was impossible that Adrian would have gone to meet Todd.

'He was a good boy,' Brian Kimber said as he gazed at Adrian's image. 'Do you know, he paid his own way through university? He worked weekends at a building firm.'

Durkin was good. Anyone less experienced than Danny would never have noticed the way the other journalist masked his reaction. For a moment Jim Durkin's face became totally devoid of expression. Then he busied himself with his notebook. Danny jotted a quick note to himself: A. Kimber – building – what?

'Was there anything –' Danny sought the right word – '*unusual* occurring in Adrian's life around the time of the murder?'

The Kimbers looked at each other. 'He'd had some problems at work,' the wife said eventually.

'What type of problems?'

Brian Kimber took over. 'Adrian was working on part of a project paid for by the University of Surrey. Not that it's got anything to do with Adrian's death. The police were quite clear about that.'

'What was the project?'

'I don't remember exactly. Adrian worked in the department of Psychology, so something relating to that. Anyway, he was very much a dogsbody. He was only really doing admin work, helping to collate the information that was coming in. I think it was called Project Round or something.'

'And what was it he was accused of?'

Brian Kimber waved his hand in a what-a-lot-of-nonsense way. 'You know how paranoid the bloody PC brigade gets about data protection and personal details; it was worse back then. Someone supposedly made a copy of files they shouldn't have; Adrian was blamed.'

Jim Durkin shuffled in his seat, clearly irritated. 'Why didn't you tell me about this at the time, Brian?'

'I told the police. But you never asked. And besides, there were enough lies being printed in the press without Adrian being branded a thief as well.'

Durkin made to answer but thought better of it. It was still Danny's show, but the other journalist's concentration had risen a notch.

'I'm glad you mentioned that,' Danny said. 'I remember at the time there were allegations in some parts of the press . . .' Danny spoke slowly, a voice designed to be interrupted. Brian Kimber didn't let him down.

'Yes, we know all about that. Bloody rubbish. Adrian was as much a man as you or I.'

His face reddened and with the same rapidity anger thickened his voice. Danny had expected this reaction. That was why he'd kept his eyes on Kimber's wife. Her lips had trembled as Danny spoke, but now she was nodding her head as Brian Kimber rose and began to bang cupboards and drawers, looking for something that would prove that "Adrian liked girls".

Living with a lie had its own way of distorting the expression. Danny saw none of the telltale signs on Mrs Kimber's face.

'There.' Brian Kimber slammed a photo album down on the table. He had opened it at a series of pictures taken at a family barbecue. Two showed Adrian with his arm around a dark-haired girl. 'Now, I'm not claiming Adrian was Errol Flynn, but you don't get a girl like that if you're a bloody . . .' He faltered, unsure of what term to use, given the neutrality of Danny's expression. 'Well, one of those.'

Danny took another look. For a moment, he thought the girl's face seemed familiar, probably because she represented a type. She was around eighteen and not strikingly pretty; her lips were too thick, the nose too broad. But she had the sort of strong, compact, curvaceous body that made men think of lust rather than love.

'What was her name?'

'Nicola.'

Beverley Kimber's head was already shaking. 'No, it wasn't.'

'What does it matter what it was? It was all over before . . .' Again, words failed him.

'Are there any other photos of Nicola?'

'That wasn't her name,' Beverley Kimber said to her husband as she picked up the tea tray.

Kimber was flicking through the pages. 'Well, it was something similar. Nickie Jane or something like that. Anyway, what does it matter? Here she is.'

The second shot was taken at the same function. It didn't help Danny much. "Nicola's" face was distorted, eyes closed, tongue poking out at the camera. Even so, the flirtatious air was more evident. You could see it in the set of her hips, the way her skirt was just short enough to show she wore stockings rather than tights. And you could see it in the way Adrian Kimber gazed at her. If you needed to explain the word "besotted" pictorially, Adrian's expression in the photo would serve admirably.

'Can you remember when Adrian and the young lady split up?'

'The year before he died.'

Beverley Kimber's voice sounded from the kitchen. 'No, it wasn't.'

'Look, you'd better speak to her, as I clearly don't know my arse from my elbow.'

'You just don't have a memory for things, darling,' his wife said, taking her seat again. 'It was about three months before . . .' Her voice faltered. 'I remember clearly because Adrian was heartbroken.'

'So it wasn't his decision?'

'He never spoke about it. But from his reaction, I would say definitely not.'

'Was this woman ever questioned by police?'

'I don't think so. They were only together a month or so. The occasion on which those photos were taken was the only time we ever met her. And I can't say she made a very good impression.'

'Really?'

'She drank rather too much for my liking. And she was very loud; one of those *look-at-me* type of girls.'

They spoke for another ten minutes. Teas were finished. Danny took the Kimbers' telephone number. As the two journalists prepared to leave, Danny noticed that Jim Durkin lagged behind. He was speaking quietly with Beverley Kimber.

They walked outside. Durkin lit a cigarette, shuffled his feet against the cold. 'So . . .' he said around a mouthful of smoke. He allowed the silence to hang. It was Danny's turn to stump up.

Danny told him everything that he knew about the bodies in Spain, both the one at the Cookes' house whose face had been bound with gaffer tape and the second at Alan Reade's. He told him about the face smeared with make-up. Durkin watched him as he spoke. He was taking short puffs at his cigarette. Danny said nothing about his conversation with O'Byrne.

'Interesting. But you've still not really told me anything that wasn't in the news articles. And you're holding something back. I can tell. That's OK, though,' he said, 'I've not told you everything I know yet, either. Want to take a look where Adrian Kimber's body was found?'

16

They went in Durkin's car, approaching Bredon Hill through the hamlet of Westmancote. It was a handful of residential streets surrounded by fields. Only one path led to the hill. They drove as far up the road as they could, then parked and began to walk.

The path was steep and uneven; Danny felt the ache of it in his thighs and ankles. A quarter of an hour later, he was pausing for breath, looking down at the flat farmland below; the Rivers Severn and Avon sparkled in the faint sunlight.

The steepness of the lower slopes began to level out as they continued the climb. They passed a series of fenced fields edged with thickets of gorse. After that came a narrow strip of woodland. It was here that the beam of Kimber's torch had been seen by a woman driving home to a farmhouse away to the right of the hilltop, Durkin explained. Danny could see the gabled roof above the undulating folds of land.

A final field filled with turnip stumps and then Danny and Durkin had reached the top. Bredon Hill was 981 feet high and Danny felt every inch of it in his legs. It was curious that it barely qualified as a bump in the ground by Spanish standards, yet Danny couldn't remember the last time he'd walked so far uphill. His mother was right; he was unfit. He felt the breeze dry the sweat at his hairline.

The view was the type you took for granted in Spain, but

there were few like it in England. From the top of the hill you could see for miles in any direction; the Vale of Evesham, the Cotswolds, the Malvern Hills. Danny was struck by how neat and ordered England's patchwork lines of hedges and trees looked in comparison with the chaotic beauty of Spain's landscape.

The square stone tower at the top was called Parsons Folly, Durkin said; it had been built to raise the total height of the hill to 1,000 feet. If you looked towards the tower, the faint incline made the hilltop seem flat. Closer up, two deep gullies became visible, running in semi-circles around the hilltop, the remains of earthworks that had defended an Iron Age fort. The gullies were four or five metres deep. Durkin directed Danny to one in particular, a deep hole filled with moss-covered boulders.

It was here that Kimber's naked body had been found the morning after he died, his hands and ankles trussed with twine tied so tightly that it had bitten into his flesh. The coroner's report had outlined the full horror of his ordeal; subdued with a blow to the back of the skull, emasculated while still alive, raped. Mascara, rouge and lipstick had been applied at some point in the process. No one would ever know when, precisely.

Or would they?

That was the question, Danny told himself, hands in pockets, kicking a stone. Was this really an isolated incident, or was Adrian Kimber's death the first link in a sinister chain? For all the similarities, there were as many differences between the Kimber killing and the Scarecrow enquiry. Kimber was a young man, but he was killed outside; he was emasculated, but the make-up had none of the grotesquerie of a clown's. He was tightly bound, but there were no words carved into his flesh.

Kimber's killing did nothing to dispel the Orson theory, Danny decided. It could easily have been a fledgling psychopath's first attempt to release the deviance within him.

'What the hell was Kimber doing, wandering up here alone at ten o'clock at night?' Danny said.

'The telephone call. That's the key. The police traced the number; it was from a call box close to Kimber's house.'

'So, he gets the phone call. Minutes afterwards he goes out.'

'And comes straight here. A witness saw him parking his car at 21:20. Roughly forty minutes later, his torch is seen approaching the hilltop.'

'And the police assumption was that he came to meet Todd?'

'Yes. That's the bit that never added up. Kimber knew Todd professionally. All that nonsense about them being lovers got blown out of proportion once the nationals got hold of the story.'

'Was Todd gay?'

'Judging from what emerged at the inquest, I don't think there is a word to describe Nicholas Todd's sexuality. Deviant, I suppose. According to psychologists, he abused both his younger brothers and sister with equal enthusiasm.'

'And Kimber knew this?'

'Of course. There was no way he would have come up here to meet Todd.'

'Why did the police swallow the Todd angle so readily?'

'Remember the timing. This was when the Cromwell Street merry-go-round was in full swing. The police were reeling, trying to explain how two total psychopaths had managed to kill all those girls, hide the bodies in a suburban house and still slip below the radar. They got a nice, quick resolution to the Adrian Kimber murder. They weren't going to start poking holes.'

'What do you think?'

Durkin lit a cigarette, looked out across the land below.

'Ever lose a game of pool on the black ball? Hurts, doesn't it? Worst way to lose, in fact. The seven balls you potted already don't mean a thing, that last damn ball is all that matters. And that's how it always felt with this story; like I fluffed the final shot.'

'You don't think Todd did it?'

'No, that's the problem; Todd *did* do it. There's no doubt as to that. But I was never convinced that was the whole story. Todd's suicide four days after the murder seemed too . . . convenient.'

'Tell me about the suicide,' Danny said, when Durkin fell silent.

'*Quid pro quo*. Tell me what it is you're working on. I can help. I've got contacts in the mental health sector. Perhaps they can shed some light on this whole mess.'

They were walking back downhill now. It was Danny's turn to fall quiet. Durkin said nothing. They picked their way through muddy fields as Danny considered the situation.

'OK,' he said eventually, 'we work on this together, all right? Any articles written are attributed to both and neither of us is to publish anything without the other's consent.'

'Done.'

'And the name Ray Taylor goes on the article, too. He was the one put me on to this.'

'Fine by me.'

They shook hands on the deal, looking warily at each other. Then Danny told him everything: Orson, O'Byrne, the doubts that existed in the original police investigation. He had to risk it, Danny decided – Durkin wasn't the only one who could tell when someone was holding information back; the other journalist certainly knew something.

'Your turn, Jim,' Danny said when he'd finished. 'What was it about Adrian Kimber's connection with a building firm that made you want to speak to the mother before we left?'

Durkin laughed. 'You've a sharp eye, Mr Sanchez. To answer that, I think it's simpler if I just show you.'

17

They made small talk while Durkin drove out onto the M5 and signalled to leave it at Cheltenham. They travelled through residential streets, Durkin checking a scrap of paper with an address on it as he drove.

'Here it is,' he said eventually, slowing the car.

Danny lowered the window. 'This is it? A house having an extension built?'

'Look again.'

Danny looked again. There was nothing remarkable about the two-storey house surrounded by scaffolding and ladders with a plastic sheet fluttering on top of the tile-less roof. Then Danny saw the sign attached to the property's gate.

'Apache Construction?'

Durkin was smiling. 'Thought that might interest you. I was having a look at some of your other articles and one about a certain builder being bashed round the head with a hammer leapt off the page at me. How are the Hackers? Charming as ever?'

'You know them?'

'Know of them, yes. They built themselves quite a reputation in this area the ten years or so they were working here.'

'I thought they were from London?'

'They were originally. They moved out here with the eighties property boom.'

'And that's the same company?'

'Sold as a going concern when they moved out to Spain.'

Danny clicked his fingers. 'Adrian Kimber. Did he work for them? Brian Kimber said he worked for a construction company.'

'Got it in one. But want to know something else really interesting? I know why the Hackers sold up and went to España.'

Danny lit a cigarette. 'Go on.'

'Quid pro quo.'

'What else do you want to know?'

'Contact details for the policeman, O'Byrne.'

'He's not going to appreciate another journalist bothering him. And it will kill any slim chance I have of speaking to him again if we need him.'

'Believe me, it's worth it.'

'OK, he lives in Newbury.'

Durkin's pen was poised. He looked up when Danny stopped. 'That's it?'

'Tell me what you've got and I'll tell you the rest. A journalist of your calibre can find O'Byrne easily enough with just the name of the town to go on, in any case.'

'Trying to win me round with flattery?'

'Why'd the Hackers move to Spain?'

'Two words: Callum Hacker.'

'What did he do?'

'Callum Hacker's gay. Not that he'd ever admit it. He's the sort will sodomise a bloke then beat crap out of him afterwards for being a "shirt lifter". He's a seriously disturbed bloke.'

'Callum? That's the one with the tattoos, isn't it? How can you be so sure?'

'Because in July 2000 Callum Hacker was sentenced to eight years in prison for doing precisely that to a nineteen-year-old bloke. They only got him on the GBH part of the business, though. Hacker's defence tried to pass it off as a drunken fight inside a flat, but the rumour was Hacker actually raped the poor sod.'

'Rumours can be just that though, can't they: rumours?'

'True. But whether the sex preceding the beating was consensual or not, it definitely took place. Plus, the Hacker clan sold up in a big hurry shortly after it happened and *long* before the case went to trial. Callum only did five years in the end. Rumour is he wasn't short of bed-friends while he was inside, either.'

'There's that word again.'

Durkin shrugged. 'Hey, I'm just hypothesising here. But if Orson exists, Callum Hacker could fit the bill, don't you think? Violent, repressed homosexual. And this business with the make-up. That's got to be some warped mother fixation. You ever met Ma Hacker? Don't tell me she provided a calm and stable upbringing for "her boys".'

'There's just one problem.'

'What's that?'

'Callum Hacker is thick as pig shit, something Orson clearly isn't. If he was, we wouldn't be sitting here debating whether he even exists.'

'Well, I'd run with it. Plus the dates match; the last Cross-Border Killing occurs when? July 1999. Early 2000 Callum Hacker is behind bars. That could be why the killings stopped.' Durkin's voice rose as he warmed to his theory.

'Jim. Remember our deal; nobody prints anything without the other's go-ahead. And all three names go on the article.'

They stopped at a pub, ordered food and beer. At least, Durkin did. Danny had mineral water. 'I'm not drinking again until I get a handle on this business,' Danny said to Durkin's raised eyebrows. 'I owe it to someone to get this right. Tell me about Nicholas Todd. What was it about his suicide that didn't add up?'

'Day after Kimber's murder, Todd was nervous. Went to work, threw up, went home. Couple of nights later, he got falling-down drunk. A neighbour heard him crying, arguing with someone on the phone. It always sounded to me like remorse, like Todd had lost his bottle. Then there's the suicide itself. Toxicology reports show he'd taken a large quantity of alcohol and sleeping tablets beforehand.'

'A bit of Dutch courage isn't uncommon in suicides, though is it? Especially if they've chosen something like hanging.'

'True enough,' Durkin said. 'But the quantities Todd had taken would have floored a rhino.'

'So someone could have rendered him unconscious, strangled him then strung him up?'

'Yep. The one final thing is that Todd's body was found dangling with a pillow case over his head.'

'A pillow case? Why?'

'Who knows with a nutcase like that? I think the police wrote it off as some sort of executioner's hood, overcome-with-remorse, just-desserts type thing.'

'And the matter wasn't pursued?'

'Todd had previous for child abuse, petty violence. He hung around play parks. I don't think the police really cared that a vague possibility existed that someone had got Todd blasted on sherry and sleeping pills then strangled the bastard before stringing him up.'

'A death like that, there would have been a coroner's inquest. What did they have to say?'

'You know how it goes if the police don't want to play ball with the coroner. They can push forward evidence that supports one theory, slow down other channels of investigation. It's subtle but it happens. I know for a fact the opinion among police officers I spoke with was good to riddance to bad bloody rubbish. The coroner recorded an open verdict.'

'We need to find out if there's any link between Nicholas Todd and Ishmael Vertanness.'

'There isn't.'

'How do you know?'

'I told you I had a contact in the mental health sector. I got her to look into it for me as soon as I read your article and noticed the reference to the make-up.'

'How did you make the connection with Vertanness?'

'Found some old scraps of news on the internet dating back to the Scarecrow enquiry, written by one Danny Sanchez, esquire. I got her phone call while you were in the bogs.'

Danny nodded in silent approval. Durkin was thorough and cunning. He could work with this bloke, he decided.

'Tell me what you found out anyway.'

'Todd and Vertanness were handled by totally separate health authorities. There's no parallel been drawn between the treatment they received, the problems they suffered or the medical staff they were handled by. The cases have been treated as totally isolated.'

'How reliable is your contact?'

'Reliable.'

'Convince me.'

'I sleep with her.'

'Meaning she's some floozy you bed?'

'Meaning she's my damn wife, all right?'

Danny bought another round by way of apology. 'Can you get her to have a dig around, see if she can unearth any –'

Durkin was already shaking his head. 'She needs a good reason to go looking through any files. Without specific names or some way to reduce the breadth of the search fields, I can't ask her to stick her neck out.'

'Fair enough. But can she check the records on one more person: Phillip Samuel Cohen. That's the guy they found walled up alive at the demolished house.'

Durkin wrote the name down, checked his watch.

'I need to get moving, Danny.'

'OK. Where do we go from here then?'

'I'll do some digging, phone round some police contacts, see if there's anything else about the Todd case we don't know. Why don't you follow up on this university project thing Adrian was working on?'

'Sounds good.'

They shook hands. 'Good hunting,' Durkin said.

'You, too. I'll phone end of play tomorrow.'

Danny phoned the university of Gloucestershire's Psychology department, got connected with a Doctor Humphries. Yes, he remembered Adrian Kimber; yes, he could spare Danny thirty minutes tomorrow at nine.

Humphries wasn't happy about it, though. As soon as Danny mentioned Kimber, the doctor's voice had acquired the reticent tone usually reserved for dental appointments involving drills.

Danny booked into a hotel in Gloucester and watched the sun set over the city's roofs.

It was only as he was debating where to eat his evening meal that he remembered there was another phone call he'd forgotten to make: to Marsha.

18

Wednesday, April 7th, 2010

Danny woke early, showered, checked out of the hotel.

His trousers didn't look so hot. The inside calves of his jeans were spattered with mud from the Bredon Hill trip. A dirty smear covered the top of one desert boot. He hadn't expected an overnight stay, so didn't have a change of clothes.

"Frosty" didn't begin to describe the way Marsha had received news the previous night that at 19:47 he was cancelling their date. She'd listened in Arctic silence to his explanation about having to interview a university professor the next day and said, 'What an exciting life you lead'. Finally they'd arranged to meet on Friday night; Danny had promised to make it up to her. Marsha sounded unconvinced. 'Last chance,' she said, before hanging up.

He arrived at the university at half-eight, knowing from bitter experience how easy it was to waste precious time blundering around a university campus. Doctor Humphries's tone the previous evening had not indicated that he would appreciate tardiness.

The academic greeted Danny at the door to his office.

'Come in,' Humphries said, indicating that Danny should be seated as he smoothed the blond hair on his round head. He was a big man, big in that way that makes men look genial and friendly. Not that his expression suggested either characteristic this morning.

'So, you're a reporter, are you?' he said for the second time, his slight sneer revealing exactly what he thought of the fourth estate. 'Well, as I said on the phone, I can't give you more than thirty minutes. Actually,' – he hoisted his sleeve – 'it's more like twenty-seven minutes now.'

Danny had already got the preliminary chit-chat out of the way: thanks for seeing me, appreciate valuable time, yes, it is chilly for April, yes, I remember our agreement, under no circumstances am I to quote you. That's where the three bloody minutes had gone. He went straight to work now. 'Adrian Kimber. I believe you worked with him.'

'And you would be perfectly correct in that belief.'

'Can you tell me something about the work Adrian did at the university?'

'It was a long time ago. But I seem to remember that Adrian was one of our post-graduate students. He stayed on and helped with research projects. Of course, I wasn't head of department back then.'

'Do you remember the project Adrian was working on at the time of his murder?'

Humphries's frown deepened. *So that's what this is all about,* he seemed to be thinking. 'You mean Project ROUNDUP?'

'That's the one. Can you tell me what it was? It's a very intriguing name.'

'A mess is what it was. And don't put too much store by the name. Every once in a while, some Whitehall paper pusher dreams up a catchy-sounding acronym then needs to make the initials mean something. Register of Undisclosed something or other. It wasn't even correct English.'

'What was it?'

'It was a first attempt at drawing together data on individuals within the health service deemed a potential danger to themselves and others.'

'You mean potential serial killers?'

'I'd prefer it if you didn't attempt to second guess what I mean when I'm describing complex issues, Mr Sanchez; I've been caught out that way before. No, I definitely do *not* mean potential serial killers. Project ROUNDUP was an attempt during the early nineties to establish some form of early warning system within the health service to flag seriously-disturbed individuals and get them the help they needed more quickly and efficiently. Obviously, given the criteria, there would be among those individuals a certain number capable of seriously harming others.'

'Potential serial killers?'

'All right, if you must simplify things to such an infantile level, yes, potential serial killers. But among a multiplicity of other potential pathologies.'

Danny hid his smile. Rattle an intelligent person's cage and it was only a matter of time before they threw big words at you.

'What happened to Project ROUNDUP?'

'The press is what happened, Mr Sanchez. Certain esteemed members of your profession decided to present the register as conclusive proof that thousands of –' he made speech commas with his fingers – '*potential serial killers* were roaming free among society. Then, when the security of ROUNDUP was breached, the press did a complete U-turn and presented it as an example of the dangers of the Big Brother state, bandying around people's personal data in cyberspace. It was only a matter of time before the Home Office funding for Project ROUNDUP was withdrawn.'

'How far did the project get?'

'Not very far at all, considering its lofty aims. There are fifty-eight separate mental health trusts in England; we managed to collect data from only five of them before we withered beneath the media spotlight and our funding was withdrawn.'

'Can you remember which five?'

'Is it really important?'

'I won't know until you tell me.'

Humphries exhaled, fumbled his glasses up from where they dangled on his chest by a cord. 'Ready?' he said. He listed the five mental health trusts quickly, too quickly even for Danny's shorthand to keep pace. Danny asked him to repeat the names. Humphries tutted.

'What do you remember of the incident that closed the project?' Danny said when he had written down the names.

Humphries removed his glasses and massaged the bridge of his broad nose. 'I have no intention of criticising former or current colleagues.'

'What about deceased colleagues? And I'm not asking you to criticise anyone. I just want to get at the facts. How did the theft occur and why was Adrian suspected?'

'Given the sensitivity of the material we were collating, the computer system where the data was being compiled kept a record of everyone who accessed it, which could only be done via a username and a password. There was also a system that logged instances of data being recorded to outside media.'

'It being the mid-nineties, I'm guessing that would have been the old floppy disks?'

'I suppose so. I really don't remember.'

'Why did suspicion fall on Adrian?'

'He was the last person to access the computer before the data theft was discovered.'

'And he recorded data?'

'According to the computer records, yes. But I reiterate what I said at the beginning of the interview, Mr Sanchez: I do *not* want any of this information to appear in public. God knows, Adrian Kimber paid for any possible transgressions a thousand-fold up on Bredon Hill.'

Danny wrote the information down, allowing a lull in the conversation. Then he asked in a quiet voice, 'Was Adrian a flighty person? Given to doing stupid, irresponsible things?'

'Absolutely not.'

'Could someone else have got hold of Adrian's username and password?'

'It's possible, I suppose. Not that it would have done much good. The computers weren't connected to the internet. To access information, the user actually had to be physically in front of the computer.'

'And that would mean coming into the Psychology department?'

Humphries nodded. 'Which would have been impossible for an outsider, as there was always someone in the computer room.'

'Was Adrian ever questioned?'

'Of course. We tried to keep the matter quiet at first, but the press got wind and then the police became involved.'

'What did Adrian say?'

'He maintained his innocence. We offered him a way out; all he had to do was return the disk with the data on it. He still maintained he knew nothing.'

'His parents mentioned he was having girlfriend trouble at the time. Do you think that might have influenced Adrian's behaviour?'

'Really, what a ridiculous question. How on earth would I know? It was sixteen years ago. Now, I'm afraid your time is up, Mr Sanchez. Good day.'

Danny sat on a bench outside, unconscious of the noisy chatter of the students passing him by, flicking through his notes. All the random scraps of information were beginning to coalesce, to take shape; a shape barely glimpsed from the corner of his eye, admittedly, but one Danny was now certain existed.

He drew a timeline, tried to find similarities between the two cases other than the M.O. and the signature. The material had been stolen from Project ROUNDUP early in January 1994. Adrian Kimber was murdered on March 28th, 1994. The alleged killer, Nicholas Todd, died in suspicious circumstances four days later. Supposing Orson had existed, had he provoked his first killing and then disposed of Todd after he'd shown remorse?

Ishmael Vertanness began killing in February 1995. Did the gap represent the lapse of time between two totally unconnected events? Or was that how long Orson had needed to find his new killer, to bring him under his influence?

Here was a problem, though; Orson had seemingly disposed of Nicholas Todd. Why had he not done the same with Vertanness? Especially if, as O'Byrne suspected, Vertanness had begun killing on his own. Wouldn't that have jeopardised Orson? Far safer to silence him. Danny circled the question. That needed further investigation.

The Cross Border Killings began in August 1999 and ceased four months later. The killer was never caught. Again, the gap, again the crimes with a similar signature. Why the delay? Because Orson was finding a new killer? Or was it proof that the events were totally separate, truly 'copycat killings', as the police and press had described them?

And then the discovery of the body at Alan Reade's eleven years later. Again, the same signature. And, in between, Phillip Samuel Cohen walled up alive at the Cookes' house, head swathed in tape. Danny thought about Todd's suicide / murder, the pillowcase covering his head. Was its purpose similar to that of the tape? And if Orson *had* moved to Spain with his new killer, would he have left a trace?

That was the question.

Danny found a café with Wi-Fi internet access, sat outside, began the search.

It took him an hour.

In May 2000, a group of hunters had found a corpse in a lonely part of the sierra in the province of Granada. The body of a Swedish hitchhiker was found dangling from a tree branch, trussed and covered in make-up. Danny read through the various ways in which the killer had sexually abused the corpse while it was strung up in chains. He felt revulsion, yet was unable to stop reading. He didn't pause until his cigarette had burnt down, singeing the tips of his fingers. Ash sprayed across his keyboard as his hand jerked in pain.

The murder had prompted a manhunt of unprecedented proportions. Hundreds of police were involved. For a few weeks the whole of Spain had been on alert. But the killer had faded into the mist. No more bodies had turned up. The usual theories were bandied around: it was the result of a satanic ritual; someone had made a snuff movie.

But Danny knew better. Orson was there.

He phoned Jim Durkin. 'Any luck on that name I gave you? Phillip Samuel Cohen?'

'Another blank, I'm afraid. Cohen was referred to the Northumberland, Tyne and Wear NHS Foundation Trust in 1991. That's miles away from Todd and Vertanness.'

'Tyne and Wear? That's close to Scotland isn't it?'

Durkin made the association straight away. 'The Cross Border Killings?'

'Yes.' Danny knew he was missing something. 'Tell me again who treated Todd.'

'Todd was first referred to the Avon and Wiltshire Mental Health Partnership in 1990 after –'

'What about Vertanness? Who was he referred to? And when?'

Durkin shuffled papers. 'Surrey and Borders Partnership NHS Foundation Trust, 1988. Does that mean something?'

But Danny was thinking aloud now. 'Where the hell have I heard those names before?' He scattered loose items in his bag, searching for his notebook, flicked through the pages.

Stopped. There they were. All three, written down during his interview with Humphries: Northumberland, Tyne and Wear NHS Foundation Trust; Avon and Wiltshire Mental Health Partnership; Surrey and Borders Partnership NHS Foundation Trust. They were three of the five mental health trusts that submitted data to Project ROUNDUP. He told Durkin, then said, 'Do you believe in coincidence, Jim?'

'No, I don't.'

'Nor do I. And this Project ROUNDUP was when, 1994? So all three, Todd, Vertanness and Cohen, would have been in the system when the data for Project ROUNDUP was sent. Christ, that's it. Kimber stole it for him. That's how Orson found his killers. He had the medical records. He knew they were all borderline psychos. Would he have had their addresses?'

'If the records were the same as the ones my wife consulted, Orson would have every last detail he needed; the medicine they took, the pathologies they suffered, their fantasies, their childhoods. In short, everything he needed to find them and win their confidence. Jesus, what a sly bastard. This is it, Danny. This means Orson exists.'

'There's more. It means Adrian Kimber knew who Orson was.'

Durkin's voice rose in excitement. 'It's Callum Hacker. I'm telling you, it's him.'

'Let's not rush into anything, Jim.'

'I'm getting hassle from my editor. Remember, I work for a daily. I've done half my normal workload during the last few days. I'm going to need to publish something soon.'

'OK. Let's at least wait until I've spoken to O'Byrne again. Meanwhile, can you get your good lady wife to look through the files and see if she can find anyone in the Gloucester area that might fit Orson's profile: someone manipulative, someone with this fixation about tying people up, the make-up. I think he might have been local to you.'

'Danny, that's an impossible task. Even if she were inclined to risk it for a third time – something I really doubt – that's so impossibly vague.'

Danny sighed as he realised the truth of what Durkin was saying. 'OK, well let's work on ways of reducing the parameters. It's my guessing that someone as disturbed as Orson would have a presence on the mental health service.'

Danny jogged to his car, headed for Newbury.

18

'I told you specifically not to bother me again.' Harry O'Byrne's voice was cold and authoritative in the the way only an ex-policeman's could be. 'Leave my property, now.'

Danny expected the reaction. His foot was inside the door long before it had closed. 'I think you were right about Orson, Mr O'Byrne. The bastard exists. And I think he's out in Spain. Will you help me?'

The pressure of door on desert boot remained. Danny waved a sheet of paper at him. 'Look at this. Three hunters found a body in the province of Granada in May 2000. I've highlighted the relevant words. *Cadaver* I'm betting you can guess the meaning of. *Sodomizado* is the past participle of a verb I think you'll probably recognise, too. And *maquillaje*. Want to know what that means? It means make-up.'

The pressure grew.

Then stopped. O'Byrne threw the door open. His eye twitched as he scanned the article, looked at the photo that accompanied the article, the clearing where the three hunters had discovered the mutilated corpse dangling by chains from a tree branch. 'Come in if you must. But my wife is back soon. I want you gone in thirty-five minutes.'

They stood in the hall while Danny explained. O'Byrne listened and said, 'What do you want from me?'

'The truth. I'm working to a theory here, but I need to get the pieces to fit. Orson uses other people to do his dirty work. But if at any point the second party endangers Orson, the stooge is disposed of. We see it here with Todd; he kills Adrian Kimber but gets cold feet. Todd drinks. He's nervous, crying. And then he's dead. Now, you've already said that Ishmael Vertanness slipped the leash on the fifth killing. Was there any evidence of Orson trying to dispose of him?'

Harry O'Byrne was staring into space. His face had gone white. 'Oh Jesus,' he murmured as he sifted the details of the Kimber case.

'What happened with Vertanness? How did you catch him?'

'It was a tip-off. The day the fifth murder hit the papers, we got an anonymous tip-off telling us Vertanness was the perpetrator of the Scarecrow murders. The very same day. This was before we'd even made a link between the fifth killing and the other four.'

'What was the tip off?'

'The classic: letters cut from newspapers, stuck to a sheet of A4. Four words: Scarecrow is Ishmael Vertanness.'

'What did police think at the time?'

'It wasn't the first case where this sort of thing had happened. People know something, are too scared to come forward or feel some loyalty towards the killer. But they eventually realise what it is they're protecting.'

'But it still doesn't prove anything. Why didn't Orson kill Vertanness?'

O'Byrne's lip trembled. 'He couldn't.'

'Why not?'

O'Byrne sighed and removed his glasses. He rubbed the bridge of his nose. 'Because by the time the fourth victim was found, we had a list of half-a-dozen men we considered strong suspects and had placed them under round-the-clock surveillance. Vertanness was one of them.'

It took a moment for Danny to realise the implications of what O'Byrne was saying.

'Then how the bloody hell did Vertanness manage to kill the fifth victim?'

'Mistakes get made. Vertanness lived in a terrace of five houses. We didn't realise the crawl spaces in the lofts of all five houses were contiguous. He was using a vacant property two doors down to come and go as he pleased.'

'Jesus. And presumably this was another reason the Orson theory was squashed?'

O'Byrne nodded slowly. 'Once the arrest was made, the instruction was to wrap things up quick smart, get the media focused on the killer and forget the surveillance operation even happened.'

'There's just one last thing I need from you, Mr O'Byrne. Phillip Samuel Cohen. Do you recognise the name?'

'Should I?'

'You're the one with the list of suspects for the Cross Border Killings. I know you can't give me the list. Just tell me if that name was on it. Spanish police have identified him as the body found at the demolished property. If he's on that list, it means Orson disposed of him, just as he disposed of Todd and Vertanness. It also means he was most likely responsible for the Cross Border Killings.'

O'Byrne went upstairs. Danny heard the creak of floorboards, then O'Byrne came back. 'He's there. Not only that, he was a Group A suspect, regarded as being worthy of surveillance.'

O'Byrne invited Danny through to the conservatory. They talked over the whole matter again, Danny making notes. When his wife returned and shot an angry look at Danny, O'Byrne shooed her away. 'I know I promised, love, but this is important. More important than you can imagine.'

The two men talked for an hour, went over all the details, backwards, forwards, tried to poke holes in their theories. It didn't work; they kept coming back to the same conclusion: Orson was real and he was operating in Spain.

They began planning how they would proceed. O'Byrne would contact the police, take them the evidence. He'd persuade them to contact the Spanish police, set up some sort of liaison with officers who'd worked on the Cross Border Killings. They were wrapping things up when O'Byrne's landline rang. His wife answered, came through, said it was for "you, dear".

O'Byrne was gone thirty seconds. When he returned, his face was pale.

'I've just had Edward Shelley from Deepmere on the phone.'

'Had a sudden change of heart about letting me see Vertanness, has he?'

'Yes.'

The flippancy was gone from Danny's voice in an instant. 'You mean I can visit Vertanness?'

'Yes. And no.'

'I'm confused.'

'Mr Sanchez, you're not going to see *him*. Ishmael Vertanness has asked to see *you*. Somehow, he knew you were coming.'

19

Thursday April 8th, 2010

Deepmere hospital was not difficult to find.

The morning was wet and grey; thick mist rose from the fields around the hospital's high red brick walls. It added an eerie element to the day that Danny really didn't need. Not when he was calling on a five-victim psychopath.

What the hell did Vertanness want with him? More importantly, how did he even know who Danny Sanchez was? He'd had a sleepless night pondering that one.

It must have been Orson, Danny decided. Somehow, he'd got a message to Vertanness and arranged this visit. It was the only explanation. Vertanness was no Hannibal Lecter. Like most other serial killers, he was a misfit, a total loser; even without the atrocious childhood, he would never have been the sharpest tool in the box. That much was made clear at the trial. There was no way he could have invented some trick to contact the outside world.

Not unless he had outside help. This was the final piece of the puzzle. Orson existed. And he knew who Danny Sanchez was.

The sudden wail of a siren from within the hospital walls nearly gave Danny a heart attack. He righted the car on the road, remembered what the press officer had told him; the escape alarm was tested every Thursday morning at ten.

Moments later, the all clear sounded. Should an inmate ever manage to escape, the alarm would be sounded to warn residents in nearby houses that a dangerously-disturbed individual was on the loose.

And yet, despite the precautions, Deepmere was a hospital, *not* a prison. It treated "patients", not prisoners. That had been something the press officer had stressed three or four times during the complex negotiations that Danny had had to make before being allowed a chance to speak with the killer: Vertanness wanted to see Danny; the hospital staff clearly did not.

Edward Shelley was there to meet him at the gates. He was a tall man with a stern expression, an attribute of which he made full use as he ignored Danny's proffered handshake. 'This is against my better judgement; I want you to know that. It is only because Mr Vertanness directly expressed the wish to speak with you that you're being allowed in here.'

Inside Deepmere, the staff had tried to give the place a homely, cheerful atmosphere. It jarred with the knowledge that the place was home to people responsible for the worst crimes humans could commit: murder, rape, pederasty. The red brick walls and buildings had been constructed thick and high, the way Victorians liked their architecture. Floodlights stood on white pillars.

They went over the safety protocols twice before they carried on to the visitors' centre.

'And he asked for me by name?' Danny said.

'No. He said "a journalist from Spain". I already knew of your existence after speaking with Mr O'Byrne.'

'Does he get mail from Spain? Telephone calls?'

'I would not breach a patient's right to confidentiality nor –'

'Mr Shelley, I saw one of Vertanness's victims: you can't imagine a worse "breach of confidentiality" than that, I assure you. If this person has asked to see me, I want to know how and why. So, please, tell me: what contact does he have with the outside world? I take it he doesn't have access to the internet.'

'Of course not. He can send letters to individuals and make and receive telephone calls.'

'Is his post monitored?'

'We vet all letters before they are given to patients.'

'And the telephone calls: are they monitored?'

'A patient like Mr Vertanness is accompanied at all times during any telephone conversation, to assess his reactions while he is speaking. At the first sign of excitement or distress, the call is terminated.'

'But you don't listen in to the other party?'

'This is a hospital, Mr Sanchez, not a gulag. I am trying to see things from your point of view. Try seeing things from mine. You don't realise what a major privilege this is for you. Apart from the occasional phone call from his brother and conversations with his lawyer, Mr Vertanness has not spoken a word in eighteen months. *That* is why we are allowing you to see him. He actually wants to *talk* to someone.'

'How did he ask to see me, then?'

'He communicates via notes, although they are infrequent at best. That is why we are so interested in seeing what he has to say to you.'

Danny took his seat in the visitors' room, an open space set out with plastic tables and chairs. It reminded Danny a little of a school dining room. Danny heard doors swing. His pulse quickened. This was it.

Ishmael Vertanness shuffled in, flanked on either side by male nurses. He'd put on weight since his appearance in court sixteen years before. His hair was cut short above a face with a pasty, doughy complexion. Flakes of dandruff peppered the shoulders of his black t-shirt. He didn't look as if he was the monster that had raped, murdered and mutilated five men.

But there was something wrong about him, something that his animal instinct had picked up on. It was as if, now that he was captive, he no longer bothered to pretend. Here, among the other monsters, he no longer wore his veneer of humanity.

Vertanness sat opposite Danny after fussily wiping down the chair with a handkerchief. He didn't look at Danny. His eyes remained fixed on the window, his face immobile as a statue's. That was it, Danny realised; that was what made him so creepy. The guy didn't blink.

'How are you today?' Edward Shelley said in a measured tone.

Nothing. Danny could understand what O'Byrne meant now. Vertanness wasn't ignoring Shelley, he was somewhere else entirely.

'The journalist you asked to see is here, Ishmael.'

Nothing.

Edward Shelley motioned towards Danny, indicating that he might speak.

Danny cleared his throat, feeling faintly ridiculous. 'Hello, Ishmael. What was it you wanted to talk to me about?'

Vertanness's lip twitched – just the once, but the effect in that ocean of immobility was like having a shark surface next to a boat.

'Why did you ask to see me, Ishmael, if you don't want to talk?'

'You've . . . come from Spain . . . haven't you?'

Edward Shelley sat bolt upright. The other members of the clinical team exchanged shocked glances. He'd spoken. Ishmael Vertannes had spoken, his voice a dry whisper, like rats' feet in straw, his moist tongue protruding as he lisped the next sentence.

'I've got . . . two messages . . . for you.'

'How?'

Vertanness's head swivelled slowly, folds of fat forming beneath his chin. For the first time, he looked at Danny. It was not a pleasant sensation: if the eyes were the windows of the soul, then Ishmael Vertanness's looked out from an empty room. The edges of his lips were sticky with spittle as he opened them to speak.

'Sigue el camino amarillo.'

Shelley's jaw dropped. Then he turned to Danny. 'What did he say? Do you understand that?' It took a moment for Danny to realise that Vertanness had spoken in Spanish. He ignored Shelley and leant forward across the table.

'What's the second message? What is it, Ishmael?'

'*¡La puta con quien vives está* muerta! ¡MUERTA!'

Vertanness's voice rose from whisper to howl in an instant. Danny recoiled as Vertanness began to slam his palms on the table, repeating two words over and over. '¡PUTA! ¡MUERTA! ¡PUTA! MUERTA!'

And then the nurses were over, restraining Vertanness, dragging him away from the table as he continued to spit the words at Danny, his eyes bright now with malice.

Danny picked up his chair and placed a hand to his thundering heart; Vertanness had scared the crap out of him.

Once Danny had recovered from the shock, his attention switched to his mobile. Christ, there was no signal. He had to get a signal.

He ran to the door, found it locked. Shelley and the other doctors followed him, yapping questions. A pass-card was produced, the door swiped. They went outside, Danny phoned his mother: it went straight to answer phone.

Edward Shelley grabbed Danny's arm, spun him round. 'For God's sake, tell us what he just said.'

Danny's eyes narrowed. 'Your fucking "patient" just said two things, the second of which was a threat to a member of my family.'

'What did he say?'

'The slut you live with is dead.'

PART III – TODAS PUTAS

He watched and waited in the darkness, feeling anticipation throb in his crotch. The woman's silhouette moved across the window again. He'd already decided what he'd do to her once the thing had killed the bitch. He rubbed the knives in his pocket. They were hard and long beneath the fabric.

The thing was anxious, excited. He could hear the way it breathed beside him, smell sour alcohol in the stillness of the night. It was new to the work. It would learn patience or he would dispose of it as he had the others; they were nothing to him, a means to an end.

They'd been here for hours now, watching. Waiting. They'd seen her outside the house, sunning herself, smoking, drinking. A slut, like all the others. He'd make her know what she was before the end.

The wire fence had already been cut in a place to the side of the house where there was no window overlooking the garden. Caution and patience.

The light in the bedroom winked out. There was only moonlight now, silvering the leaves of the olives. Soon they would be tinged with red. He touched the knives again. It was a good place to work; isolated. Like his old house. He had something special planned for tonight. Tonight there would be no secrecy. He would leave them a message, a message that he was not to be trifled with. He could taste it already.

They moved towards the fence. The thing carried the bolt croppers for the door.

Wouldn't be long now.

1

Friday April 9th, 2010

For the twentieth time Danny called Paco Pino as he rushed through the darkness toward Gatwick's departure building. He let the phone ring, waiting for it to go to voicemail *again*, and almost jumped when Paco's voice said, '*¿Hola?*'

'Jesus, at last, Paco. Have you –'

'Danny, I'm really sorry.' Paco's silence seemed to last an age. Danny filled the time with a thousand bleak thoughts, then realised that the photographer had been yawning. 'I can't find your mother anywhere. There's no sign of her.'

Danny's heart began beating again. 'Have you been to the house?'

'Three times, *amigo*. There's no one home.'

'Did you see any sign of anyone tampering with the windows or the doors?'

'No. But then again it was pitch black. I couldn't see much.'

'Jesus, Paco, why didn't you take a fucking torch?'

'Hey, take it easy. I spent half my anniversary watching your house and now you're shouting insults at four in the morning. Lourdes and I had a hotel suite booked. Know how much use of it I've got for my 120 Euros? About three bloody hours. And that's three hours of *sleep*, if you catch my drift.'

People in the check-in queue were staring at Danny; his

voice had risen sharply. He calmed himself. 'I'm sorry, mate. Thanks for everything. Really, I appreciate it.'

Paco left a pause, one Danny knew could only precede bad news. 'There was one thing, Danny . . . I don't want to worry you but Lucky wasn't there. Not in the garden, not in the house.'

Fuck.

If anyone wanted to get into the house, the dog was the first obstacle they would have to overcome. Paco read Danny's silence. 'The good news is a friend's cousin is a *policía local* on your beat. I explained the situation to him; he promised to keep an eye on the property, make sure there's a visible presence there every couple of hours throughout the night. I've also pushed a note under the door telling your mother to contact me at the hotel as soon as she gets home.'

If Danny had called Paco twenty times, he'd called his mother a hundred... and got voicemail every time. What was the name of that stupid boyfriend in Mojacar? The French one. He wracked his brains. It was no good.

He'd argued bitterly with Edward Shelley at Deepmere, kept insisting the man look at the telephone logs and find out when Vertanness's brother had last called and where he'd phoned from. When Shelley finally relented, Danny quickly wished he hadn't.

'Here's the number: 0034 950 343296.'

The first prefix was the international code for Spain. The second, for the province of Almería. Danny dialled the number, kept ringing until someone answered, a cautious voice speaking in Spanish. The number was a callbox in the town of Los Membrillos.

Danny queued and passed through security, a red raw bundle of nerves. Every second seemed a minute, every minute an hour. The plane took off in total darkness at 06:15, and crossed the Bay of Biscay as the sun was rising above blood-red clouds.

Danny prayed it wasn't an omen.

He sat as close to the door in the plane as he could, ran the short distance from the stairs to the terminal building, ignored the cries of airport staff. He hurried through passport control, jumped into a taxi. The ten-minute ride seemed to take forever. He flung a 20 Euro note at the taxi driver and raced through the olive groves toward his house, calling for Lucky as he went.

Paco was right. The dog wasn't there.

Danny's guts turned to water as he saw the door to his bungalow was wide open. His bag dropped to the floor. He broke into a sprint.

'*¡Mamá*! *¡MAMÁ!*'

He kept his back to the wall as he entered the house. The window shutters were all closed. Inside the house it was pitch black. The light switch didn't work. Cold hands clenched his heart as he entered the darkened living room and threw the shutters open.

Nothing. Furniture, table, television; everything was as it should be. But no dog.

He turned just in time to see the figure slip into the house through the front door, come straight at him. Danny screamed, tumbled backwards over a stool.

The figure screamed back.

There was a moment's silence before Adriana Sanchez's anger got the better of her shock.

'Danny, what in *God's* name are you DOING blundering around in the dark? You scared the daylights out of me. Get up off the floor.'

'Mum? What are you doing here?'

'I bloody well *live* here, that's what. You're not supposed to be back for another two days.'

'Where's Lucky?'

'I've got better things to do than run round after that malodorous mutt. I left her with that nice man down the road. I've been away for the last few days.' Her hand was still pressed to her heart. 'Is this your way of getting back at me for the argument we had? If so, you've made your point.'

Danny couldn't help but laugh. It was either that or burst into tears. 'God, Mum, you don't know what I've been through in the last twelve hours.'

'What *you've* been through? I come home to a house without electricity. I go outside to check the fuse box, I hear you screaming my name then you leap on me in the darkness. And another thing...' She was waving a piece of paper at him now. 'Tell your friends if they wish to proposition me, I'd rather they had the gallantry to do it to my face. Look what I found pushed under the door: *Adriana, contact me as soon as you read this no matter what time it is. I will be staying at the Hotel Almería. Paco.*'

Danny rose to his feet, laughter hysterical now, the hours of tension finding release.

Adriana Sanchez's hands rose to her hips. 'Are you drunk? What the bloody hell are you playing at? You're acting like a madman. Lucky for you Jacques wasn't here. He might have clocked you one round the head. He's the jealous, protective type.' Danny opened his mouth to explain, but his telephone rang.

The name on the screen silenced his laughter in a moment: Marsha.

He walked outside to take the call.

'I'm really sorry to bother you, Danny, but I just wanted to check what I should wear for tonight; smart, smart / casual or jeans and a blouse? Don't tell me where we're going, though. I want it to be a surprise.'

Danny put a hand to his head. He could hear Marsha's voice saying his name, asking if he was there. He steeled himself for what he knew was coming.

'Listen, Marsha, there's been a change of plan...'

2

'Danny.'

'Jim.'

'All you all right? You sound a bit overwhelmed.'

Overwhelmed. Was that the right word for his mood after the tongue-lashing Marsha had given him? Gutted would be another suitable adjective. He'd lost her now. There could be no going back, not after what she'd said to him.

'Don't worry, Jim. I'll get over it.'

'The line's pretty bad.'

'Yeah. I'm back in Spain.'

'Right. OK.' Durkin spoke without intonation, the way people do when they need time to think. 'Are we still working together?'

'More than ever. I need your help.' Danny explained what had happened.

'Jesus. I'm so sorry. So the Vertanness meeting was a set-up? I thought it seemed too good to be true.'

'Don't worry, my mother's OK. But yes, it was a set-up. Someone got a message inside the hospital to Vertanness.'

'It proves Orson is real though, doesn't it?'

'Yep. And it proves he's in Spain. At least, he was two days ago when he rang Vertanness. I got the number. It's a phone box in a small town about an hour from where I live. Also, Orson knows about the police operation. Vertanness said: Follow the Yellow Brick Road. That's got to be a reference to the Dorothy nickname.'

'You think it means something?'

'No. I think it means Orson wants us off chasing our own tails.'

'Of course, this does mean something else, Danny,' Durkin said. 'He knows who you are.'

'Yes, but thank God he doesn't seem to have followed through on his threat. I think we've got him rattled, Jim. Listen, Vertanness spoke to me in Spanish. Now, I'm assuming the guy was doing what he seems to have a talent for, parroting what other people have said to him – which means Orson speaks Spanish. Would that help narrow the parameters for your wife at all?'

'Not really.'

Danny hadn't held out much hope.

'What should I do now?'

'Let's stick to our guns, Jim. Keep digging, doing what you've been doing. Orson was masquerading as Vertanness's brother. Find out about Vertanness's family. See if they can shed any light on this. Find out where his brothers are, if there's any connection with Spain.'

Durkin was quiet. Then he said: 'Danny, I have to say, I still think it's Callum Hacker.'

'No. And this proves it: two days ago Callum Hacker was safely behind bars. Don't you see? He couldn't have made that phone call if he was in prison on remand.'

Durkin's silence indicated strong disagreement. Then he said: 'I've been doing some research on serial killers. Sexual psychopaths run on a clock. The more they murder, the tighter the clock is wound, the faster the hands turn. Once they start, they don't stop, Danny.'

'Meaning?'

'If Orson has been in Spain all this time, there is a serious lack of bodies between May 2000 and the body found at Alan Reade's house, who they reckon was killed at the end of 2009. Callum Hacker was banged up most of that time. The facts fit. That explains why there aren't any more bodies;

he was inside. And this business about Callum being dumb. Well, doesn't the fact that he walled up his victims in houses connected with himself *prove* that stupidity?'

'I still don't buy it.'

Durkin gave him more silence. 'Let's talk tomorrow,' he said eventually. It was clear from his tone of voice what they would be talking about.

Danny began phoning round, catching up on the news. First, he called Paco Pino. No, still nothing on either of the bodies; the police were stonewalling everything. Charlie Hacker was still in hospital, though he was out of intensive care now. Then Danny phoned Niall, told him he was back. He could tell from the youngster's tone something was wrong.

'Danny, I'm sorry, I forgot to phone you.'

'What's the problem?'

Niall swallowed. 'The Hackers are out on bail. All three of them.'

'When?'

'Two days ago.'

Danny hung up. *Now* he felt overwhelmed.

3

'Thanks for seeing me at such short notice, Señora Perez,' Danny said.

The woman shook her head. 'I'm afraid Señora Perez is too busy to attend you. My name is Dolores Donaire. '

That explained it: Danny had thought the woman far too young to be the *decana*, the dean of the University of Almeria's Psychology department. She caught Danny's faint look of disappointment. Her tone became defensive. 'I have ten years' experience and run the university's course on criminal psychology.'

Danny smiled. 'I'm sorry, I'm a little stressed. I'm sure you'll be extremely helpful.'

Donaire showed him to her office. She was dark even for a Spaniard, short, slim and attractive. 'So, Mr Sanchez, you told the university's press officer this was extremely important. How can I help?'

Danny took a deep breath, then explained everything that he'd discovered in the UK. He went on to outline his suspicions, watching a range of expressions cross the woman's face: surprise, incredulity, then the one he'd been hoping for – curiosity.

'So,' she said, weighing her words, 'you think this person, this Orson, has relocated from the UK to Spain?'

'Yes.'

'Fascinating. But how do you think I might be able to help?

Isn't this a matter for the police?'

'The UK police will be contacting the authorities here in Almeria. I've come to you because I want you to tell me who Orson might be.'

Her eyebrows rose. 'That's a tall order.'

'I know and I'm sorry. But could you at least give me some ideas about his background?'

Her eyebrows disappeared beneath her fringe. 'You want me to do it *now*? Impossible. Despite its name, forensic psychology is not an exact science. We deal in carefully deliberated probabilities and that is something that cannot be rushed.'

'I'm sorry to be pushy, but I'm desperate. People are dying and I don't think anyone is even looking for the real culprit. Is there anything you can give me? Just some broad brush strokes.'

Danny gave her his best winning smile.

'OK,' she said. 'But I don't want you to quote me on anything that is said. Not without due time to consider my opinions. You've forced me into a corner here. Those are my conditions.'

'That's fine.'

She extended her hand. 'You mentioned you had photographs of the victims in the UK killings, the Scarecrow enquiry. Can I see them?'

Danny showed her the photos of the Vertanness killings, the photos he'd taken at O'Byrne's house. Then he showed her the photo Paco had taken of the victim found at Alan Reade's house. She looked at them, considered each in turn, began scrawling notes. After a couple of minutes she looked up at Danny. 'You might as well take a walk around campus, Mr Sanchez. This will take me at least an hour. Leave your notes as well. I speak good English.'

Danny walked across the seafront campus and crossed the road to stand before the wall of huge brown boulders that served as a breakwater. Wind stirred the palms that lined the seafront promenade; the sea rolled in long foaming lines of white. The late afternoon sun was sinking towards the waves. Nowhere in the world had a sunset quite like southern Spain's.

He smoked a few cigarettes, drank a coffee and walked back to Donaire's office. Danny had caught her on the hop before, he realised; now she'd had a chance to mull things over, Danny could see she was excited by the challenge.

She invited him to sit, asked Danny to clarify a few points and began talking. 'OK, from what I've seen and been told Orson is *probably*' – she stressed the word – 'a cunning, ruthless and intelligent individual in his mid thirties from an abusive family background.'

'How can you determine the age?'

'People like Orson get all twisted out of shape during infancy; then comes adolescence and hormones and the mangled part of them begins to feel the need to express itself. That is one of the tragedies; the abused often becomes the abuser. Deviant behaviour like this normally manifests itself in late teens or early twenties. Ergo, if Orson started in 1994, he must now be mid-thirties. This is also a person who is outwardly confident and used to being obeyed. Look at the ease with which he gets others to do his bidding.'

'So Orson uses these surrogate killers to help protect himself?'

'I don't think so. I would say Orson involves a second person due to a strong desire to *see* the victim humiliated. The use of the surrogate killer, as you described it, means Orson is able to stand back and enjoy every moment of the spectacle uninterrupted. I would hazard a guess the emasculation takes place as the final act of domination and is actually undertaken by Orson once he is alone with the body.'

That all sounded very plausible. Danny made notes. 'Anything else you can tell me about him?'

'He has proved himself to be utterly ruthless and single-minded. Whenever an accomplice has seemed troublesome they have been dispatched without any qualms. However, he seems to possess some reticence about the actual act of killing.'

'Really? Why do you say that?'

'This mask of tape you described. It wasn't to silence. That would merely require tape over the lips. Look how it covers the entire head; the person is shorn not only of speech but of sight and hearing, too. And with the features covered, the victim is converted into an object, an un-person if you like, something to be controlled, humiliated. I think you mentioned Nicholas Todd's face being covered with a pillow case.'

'What does it mean?'

'I think it shows that Orson knows what he is doing is wrong.'

'Better?'

'Worse. Far worse. This is not a person whose pathology controls his actions, forces him to act. This is a person in complete control of himself. This person *chooses* when to act this way. And that makes him far more dangerous than a normal serial killer. The chances of this person making a mistake after so long a track record are minimal.'

And the bastard knows who I am, Danny thought. That was precisely what he didn't want to hear.

4

William Fouldes stared at the greens, greys and browns around him, stifling a yawn as he followed the snaking road south through the *Valle de los Despeñaperros*, the series of gorges that linked the Castilian plains with Andalusia. It was beautiful in a bleak Spanish way; the sun was setting above sheer faces of splintering rock, trees and bushes that burst from the gaps between boulders.

Not that William Fouldes really cared. The early morning flight had taken seven hours: Bordeaux to Amsterdam, then a two hour wait for the Amsterdam-Madrid flight. And now the long drive from Madrid to Almeria; five hours if you were unlucky enough to hit traffic, which he had been. It would be eight o'clock before he got home.

Fouldes changed the CD and fought sleep as he turned onto the *autovia* that would take him through the province of Granada and toward his home in Huercal-Overa. The Bordeaux meeting had been a total bore: the editors of all fourteen of Ms Pelham-Kerr's Spanish, French, German and Italian publications stuffed together in a conference room for hour after hour of corporate nonsense. Still, things were not as bad as Fouldes had feared. The staff of each had been ruthlessly pared down, but the company was still holding its heads above water. Of course, it meant far more work for the remaining staff, but that didn't really bother Fouldes. Who cared how much work there was when you were in charge of delegating it? Plus he'd got the telephone number of a very attractive Italian woman he'd met at the hotel.

And it was good to show your face at this sort of thing. He knew for a fact the editor of the chain's largest paper in Spain was earning nearly a grand more a month than he was. That was where Fouldes wanted to be in two years, up at head office in Valencia, sitting pretty, nice and close to the powers that be, not stuck in Almeria. The overnight stay had bothered him, as well; it was never a good idea to leave a woman like Jeanine alone, even for a night. That was how her previous boyfriend had lost her to him.

Three CDs later and he was home. He pressed the electronic key, watched the gates to his rural property swing open.

Jeanine was in bed already; the bedroom light was on but the curtains were drawn. At least she'd waited up for him. The headlights of Fouldes's car swung across the grey trunks of olive trees; wheels crunched on gravel.

It wasn't until he was inside and taking his shoes off that he noticed something was wrong. A large red arrow was drawn with a waxy substance on the white tiles of the floor, pointing towards the staircase. For a horrible moment he thought it was blood. Bending down, though, he saw it was . . . lipstick? Or greasepaint?

'Jeanine? What the bloody hell have you done down here?'

Another arrow was drawn on the wall of the staircase. A third pointed left at the top of the stairs, towards the bedroom. Irritation fought the sudden flush of blood to his crotch. It was a pleasing little game, but she'd ruined his bloody wallpaper.

William Fouldes sniffed the air. It smelt of food. He looked into the living room. The plasma screen showed children's cartoons. A ketchup-smeared plate lay on the coffee table. The floor was spattered with red dots. He tutted as he carried it through to the kitchen and stopped dead in the doorway.

It looked like a bomb had gone off inside. The fridge door

stood open; broken egg shells covered the work surface, stuck to it by congealed egg white. Packets of cereal stood on the worktops, ripped opened. From the crumbs that had been spread across the kitchen work surfaces, it looked as if Jeanine had simply been digging her hand in and helping herself.

This was too much.

'Jeanine? Why the bloody hell won't you answer me?'

William Fouldes gripped the banister, took the stairs two at a time.

5

Eight o'clock. Danny drove round to Paco Pino's house. Paco lived in the sort of enclosed condominium most Spanish couples aspired to; although the flats were small, the communal space was large and contained a swimming pool, tennis court and plenty of benches for the inhabitants to gather and chat in the evenings while their kids hared around making noise. This was one thing the Spanish did right and did well; children were the focus of Spanish life, the axis around which everything else turned.

Danny rode the lift to the fourth floor. Upstairs, Paco was preparing his two daughters for bath time. 'How was it in England?'

Danny stared down at the two beaming kids' faces, stroked their hair. 'I'll tell you later on, mate.'

Paco's wife, Lourdes, was in the kitchen preparing the evening meal. Danny chatted with her while Paco bathed the children. She invited him to eat. Danny wasn't hungry but he said yes anyway. Having filled his mind with the horrific consequences of belonging to a dysfunctional family over the past few days, it was good to see such a happy, natural dynamic between parents and children, husband and spouse.

Bath-time here was a chaotic time: sounds of banging, splashing and laughter came from behind the closed door. Then Paco's voice rose, trying to impose some order on the watery mayhem behind the door, telling his daughters to clean themselves, to get out of the bath, to dry their –

Lourdes was explaining the children's nursery routine when Danny froze, his reaction so swift that Lourdes frowned and took his arm. 'What is it, Danny?'

The second time Paco said the word, Danny turned and hammered on the door. 'That word, Paco. What you just said. How do you spell it?'

Paco's voice rose in irritation. 'Got my hands full here, Danny. What word are you babbling about?'

But Danny already knew how it was spelt.

Isabel, clean yourself down there.

Be a good girl, Alejandra.

Dry your *toto*.

The pronunciation was so different, it would never have occurred to him until he heard it said by a Spaniard. Spanish vowels were pronounced dry and clipped – they didn't say "toe-toe". The two syllables were pronounced like the word tot without the final t: TO-to.

Danny was remembering his own childhood now. It wasn't even a real word, not one you would find in any dictionary. Girls had a *toto*, boys a *colita*. The innocent words Spanish parents used to talk about children's genitals. What would English parents say? Winkle? La-la? The sort of word you could only learn if you were brought up in a language.

He thought about the photos of Vertanness's victims, the word TOTO carved into the lower belly. Christ, the answer had been staring him in the face all along.

He went out onto the balcony, slid the patio door shut and phoned Jim Durkin.

'Jim, tell your wife I can narrow the parameters. Tell her to look for native Spanish speakers. Anyone with a connection to Spain or South America. Or with a Spanish parent. Orson doesn't just speak Spanish, Jim. I think he *is* Spanish.'

Danny's strange behaviour required an explanation. Lourdes took the children into the bedroom while Danny and Paco sat on the balcony. It took him 20 minutes to explain everything. Paco blew air.

'I've always trusted your instinct, Danny but I have to say – there seem a lot of ifs, buts and maybes in your theory.'

'I know. But I'm working with an English journalist on this. It could be a really decent exclusive.'

Paco wasn't thinking about exclusives, though. A frown wrinkled his nose as Danny explained about Vertanness's threat, the hurried return to Spain. Paco's chestnut eyes strayed toward his children.

'I don't know, Danny. I say let the police catch the bastard first – *then* we publish something.'

'Don't worry, I'm not going to jump the gun. There's a British ex-policeman who's going to organise something, get someone to liaise with the police here in Almeria. But the more we find out about this bastard, the less we'll have to worry about when the arrest is made and the race is on. Plus, it's in my own interests, too. I want the bastard caught. I don't want to spend the rest of my life looking over my shoulder.'

After that, Danny drove home. It was barely nine-thirty when he dumped his shoulder bag on the sofa but still he showered and prepared for bed. He felt drained. All he wanted was to sleep. His mother had gone to stay with Jacques. Danny didn't want the added distraction of having to worry about her.

He checked that all the windows were closed, pushed the sofa up against the door, bolted it. Then he got a large knife from the kitchen and put it on his bedside table. As a final precaution, he dragged Lucky inside the house and put her bed beside his own.

If Orson wanted to come sniffing round, Danny wasn't going down without a fight.

The dog looked at him, bemused, then curled herself round

and settled down with a sigh. Danny checked once more that the front door was locked and bolted. Then he allowed sweet, honeyed sleep to wash over him.

6

Inspector Jefe Andrés Bosquet walked down the stairs holding the banister, afraid his legs might buckle. He'd seen a hundred murder scenes in his twenty years of service, but nothing like this. He could still smell the blood, taste it. The air in the bedroom was thick with it.

The walls, too.

Forensic officers chatted nervously as they donned their white overalls. One who had actually been upstairs and photographed the crime scene was warning his junior officers about the level of depravity that was about to confront them .

Bosquet's telephone rang. It was that damned politician again. He walked outside to answer the call, glad of an excuse to be away from the bedroom. His hands were still shaking.

Gutierrez launched into the conversation without bothering with pleasantries. 'How bad is it?'

What a question.

Bosquet's voice failed him the first time he tried to speak. 'The worst I've ever seen.' Five words, but Bosquet stammered twice in saying them.

'Is there any possible link to this other business?'

'It's too early to say. There's no make-up on the face. But the genitals are cut about.'

'I don't want a word of this getting out to the press, OK?'

'They're already here. A photographer has been sniffing round, asking questions.'

'¡*Joder*! What's he learnt?'

'Nothing. But he'll begin phoning chums. Reporters will be here soon. They'll start knocking on neighbours' houses. One of them will know someone: an ambulance driver, a cousin in the Guardia.'

'I don't want a word of any possible connection to the other murders getting out. Nor to that business with the hunters in Granada, either.'

'They're not stupid.'

'OK, I'll get on the phone to the local editors, give them an exclusive. There's still time if I hurry. But as far as police are concerned, it's a burglary gone wrong. I don't want any mention of the severity of the attack leaking out.'

'There's only so long we can keep this hidden.'

'And that is all I am asking you to do, *Inspector Jefe*. Keep it hidden for a few more days.'

'There's something else we need to take into account.'

'What?'

'There is a seriously disturbed individual on the loose here in the province. Dead bodies in walls are one thing; this was done within the last 24 hours.'

'That's your concern, not mine, *Inspector Jefe*. Do what you must to find him, but I want this locked down, watertight. And keep that cocky English reporter as far away as possible. The Spanish papers will play ball – they know what's riding on this – but he's a loose cannon. He's dangerous.'

'Why?'

'Because the dumb bastard's capable of printing the one thing we can't afford to disclose at the moment: the truth.'

7

Danny's phone. It was ringing.

He sat up in bed, fumbled the mobile to the floor, hissed as he swung bare feet onto cold tiles.

What time was it?

03:13.

'Danny?' Paco said when he answered.

'Where am I headed?' Danny was already looking for his clothes: a call at this time from the photographer could only mean one thing.

'Huercal-Overa.'

'Is it big?'

'Yes.'

'What is it?'

'Murder at a rural property. I got the call just before midnight. I didn't think you'd be interested, but rumour has it one of the victims is English.'

'I'll be right there.'

An hour later, Danny met Paco on the darkened forecourt of a petrol station close to the *autovia*. The photographer was pale.

'Whatever's happened is big. I've never seen so many police vehicles called to a crime in Almería. It's as if they'd found a bomb up there.'

'How'd you find out?'

'Ambulance contact. The agency pays him a monthly fee to

give us a heads up on anything involving a fatality. I reckon the local papers will already know about it, but we should have a clear run at selling it to the UK nationals.'

'Any news on the victims?'

'Victim, singular. An English woman – that's confirmed now. The husband / boyfriend / partner – that bit isn't clear – came home, found her.'

'So it could be a domestic?'

'That's what I thought at first. A neighbour heard the screams and phoned the police. The bloke was half-crazed apparently.'

'That sounds like remorse, doesn't it?'

Paco shivered. 'Whatever it is, it's bad. I've worked nineteen years as a photographer now and done everything from shootings and stabbings to explosions and motorway pile-ups. But I've never seen Guardia officers as shaken up as I did tonight.'

They climbed into their cars. Danny followed Paco past the edges of the town into winding rural streets lined with walled villas and chalets. He rounded a corner, saw Paco's brake lights flare. Two Guardia Civil officers stood in the middle of the road. Paco spoke with them, came back shaking his head.

'They've set up a road block. Can you believe it? The property's a good kilometre further on down the road. I've never seen them this jumpy.' He looked into the darkness. 'I need to get some daylight shots of the property.'

'Looks like we'll be hoofing it, then.'

They drove to an all-night garage, ate tostadas, drank coffee. There was plenty of time before sun up. They ordered *bocadillos* wrapped in clingfilm and a bottle of water – who knew how long they would be out there? – then headed back. They parked up far from the roadblock, scrambled down a dirt bank, then began the long walk towards the house, crossing unfenced groves of olive and almond trees, swearing occasionally as they stumbled over the black plastic irrigation tubes that criss-crossed the earth.

It wasn't difficult to find the property. Despite the darkness and absence of streetlights, the number of police vehicles and ambulances around the house meant it stood out like a Las Vegas casino. Lights blazed in all the windows. The surrounding cortijos were lit up, as well.

They found a suitable vantage point and waited.

Dawn began the way it always did in Spain: pale light crisping the rocky skyline, the milky colour deepening to midnight blue before a sliver of blood red sun peeked above the horizon, suffusing the foothills with warm brown light and creeping shadows.

An elderly Spaniard appeared from out of the darkness, walking with a short-handled hoe over his shoulder, his head covered by a black beret. The sudden appearance of two men from a darkened olive grove didn't seem to faze him in the slightest. Danny spoke with him. No, he knew nothing about what was going on at the big house but, yes, the owners were foreign.

He offered Danny and Paco his wineskin, rubbed his wrinkled hands. 'So, they're English? I always thought they were Germans. But what do I know? I never spoke with them.'

The outline of the house became visible. It was a big one, a two-storey villa.

The sun had risen fully now, blinding them. Paco cursed. 'We'll have to move round, Danny. I'm taking shots directly into the sun here.'

Danny wasn't listening, though. He was staring at the house, at the ramparts that surrounded the rooftop patio, the clock tower atop its peak.

He ran after the Spanish man, caught up with him.

'The owner of the house,' Danny said, breathless from the run. 'Did he drive a big, silver car? A4x4?'

The old man was hoeing the earth. He stopped, straightened, considered the matter in the slow, careful way Spanish *campesinos* considered everything. 'Yes. One of those with the bars on the front.'

Christ. Danny was right, then.
It was William Fouldes's house.

8

Saturday, April 10th, 2010

The staff of *Sureste News* gathered in the newsroom at ten. They'd all heard the rumours. Sandra had been crying.

'Is it true, Danny?' she said between snuffles when Danny walked in.

He took a deep breath. 'Yes. The police aren't saying much. All I know is a woman has been murdered inside William's house and a man – William, probably – has been taken to hospital suffering from shock. I think the only logical conclusion is that the victim is his girlfriend, Jeanine.'

Sandra began crying again. Niall stared at the floor. Leonard gripped his walking stick.

Danny was numb with exhaustion and yet had never felt further from sleep. As soon as he had realised whose house it was, Paco had phoned his ambulance contact. He'd listened in silence and hung up shaking his head. 'Cold-hearted son of a bitch went downstairs and made himself an omelette afterwards.'

'What?'

'What you heard. Watched some TV, too, by the sound of it. Kitchen was dirty – broken egg shells and saucepans all out. They found the plate with sauce on the coffee table, with the television on.'

Christ, just like Ishmael Vertanness smoking his cigarettes.

Killing time while Orson did his work.

'What about the body?' Danny said. 'Was the face covered in make up?'

'He doesn't know. He took your boss to the hospital. But he heard Guardia officers talking outside. Apparently, she'd been gutted. There was blood all over the walls.'

'We need to establish a solid link between this crime and what I've discovered in the UK.'

Paco had looked at him, indecision writ large on his face. Then he said, 'Why do *we* have to do it?'

'Because, apart from us, no one else is looking for the bastard. Don't you see, Paco? This is how he operates. Police are looking for *one* person, the person that killed Jeanine. But there's someone else involved, the person that instigates these crimes. He's always there, in the shadows, hiding behind others. All this time he's been getting better and better at what he does, refining his technique. Look at the victim we found at Reade's house: it's been a week or more; they still don't know anything about him, apart from the fact he's "probably" of North African extraction. And here in Spain Orson has found the perfect hunting ground; a transient population, separated by language and culture. Christ, the guy could have killed dozens.'

'But where are these people coming from, Danny? Where is Orson finding people who disappear without a trace?'

'There are thousands of people mooching around in the province illegally.'

'Granted. But they all have families somewhere or other. And the bodies, Danny. Why haven't the police found more bodies? You know as well as I do, if someone gets killed, the body always turns up.'

Danny had more pressing concerns at the moment. He had to take charge of the paper. He drew a deep breath. 'I appreciate this is a difficult time for everyone, but we need to focus. William was away in Bordeaux when? All day Thursday; and he returned at some point late on Friday night. Jeanine – it has to be her – was killed during the time he was away. Now, I want everyone to stay as calm as possible, but I don't think this was a random attack.'

Sandra drew her breath, wiped snot from her nose. Her eyes bulged.

'That's quite a bold assertion,' Leonard said, knuckles white on his walking stick. 'One that requires an explanation.'

'I've discovered information in England. Someone here was communicating with a serial killer in Deepmere high-security psychiatric hospital. Did anything unusual happen at the newspaper while I was away?'

Blank looks were exchanged.

'Unusual in what way?' Niall said.

'I don't know. A threatening letter? Someone doing heavy breathing on the phone?'

No, there'd been nothing like that.

'What about unusual visitors? Did anyone come into the office? Speak to Fouldes alone? Or telephone? Anyone out of the ordinary?'

For some reason, Niall put his hand up before speaking. 'There was a woman from *The Sunday Times*.'

'And what did she want?'

'She wanted to speak to you.'

'Why?'

'About the article you wrote on the killings.'

'How did she know it was me? The article was attributed to Staff Reporter.'

'I told her that. But then William took the call.'

'And what did he say to her?'

Niall shrugged. 'No idea. He told me to close the door and he never mentioned it again. But he did give me a number he told me to keep trying, a local number.'

'And did you?'

'Yes. Someone answered eventually. It was a call box in –'

'Los Membrillos.'

'How did you know that, Danny?'

Christ. What was the betting Fouldes had claimed . . .

'What was her name? The journalist from *The Sunday Times?*'

Danny called *The Sunday Times*, got the answer he knew he would receive after thirty minutes of faffing about. There was no one of that name employed on the paper. Danny put the phone down, trembling. Orson had a female accomplice. Sudden doubt assailed him. Was it Hacker? The accomplice could have been his mother.

He explained to Leonard. For once, as he listened, the old man's face was devoid of its habitually sardonic smile. 'You know what it means if Fouldes did claim to write your article himself, don't you?'

Of course Danny did; he could think of nothing else. Whoever attacked Fouldes had meant to attack him.

9

Danny stood before the news kiosk, shaking his head as he examined the morning's Spanish papers. Jeanine's murder hadn't been reported on the front page anywhere.

He could understand that it might have not made it to the nationals – *El Pais, El Mundo, ABC* – but the locals? There were maybe ten murders a year in the whole province and most of those were either the result of domestic violence or stupid squabbles that had got out of hand; Jeanine's murder was one of the biggest news events of recent years and yet it was buried among the middle pages, the traditional dumping ground for low-priority news.

Danny bought all three local newspapers and sat in a bar to read them. All three followed the same line: that Jeanine's death was the result of a burglary gone wrong.

What really bothered Danny, though, was how the hell they had got hold of the story at all. Danny and Paco had been the only journalists there. Plus Paco hadn't even found out about the incident until midnight. That was long after the Spanish papers got put to bed.

Spanish television and radio were following the same slant on the story. A television above the bar caught Danny's attention; Tomás Gutierrez's beaming face, smiling in the way that politicians do when they are about to candy-coat a turd.

'The situation is completely under control and there is no reason for panic. All I can tell you is that police are investigating a British woman's death in Huercal Overa and that they have already identified a man they wish to question in relation with the matter.'

There it was again, that neutral language: a British woman's death; the matter. Danny knew a Spanish journalist who'd written one of the articles. He phoned him.

'Julio? What the hell's going on?'

'The murder story? I know about it.'

'So you admit it was a murder? You'd never be able to tell from the headline: British woman dies in burglary. *Dies*? Not killed? Or slaughtered? Dies? You make it sound like she keeled over from a heart attack.'

'Hey, I didn't write the headline, OK? And for your information I do think it was a murder and I wrote it as such. But word came down from on high late last night to change the headline.'

'How did you find out?'

'About 22:45 last night, the editor got a phone call: big story breaking; everyone stop what they're doing.'

'Who phoned?'

'I don't know. But the press release we got was from the Junta.'

'Why from the Junta? It should have been from the police.'

Julio's voice dropped to a whisper. 'Don't be naïve, Danny. There are interests at work behind the scenes here. No one wants the province to look bad. At least not this week.'

'Interests? Three dead bodies turn up in a week and you talk about interests?'

'Things are bad here and they're going to get worse. Unemployment is currently at 30% and rising. No one knows where this thing is going to bottom out. In short, things are fucked. Seriously. People are blaming governments. The regional government here has existed since 1978 and it's *always* been run by the socialist party. They've won every election. Andalusia is their great bastion. Within eighteen months there will be elections and for the first time it looks like the socialists could lose. Not only that, the conservatives could get an absolute majority. The socialists are working flat out to avoid that. That's why certain prestige events have become so vitally important.'

The penny finally dropped. 'Christ, you mean to say this secrecy is all because of the powerboat race?'

'No, I'm talking about Almeria's *bid to host* the powerboat race. I'm talking about a four-day international event with the world's jet set guaranteed to descend en masse. I'm talking a lifeline for thousands of local businesses, hotels, free publicity for the province's exports and, most importantly, a little ray of sunshine for the socialists in a period of unrelieved gloom.'

'So they don't want murders investigated because of bad publicity?'

'No. The murders *are* being investigated – but as separate entities.'

'Why?'

'Because murders happen all the time. Like rainy days and traffic accidents, murders are an unfortunate, unavoidable fact of life. But a serial killer? That's a different story altogether. Serial killers get reported internationally. And serial killers, by their very nature, imply incompetence on the part of the authorities, simply because to have become one they have to have killed more than once. The question is always "Why weren't they caught earlier?"'

'Can politicians put that much pressure on the police?'

'For your information, yes they can. But do you seriously think this is just politicians? This is everyone. It's national government, regional government, councils, chamber of commerce, business magnates. No one wants to hear about a possible serial killer running rampant in the province the week before the judging committee is due to assess Almeria's bid.'

Danny hung up. The Junta had fed the burglary story to the Spanish press.

Well, Danny Sanchez knew different. He knew Jeanine's death was part of something else and he was going to prove it. But to do that, he needed to know exactly what had happened inside Fouldes's house.

There was only one person who could tell him.

10

He spread the newspapers before him and smiled; a burglary gone wrong? They'd got the message. They were scared.

He thought back to another time, a time when he'd made headlines. That had been a thrill, walking to the paper shop each morning, seeing photos of his work spread out across the racks.

They'd got the message that time, too. People were right to fear him.

All of the stories used the same photo, a night-time shot of the house's exterior. He traced a finger across the picture, lingered by the bedroom window thinking of what was behind the curtains. Women weren't really his thing, but she'd been a piece of work. His finest yet.

He closed his eyes, revisited the scene, heard the rustle of the bin bags he'd wrapped around himself as he worked, his lovely, wet work, cutting and unpeeling. He'd opened her out like a flower, left her posed atop the bed, arms spread to receive that prick journalist when he returned home.

But he'd left his wigs and make-up at home. Just as well. The temptation to smear the bitch as he worked her had been overwhelming. He'd scrawled a little memento, though. For old time's sake. Caution and patience. That was how to turn the trail cold. Change. Keep them guessing. He'd learned that early on.

Dorothy, they'd called him once. He liked the name. It made him think of pigtails and ruby slippers, sparkling wet and red.

He'd got that from a policeman. It had been easy making him talk; he knew what little boys wanted.

After that they called him Orson. That didn't please him as much; he'd never been fat.

The new thing was good. It had worked well, even though women weren't its thing either. But they would work together again, and soon: he had another fish he was reeling in.

11

William Fouldes sat a little distance from the entrance to the UCI. Two uniformed Guardia Civil officers were interviewing him. A female officer sat beside him, listening with a sympathetic expression. Her male companion stood in front of Fouldes, writing down his replies on a notepad.

Fouldes was deathly white. He trembled, despite the blanket wrapped around his shoulders. The muscles of his face twitched constantly. Seeing him like that, all the harsh thoughts that Danny had ever had about William Fouldes dispersed. Christ, the poor bastard: to walk home to that.

Danny watched, bided his time. When Fouldes got up to go to the toilet, he followed him in.

'William.' Danny put a hand on his shoulder. 'I'm sorry.'

Fouldes turned slowly, raised his eyes to Danny's. He didn't recognise him at first. Then a faint sneer creased his upper lip. 'Sanchez. What are you doing here?'

What to do? Ask him direct? Make small talk?

Be honest.

'I'm here to offer my help and support, William, and that of everyone else at the newspaper. But I'm afraid I need to ask you a difficult question first. Was Jeanine's face covered in make-up?'

He wondered whether Fouldes had heard him. The man's lips moved but he seemed to be whispering words to himself.

'William, are you OK?'

Fouldes sneered. 'OK? How the fuck could I be OK? Have you any idea what . . .' Some of the fire returned to Fouldes's eyes. His voice rose in anger. 'And, no, there wasn't any *fucking* make-up. What are you doing, Danny boy? Looking for the angle, are you? Want to make a story out of it? Sell me to the tabloids back home? Another Alan Smithee exclusive? You think I don't know that's you? You prick. You disgust me. Do you hear? You disgust me.'

Fouldes spat at him, but only a thin dribble emerged and dangled from his bottom lip. He wiped it with the back of his hand, staring at it stupidly. Then Fouldes unravelled before Danny's eyes; he sank to his knees, sobbing and moaning.

The raw display of emotion caught Danny by surprise – but only for a second. He'd seen this before in his career. He knew what to do. He knelt beside William Fouldes, wrapped his arms around him, pulled his head into his shoulder and rocked him, whispering words of comfort. They stayed that way until Fouldes quietened; then Danny helped him outside.

'He gutted her,' Fouldes said as they walked. His jaw trembled as he spoke. 'Like a . . . pig in a butcher shop window.'

'Try not to think about it, William.'

Fouldes wasn't listening. 'He wrote letters on her stomach.'

Danny stopped in the corridor, glanced at the Guardia officers. They hadn't noticed Fouldes was talking to anyone, yet. He fought the impulse to rush at the question. He patted Fouldes's arm, calmed him, then said, 'What did the letters say, William?'

'Toto.'

Danny felt the world spin. It *was* him.

The Guardia officers chased Danny away when they saw him helping Fouldes. Danny was glad to have got away so easily. Part of him wanted to stay, share Fouldes's burden, but he knew he had work to do. First, though, he needed a coffee. He headed out to the stairwell, taking the steps two at a time.

The stench of perfume hit him first. Then he heard the

clatter of high heels. It took him a split second to realise what this combination of sensory impressions might mean: Mrs Hacker.

But not alone. Muscle-beach Hacker was with her, wearing the same weightlifter's vest, the same tight jeans, the same dumb look. Despite being eighteen inches bigger than his mother along both the x and y axes, he wore a curiously cowed look as he lumbered along behind her.

Adam Hacker recognised Danny in the same moment that his mother's eyes narrowed. She hissed something. He shook his head; then his expression clouded as realisation dawned. His raised a stubby finger. 'Consulate, my arse. Come 'ere, you lying bastard.'

Danny spun on his heel and hurried back to where Fouldes stood with the Guardia officers. Adam Hacker charged round the corner, sliding to a halt. 'Copper's cunt,' he said as he strode past. Mrs Hacker held his gaze in a cold stare of hatred. 'You've ruined us, you bastard. My boys'll see you pay.'

Danny took a seat opposite the Guardia officers. Coffee could wait.

12

The four-storey *Palacio de Justicia* in Almería is located at the union of the city's two principal streets, the Paseo de Almería, with its shops and lines of rounded bay trees, and the Avenida Federico Garcia Lorca, a wide pedestrian esplanade tiled in white marble. Lawyers and bureaucrats mingled on the steps outside. Danny showed his press card, said he had an appointment with *Inspector Jefe* Andrés Bosquet. The uniformed officer on the door checked and waved him inside.

Bosquet sat behind his desk. He did not rise as Danny knocked and entered.

'You wanted to see me, Señor Sanchez,' he said, placing papers in a tray on his desk. 'Provided that this is important, I can spare you five minutes.'

'Made any headway on last night's murder?'

The policeman gave a thin smile. 'If the sole purpose of your visit is to try to crowbar exclusive titbits from me, I am going to take great pleasure in having you forcibly ejected from this building.' He lifted the receiver of the telephone on his desk.

'It's happened before. The killer has come from England. He's been murdering with impunity since 1994, *Inspector Jefe*. And I think he's been here in Almeria since 2000.'

The receiver clicked as it went down. Bosquet gestured towards a chair.

First of all, Danny asked if the British police had been in contact and saw the faint sneer on Bosquet's lip. For all they tried to hide it, that the British and Spanish police forces did not get on with each other was an open secret. Gibraltar remained a constant barrier to warm relations between the two countries. The Royal Gibraltar Police did little to improve the situation. Only recently, a Guardia Civil launch had chased drug smugglers into British waters. The RGP had arrested the drug dealers *and* the Guardia Civil officers.

Danny explained everything; Adrian Kimber, Nicholas Todd, the Scarecrow enquiry, the Cross-Border Killings, the body found by hunters in Granada. Then he explained what Project ROUNDUP was.

Bosquet steepled his fingers. Danny had caught his interest, that much was clear. 'And you think the murderer is still at large?'

'No. I think the *instigator* of these murders is still at large. He uses others to commit the actual killings. That's why he's not been caught; no one's been looking for him. In each case, the actual perpetrator of the killings has betrayed himself to such an extent that the UK police have never looked for anyone else. But after the final series of killings, the police deployment of resources became too much for him. So he upped sticks and moved to a safer country.'

'Safer?'

That had been a poor choice of word; Bosquet frowned at the implication of the UK police being more competent. 'Safer because no one knew of him, I mean.'

Bosquet mulled over Danny's words. 'I must admit you present a very persuasive case, but I'm afraid this office cannot investigate convincing suppositions. If there is, as you claim, a maniac on the loose, where are the bodies?'

'You've found two hidden within the walls of houses. There could be more.'

'I agree. And that is precisely why we investigated every single house Apache Construction has built or worked on in the province since the company was established. We found nothing.'

'Are you sure?'

Bosquet frowned. His voice hardened. 'Yes, we are sure. We consulted architects' plans, we measured, we drilled. Some of the homeowners have been tearing their own properties to pieces in an effort to ascertain whether they are living with dead bodies in their walls.'

'What about the houses under construction?'

'Those were the first ones we checked.' Bosquet saw doubt creep into Danny's face. 'I see another problem with your theory besides the lack of bodies. People rarely go missing without someone realising.'

'What if Orson were preying upon the immigrant community? People without an official presence? The body at Reade's house was north African.'

'Granted, that would increase the chances. But still, someone would notice. Immigrant communities here tend to be close-knit, simply because they have no one else to turn to. But that is a minor quibble. Your involvement worries me.'

'In what way?'

'You're a journalist, Señor Sanchez. Were I to admit a link between these killings – no matter how tenuous – it would be easy for you to write a story decrying the blunders of the Spanish police.'

'That's not my angle here.'

'What is your "angle"? I think that is what needs to be established before we go any further.'

'Christ, there's a maniac on the loose and you're asking me about angles? My angle is I want the bastard caught.'

Bosquet removed his glasses, polished the lenses with his tie, looked at his watch. 'What is it you want from me, specifically?'

'I saw Gutierrez on the television earlier. He said you had

found evidence implicating a British man. What did you find?'

'Semen-stained underpants, underneath the bed.'

'And you know the man's name?'

Bosquet thought before answering. 'Yes.'

'How?'

'We have a positive DNA match.'

'That's mighty quick for a DNA analysis.'

'His name was stitched in the waistband of the garment.'

'Oh, come off it. A guy commits murder then leaves his semen-stained underpants at the scene of crime with his *name* stitched in the waistband?'

The convenience of the discovery worried Bosquet, too, that much was evident. Doubt was writ large on the man's features. Danny fished in his bag, withdrew a folder.

'I can give you this. It's everything I found out in England. I have photos. And I've also translated all the relevant documents into Spanish for you. I have contact numbers for the UK police.'

'In return for?'

'The name the DNA match gave you. I want to know who you are looking for. I think he's being framed.'

The policeman leant back in his chair, tapping his thumbs together as he considered the matter. 'Do I have your solemn promise that none of this will be used with my name attached? And that you won't print the name?'

'If you want me to put it in writing, I'll do it now.'

'An unfortunate choice of phrase; putting it in writing is precisely what I am afraid of.'

'I don't stab my sources in the back.'

'Your ethics are very admirable, but it'll take more than that to convince me. If you can't print the name, what will you do with it?'

'I've contacts with the mental health service in the UK. If you give me the name I can get in touch with them, try to find out more, see if there's some connection. I've been a journalist long enough to know these bastards are only ever caught because of solid, methodical police work. I'm just saying I can explore a different angle without any of the usual jurisdictional snarl-ups.'

Bosquet nodded slowly. He fished in his drawer, then wrote something on a piece of A4, folded it in half, slid it across the table.

'I repeat: I don't want to see this name in print,' he said without taking his fingers from the paper. 'Is that understood?'

'Perfectly.'

Danny made to unfold the paper but Bosquet's finger remained there. 'Make sure it is. If you mess me around, I will see to it you regret it.'

Danny unfolded the paper, read the name, stood to hide his reaction.

Alan Reade.

13

First Danny checked online. It was precisely what he had guessed: semen was still valid for DNA testing months after ejaculation. Then he sent an SMS to Alan Reade's phone. 'Had unprotected sex in the last month or so? We need to speak. You're being set up for last night's murder. Danny. *Sureste News*.'

Then he phoned Durkin. 'Man, it is all kicking off out here, Jim. You wouldn't believe –'

'Danny, I know who Orson is.'

'What?'

'My wife found a perfect match: Tomas Enrique Cain. Mother was Spanish, father Scottish. He grew up in the Gloucester area and first came to the attention of the authorities when young Tommy – wait for it – "immobilised another boy with twine and sexually assaulted him after spray-painting his face white". That's taken verbatim from a psychiatrist's report that was quoted during his trial.'

'How did you find him?'

'I went to see a guy who used to work for us as court reporter at Gloucester Crown Court back in the early nineties. I asked him if he remembered anything about cases of sexual abuse involving Spaniards. The guy's in his seventies, but he's got a mind like a steel trap. He remembered something straight away – mostly because the defendant's mother had a full-on Latin meltdown in the courtroom. Then

I checked the newspaper files. I've sent you scans of them. Have a look, see what you think.'

There were three articles relating to the trial of Tomas Enrique Cain and his mother. The first article detailed how, in 1992, eighteen-year-old construction worker Tommy Cain was accused of raping a minor and his mother of aiding and abetting him. The second article described an incident during the two-day trial. Cain's mother, one Inmaculada Cain, née Cruz, had been removed from the courtroom after a "violent outburst" in which she "verbally abused and spat at the prosecution's principal witness".

There was a note from Durkin here: *Prosecution's principal witness was Cain's own sister, i.e. Inmaculada Cain's daughter. She couldn't be identified, owing to anonymity laws governing victims of sexual assault, but that her brother had abused her was an open secret in the town.*

Jesus. Her own daughter. What sort of mother would do that?

The answer was in the third article. It detailed the Cain family's miserable existence: the mother, addicted to drink and drugs, scratched a living as the lowest kind of prostitute whilst subjecting both children to psychological and physical abuse. Although Tommy had received his fair share, it seemed the mother reserved her greatest spite for the daughter, and encouraged her son to abuse the teenage girl. Inmaculada Cain had photographed some of the assaults, her teenage daughter smeared with make-up, hair tied in pigtails. The nature of the abuse had eventually changed: the mother's clients had been allowed to participate, with Tommy Cain lurking in the shadows, watching, waiting his turn.

There it was: the final piece in the puzzle. That was where Tommy Cain had acquired his taste for voyeuristic spectacle.

Danny phoned Durkin. 'Jesus. That's it. That's him. It's got to be.'

'Oh, it gets much better, mate.' Durkin could barely contain the excitement in his voice. 'Want to know the best thing of all? Tommy Cain worked for Apache construction. It all fits.'

'Got a name for the sister?'

Durkin laughed. 'Give me a chance, pal. I thought that was pretty good going for a morning's work.

Danny could feel himself being carried away by the excitement of it all. But he couldn't ignore the buzzing of one little fly. It took him a moment to place it.

'Was Cain found guilty?'

'Of course.'

'But if this is from 1992, Cain was most likely in prison during the Scarecrow killings. And the Cross Border Killings.'

'Perhaps. I'm still trying to find out what happened to him, how long he served. But perhaps he escaped, Danny. Perhaps his appeal was successful. Even so, it still works. Imagine this: Cain works with Callum Hacker, describes what he used to do to his sister, maybe taught Hacker the "toto" word. Hacker likes the sound of it, gets Kimber to steal him a list of loonies, befriends Todd and off you go. He could have rung Adrian Kimber on the pretext of work the night of the murder.'

'I don't see it that way, Jim. Callum Hacker is violent. Don't you see? He doesn't need someone else to do his dirty work. He would do it himself. Plus, he's shown on more than one occasion he is thick as the proverbial.'

'I don't agree. We're not the police, Danny. It's our duty to put this information into the public domain ASAP so the police *can* do something about it. For my money, I've got enough information to publish.'

'We've got an agreement.'

'And I've stuck to it. But this is where I'm getting off, mate.'

'What?'

'I've done so much legwork on newspaper time, I need to print something. My editor is going spare.'

'You son-of-a-bitch.'

'I know. I feel bad about it, really I do. If it means anything, I am truly sorry.'

'That's too late.'

Durkin hung up.

Bastard. Never trust another journalist – at least, not one from another newspaper. How many times had Danny fallen foul of partnerships of convenience during his career? Too many.

On the way back to his car, Danny noticed he had two missed calls from the office.

'What is it?' he said when Leonard answered.

'You don't sound very happy.'

'I'm not.'

'You're going to love this, then. We've just had an anonymous phone call offering, and I quote, "secret information on the Hackers and the murders".'

'Jesus, that's all I need. Did it sound genuine or was it a time-waster?'

'As the entertainments correspondent, all this cloak and dagger nonsense falls a little outside my remit, don't you think? But, yes, I think he sounded genuine. Genuinely nervous, anyway.'

'OK, where and when?'

Leonard gave him the details: the Cabo de Gata lighthouse, four o'clock. 'There's one final proviso: you're to take some food and drink with you.'

'What?'

'Preferably a Big-Mac meal, large, with normal fries, though sandwiches and crisps will do. Coca-cola to drink.'

'You're having me on.'

'As the Lord is my witness, those were the informant's exact words – *sans* grammatical errors and a terrible Liverpudlian accent.'

'Liverpool?'

'Without a shadow of a doubt. He sounded a regular Ringo Starr.'

It was Reade.

Alan Reade had phoned.

14

The lighthouse that marks the *Cabo de Gata* cape, the point where Spain's eastern and southern coastlines pinch together in a crooked black finger of rock, is one of the country's most desolate spots. Elsewhere along the coast, the Mediterranean is usually like a mill pond, but around the cape the sea surges and foams against the base of steep, angular cliffs. Off-shore, the shadow of jagged reefs can be seen below the surface of the angry water – hence the lighthouse.

It was a good place for a meeting.

Or a trap.

The lighthouse is situated beyond a series of inland salt marshes where flamingos live for part of the year. It can be reached only by a steep road that winds up and around the face of the cliffs. It is the sort of road that exists only in Spain; on one side, mountains of three-billion-year-old rock; on the other, a hundred-metre drop to the sea. To make matters worse, the road is only wide enough for one car to pass and has about twelve blind corners.

Danny loved the lighthouse, but loathed getting there. Just the thought of that road made his heart jump into his mouth. He stopped at a garage, bought sandwiches, crisps and a bottle of diet coke. He looked at his watch. He'd need to get a move on if he was to be there by four.

Danny drove as fast as prudence and the single-lane roads permitted, but a coach-load of Dutch tourists disembarking at the beginning of the lighthouse road sealed his fate. By the time he arrived at the lighthouse he was a full twenty minutes late.

An obviously Spanish couple stood at the railings, looking down at the churning white water at the base of the cliffs, wind blowing their hair and anoraks taut. It was always windy here.

There were only two cars; a saloon car and a clapped-out purple van.

Danny was about to ask the Spaniards if they'd seen anyone when he heard a loud 'pssst'. A man emerged from behind a large rock, arms wrapped around his shivering chest in a vain effort to keep out the cold. He was dressed in an unusual collection of clothing: pyjama top beneath a ripped and paint-spattered body warmer and jeans that Danny could have sworn were meant for a woman.

And sandals.

And one sock.

This was Reade. He recognised the man's face: blonde ponytail, scarred lip.

'You from the paper?' Reade said.

Danny nodded.

'Thank fuck. Did you bring food?'

'It's in the car.'

Reade headed towards the Golf, stopped when Danny held up a hand.

'Not so fast. I want to see your arm first.'

'What?'

'Your forearm. The one with the dates on.'

Reade shook his head, rolled up his sleeve. Danny approached gingerly, read through the dates, five of them, found what he was looking for. June, 1996 – January, 2001; Reade had been in prison when the Cross Border Killings occurred. He wasn't Orson. Danny already knew that, but you couldn't be too cautious.

They sat in Danny's car, the heater blowing. Reade grabbed

at the food hungrily, stuffed crisps and sandwiches into his mouth. He smelt like he'd spent the night sleeping rough.

Reade saw Danny's nose wrinkle. 'Hey, I don't normally dress like this, OK?'

'What happened?'

'The Hackers found me at my girlfriend's house up in San José two nights ago.'

'And you got out in one piece?'

'Just. Luckily for me, I was awake when they turned up. I was out the back door and over the fence before they started knocking, so I had to grab what clothes I could. And I can't go home: the Hackers have got the old bitch across the road watching out for them.' His face clouded as he thought about it. 'I wonder who it was told the police about the fucking dead body? The Hackers must have grassed on me. I've been thinking about it. I mean, it's the only way. The police wouldn't have just gone to my house at random and started drilling holes, would they?'

'No way.' Danny busied himself with his shoulder bag until the guilty look faded.

His hunger partly sated, Reade got down to business. 'What's this bollocks about me being framed for murder?'

Danny explained what had happened at William Fouldes's house. Reade's mouth gaped. Then he became angry.

'Do I look the sort of twat would sew his fucking name in a pair of boxer shorts?'

'I think the name tag is the least of your worries. There's a semen stain the Spanish police have matched to your DNA records back in the UK.'

Reade's face paled.

Danny shifted in his seat. 'Look, I know you didn't do it. But you need to level with me if you want my help.'

'You got it.'

'How did you get Craig Thorndyke's cash card?'

Reade gave a practised shrug. 'No idea what you're talking about.'

Off to flying start.

'Look, I saw you at the cash point on Mojacar Playa, a touch after seven-thirty. I never forget a face, Alan, especially not one with a scar on the upper lip. Come on, how do you expect me to believe you about anything else if you won't play straight? Where did you get it?'

His mouth became sulky. 'I found it. And that's the God's truth, so help me.'

'Where?'

Reade wriggled in his chair. 'About two months ago, I pulled this bird. Or rather, she pulled me. She was real dirty. We went back to my house, she spent the night. In the morning I found this on the floor. Must have fallen out of her bag.'

'How'd you get the PIN number?'

'It was wrapped up in a sheet of paper. The PIN was written on it.'

'Come off it.'

'It's the truth. As God's my witness.' Reade's eyes were wide with sincerity.

Danny thought of something. 'Did you have unprotected sex with her?'

'That's none of your business.'

'Jesus, now's no time to be coy. Did you wear a condom?'

He shook his head.

'And did you –'

'Yes. I did.' Reade was following Danny's train of thought now. 'Oh, Christ.'

'Yes, mate. It's like I said, you've been set up. Tell me about this woman. How'd you meet her?'

'In a disco.'

'What did she look like?'

'Pretty average. Dark hair, shortish, quite fit.'

'How old?'

'Late thirties, I think.'

That was the Ma Hacker theory out the window. Who the

hell was this woman who was prepared to sleep with a scuzz like Reade? A prostitute, paid by Orson to implicate Reade? That was the most likely explanation. By using the cash card, Reade had implicated himself in the crimes; not only did he have a dead body in the wall of his house, he was using a cash card that belonged to a missing youth.

'Where was she from, this woman?'

'She was English. She had one of those bumpkin accents. Bristol, something like that.'

'What happened with the cash card?'

Reade's face became sulky. 'I went down to see if I could get any money with it. Satisfied? I fucking admit it. I stole money from the account. But that doesn't make me a murderer, does it?'

'And you went back every month?'

'Yes.'

'Why go back three times?'

'The cash point had a limit on it: 300 Euros a day.'

'And why go to the cash point in Mojacar?'

Reade bristled. 'I wasn't going to pay a six Euro bank charge for every withdrawal. If you ask me, they're the real thieves. Fucking banks.'

A stingy thief; Danny had heard it all now. A lump of mushed bread flew from Reade's mouth as he said the last word. He wiped it from Danny's dashboard with a grimy finger.

'Answer this one with your head. Did you attack Charlie Hacker?'

Reade's head shook violently. He swallowed a lump of bread. 'As God's my witness, I never touched a hair on his head.'

'Can you think of someone that might have?'

'I put some feelers out when the bastards starting hunting me. Guess what? About three weeks ago there was a Bulgarian guy got his hand mangled while working for Charlie Hacker. There was a big bust up because Hacker wouldn't take him to hospital. The poor bastard was sat there dripping blood with his hand turned to Pedigree Chum while a taxi turned up. Taxi driver took one look and told them where to stick it. Hacker took him in the end, but dropped him a good half mile from the hospital. Seems the guy's brother wasn't too impressed when he turned up last week.'

So that was the answer. It was a common enough phenomenon in Spain. There were thousands of companies like the Hackers', employing cheap, cash-in-hand immigrant labour. They got nervy when a worker was injured. In one infamous case, a worker's arm had been ripped off and his Spanish "boss" had dropped him 100 yards from the doors of the hospital with strict instructions not to mention where or how the accident had occurred.

'Where are these Bulgarian blokes now?'

'How should I know? You think I want to go near someone mental enough to crack Charlie Hacker round the head? Those east European blokes don't fuck about. I mean, there's hard and there's ex-communist hard.'

'OK. Now what's this secret information you mentioned on the phone?'

Reade smiled. 'I've been following the story in your paper. I read how the police were checking houses built by the Hackers, ripping the walls out to see if there were more bodies. Well, there's one house the police have missed.'

'Are you sure?'

'Sure I'm sure. Where do you think I slept last night?'

15

Dust rose as Danny's car rumbled down the dry riverbed. They were back in the Almanzora Valley now, in Los Membrillos; it was an hour's drive north from the lighthouse. The early evening sun was low and hot.

How did Reade know about this house? That was the first question Danny had asked. The answer was simple enough; Reade had been in the process of installing the plumbing when the project was stopped. He'd known it was one of the Hackers' dodgy jobs, had revisited the place on a number of occasions for "bunk ups" he didn't want his girlfriend finding out about.

Danny saw Reade's purple van turn left, checked in his rear-view mirror that Paco was still with them. He'd phoned the photographer, found out he was working somewhere close, got him to come along. Safety in numbers.

Reade's van slowed to a halt. Here it was. The three men parked.

The villa would have been an amazing property if it had been finished. It was similar in size to the Cookes' villa and also two storeys high. The exterior walls were finished but lacked rendering. Danny estimated it had a good 8,000 square metres of land, surrounded on two sides by grey-brown walls of mud and rock that had been carved out thousands of years ago by rushing water. The ground was stippled with esparto grass and cacti. Lines of dried-out olive and almond trees covered the sandy ground to the left of the house and fell away as it dropped towards the riverbed.

There were no windows, but crosses of yellow and black tape bearing the word SEPRONA – the name of the Guardia Civil department that dealt with environmental crimes – fluttered in some of the holes. A low stone wall delineated the edge of the property. A bank of sandy scree ran behind the house; it was ten metres high and had been built on with dozens of houses.

Paco shaded his eyes against the evening sun as he stared up at the houses. 'It's not a particularly isolated spot for a murderer to work in.'

Danny shook his head. 'I checked with Reade. All those houses up there are new. Two years ago there was nothing here for about a quarter mile apart from this building.'

'Why'd the building work get stopped?'

'It's built on land prone to flooding.'

Piles of unused building materials lay off to one side. Weeds grew through the holes in breeze blocks and through the gaps between pallets of bricks.

Stairs zigzagged through the centre of the construction, most of which was still surrounded by scaffolding. Iron poles supported one section of roof.

'Now what?' Paco said. 'We've found a half-built house. How are we supposed to sell that?'

It was a good question. Danny looked at the walls of grey breeze blocks. There was no way of telling whether the walls were too thick for the interior dimensions of the house. Paco leant a hand against one of them. 'If you think I'm going to waste the rest of the day drilling holes in walls at random, you're sorely mistaken.'

Paco had a point. It had taken them the best part of twenty minutes to knock out one of the bricks at Reade's house. If they were to attack this place at random, it could easily take them all night.

'We need the architect's plans,' Danny said.

'I. .got . . . plans,' Reade said in faltering Spanish.

Danny smiled, switched to English. 'Where are they?'

Reade's face fell in a *me-and-my-big-mouth* way. 'No way. I'm not going to my house. Not if the Hackers are out on bail again.'

'Give me the keys, then, and tell me where they are.'

'I'm not having you wandering around inside my house.'

'Jesus, pal. It's your neck that's on the chopping block here.'

Reade swallowed, fumbled in his pocket, produced the keys. 'In the corner of my bedroom, underneath the cabinet, there's a tile that's not grouted. Lift it up, there's a floor safe. That's where the plans are.'

'You got a tape measure in your van? Good.' Danny threw him a pen and a notepad. 'Start measuring the rooms, width and length. Paco? Take a walk round those houses up top, see if anyone saw anything.'

'Like what?'

'People coming here late at night, suspicious activity, that sort of thing. Just have a dig; you never know, we might get lucky.'

It was a twenty-minute drive to Reade's house. Danny parked at the end of the road, walked along the back of the property and hopped over the wall. The last thing he wanted now was hassle with the Hackers.

He let himself in through the patio door and found Reade's bedroom. All the files and papers on the shelves were gone. The police had taken them.

Reade's bedroom had been searched by the police: the bed had been shunted to one side, the cupboards emptied, the clothes piled on top of each other on the bed.

They hadn't found the floor safe, though; it was well-hidden. Danny lifted the tile up, opened the safe. This was obviously where Reade kept all his illicit stuff. There was a bag of white powder, four or five grams in weight, and a big bag of skunk marijuana; there was no mistaking the cat piss scent it gave off. Underneath were lots of files containing details of all the cash-in-hand work Reade had carried out. He was obviously a cautious man.

Danny searched through the pile of papers and found the plans relating to the house. He took photos of all the documents; they would be evidence when he came to write the article and he couldn't bank on Reade's letting him keep the originals. Then he wrote down in his notebook the measurements of each room's size in square metres. Fully spread out, the A1 plans covered a good third of the bed and he didn't want to have to mess around with them back at the house.

He was three-quarters of the way through noting the information down when a key could be heard opening the front door. Danny froze; seconds later, the patio door slid open. The light in the living room flicked on as someone shouted in Spanish, 'Bedroom. In the bedroom.'

Danny was still standing motionless as a tall, muscular man ran into the room. Then the file fell to the ground and his hands shot up in the air.

Danny was staring down the barrel of a gun.

16

He sat before the mirror, staring at his reflection, readying himself for work. He liked this part of it, covering himself up, hiding. No one ever suspected. He stretched his lips, practising his smile, admiring pearly-white teeth. He wished his hair were longer. He would be able plait it into pigtails if it were. He did that sometimes, stood in front of the mirror, re-created those whimpering, whining faces he'd observed so many times. Not tonight, though. Caution and patience.

The files from the brothers' building company were no use to him now. The police were on to them. They hadn't found his house, though. He'd been careful to remove every trace of it. The house was too sacred for him to run any risks. They were chasing the plumber now. If that failed, he could point them in the direction of the builder, the fat one, Callum. Callum was the main reason he'd settled in this part of Spain. Thousands of half-built houses and a violent rapist building them; that was too good an opportunity to pass up. He remembered Hacker from the old days, back in the old country. He knew what had happened, what he'd done to that boy. It was good to hide near a man like that.

He had another fish he was reeling in. He'd won his confidence. He could hear the man's voice now, speaking clumsy Spanish on the phone and tried to imagine the features that belonged to the face. What language would he scream in? He'd soon find out. The thing was hungry to get back to work. It had been pestering. But mustn't rush these things. They needed to find somewhere new, somewhere they could work in peace. After so long preparing, he wanted to savour the pleasures in silence.

As always when he thought of the property, he wanted to look at it.

He didn't realise anything was wrong until he had stepped out onto his balcony, lit a menthol cigarette and looked down at the gully below where the grey brick construction mouldered.

Cars.

Three cars were parked outside.

He ran inside, grabbed binoculars.

The reporter. It was that fucking *reporter.*

And Reade.

How dare they? That place was sacred. He trembled all over. He would make them pay.

Who was the third? Fat with cameras round his neck. Where did he know him from?

He rushed back inside. His lip curled as he realised he did recognise the photographer, remembered where he'd seen him before.

He reached for the phone. 'Hello, something's come up. I might be a little late for work.'

17

Danny was so preoccupied with the damned Hackers that he'd forgotten the police would be watching Reade's house. It was logical, really; the man was suspected of committing one of the worst murders the province had seen.

That said, it was a relief to hear the guy with the gun shout '¡*policia*!'.

The police had searched him, looked at his documents, at his press card. Then they'd all waited for more than an hour for Bosquet to turn up. Danny was sitting on the edge of the bed, his hands cuffed behind him.

That had been twenty minutes earlier. The reprimand had died on Bosquet's lips when Danny had said, 'The Hackers. There's a house you didn't check.'

'Take us there. Now.'

'Once you take these cuffs off me, I'll be glad to.'

They went in three cars; two unmarked police vehicles and Danny's. Danny travelled in the second police car, Bosquet in the first. No one had said whether Danny was under arrest or not.

It was dark now. Headlights formed pools of light against the bare bricks of the half-finished house. And then they saw a flicker of motion, away to the left, at the edge of vision; a man, running between the trees.

Danny saw Paco Pino standing in the headlights, shielding his eyes. The photographer said, 'Where the hell have you bee . . .' then his voice died as he realised it wasn't Danny who'd gotten out of the car.

Inspector Jefe Andres Bosquet pointed towards the olive trees. 'Who was that running away?'

Paco had no reason to lie. 'Alan Reade.'

Bosquet spun round and ordered the other car to follow Reade; he put out an APB. Then he returned to the second car, in which Danny was a passenger. 'Why didn't you tell me Reade was here?'

'You didn't ask.'

Bosquet slammed the roof of the car.

'No more games, Señor Sanchez.'

'This business is nothing to do with Reade. He's being set up.'

'Damn it, that's *not* for you to decide.'

Danny was pulled roughly from the car. He'd known Reade would bolt, known it would piss Bosquet off. But it was a calculated risk. The last thing he wanted now was for the police investigation to focus on grilling a false suspect. That was precisely what Orson wanted.

Danny shuffled up to Paco. 'I got the measurements from the plans,' Danny whispered, lighting a cigarette.

The photographer patted his pocket. 'And I've got Reade's measurements here.' His face was serious. 'Look over there.'

Something glistened in the darkness. It took Danny a moment to realise what it was; a hook, a foot long, an inch thick, the sort butcher's used to hang whole pigs from. Lengths of rope were coiled near it.

'I found it inside the house, in a windowless room at the centre. It's the only room in the house with a door. There's a hole in the ceiling from where the hook was removed.'

Danny nodded towards the twinkling house lights on the ridge above them.

'Have any luck speaking to anyone?'

Paco shrugged. 'Not much. Most of them were English. But there was one Spanish woman. She gave me a right grilling, demanded to see my press card, asked me my name, who I worked for.'

'She have anything to say?'

'Not really. She said she'd only lived there for a while.'

The police questioned both men for what seemed like hours. It was nearly 10 p.m. before Danny and Paco could talk to each other again.

In the meantime, the police activity had increased. It had begun roughly twenty minutes after they'd arrived. Bosquet had emerged from the house looking pale and angry as he talked into a radio and requested a forensic team.

So, it was true. There was another body.

Back up teams arrived; lots of back up teams, their swirling lights filling the gorge with neon light. Scene of crime tape was stretched across the entrance; police with construction equipment arrived and began knocking down walls. Then more policemen arrived.

And more.

Paco whistled as surreptitiously he took another photo. 'What the hell have they found in there?' More than twenty Guardia Civil officers were inside the property. Bulb lights blazed inside the house. It was impossible to tell where exactly the police were working. The sound of drilling seemed to come from everywhere at once.

Now Danny listened; he was sure the drilling *did* come from two places at once.

'Let me see Reade's measurements. Let's see which room it is.'

They took the two notebooks, began comparing the lists. It was a tough task; neither Danny nor Reade had written them down in any particular order. Both men rearranged their lists, largest to smallest. Then they compared the lists again.

'Oh Jesus,' Paco said as his eyes flickered from one list to the other.

It wasn't one room.

It was every room. Every single room was smaller than the plans said it should be.

Christ, the walls of the house were full.

18

It was over. He watched from the window above, watched the lights sparkling on the walls of his house. It was time to move on again. He felt nothing now. Not anger, not fear. They would only cloud his judgement. Caution and patience. The work came before everything. He would run now, sink beneath the surface. He could wait.

But there was something he had to do first. He must cover his tracks. They'd got too close this time.

He hefted the Jerry cans into the back of his car. He would get everything ready tonight. Tomorrow he would tie up the loose ends; reporter, photographer and thing.

19

Sunday April 11th, 2010

There was a sleeping bag and camping mattress in the storeroom at *Sureste News*. Danny worked until 04:00, sent the special article to head office and made up a bed on the newsroom floor. He lay down, using his rolled jacket as a pillow.

Bosquet had released Danny and Paco at around 10 p.m. Correction: Bosquet had turfed them out at around that time. The last Danny had seen of him, the homicide detective was storming up and down outside the house, arguing on the phone. 'Not this time. Goddamn it, there are too many. We can't pass this off as a burglary gone wrong. Or as anything else. We'll look fools if we tell lies again.'

Then he'd looked up and seen Danny and Paco staring at him. 'What the hell are they still doing here? Get rid of them.'

At about 11.30 p.m., Danny had received a phone call from the newspaper owner, Leonie Pelham-Kerr, the White Witch herself.

'Mr Sanchez. What's going on down there? Is it true?'

'Yes.'

'How many bodies are there?'

'No one knows. Lots.'

'What's your involvement?'

Danny explained, being careful to stress that most of the information had been discovered during his holiday. Danny felt her displeasure rising from the phone like a chill draught.

'And this bid to stage the powerboat competition is the reason the authorities have been dissimulating up until now?'

'I believe so.'

'What do you intend to write?'

'What do I . . . ? I intend to write exactly what you pay me to write, Ms Pelham-Kerr; the truth.'

The White Witch said nothing at first. 'Can you explain,' she resumed, after the silence had become sepulchral, 'why I have had an anonymous phone call threatening to pull 150,000 Euros worth of advertising from the chain if we publish this news?'

'Because some people here are stupid enough to believe Canute really could turn back the tide as long as he threatened and bullied enough.'

'And is it that? An unstoppable force of nature?'

'The truth tends to be, doesn't it? Sooner or later, anyway. The Spanish papers will be sniffing around here tomorrow. Word always gets out on something like this. They'll have bodge-jobs ready for their online versions by midday tomorrow. Let's do a special edition for our online edition tonight. Let's make sure people know this is our story.'

'My story, Mr Sanchez. I'm the one who stands to lose 150,000 Euros of advertising.'

'Someone is going to break the story. I have all the facts.'

'I'll organise things here. Just make sure you're right, Mr Sanchez.'

About eight a.m. Danny was woken from a troubled sleep by the ringing of his mobile. He'd barely had time to say hello before the voice at the other end said, 'Wherever you are, you cunt, I'm going to find you and then I'm going to kill you. Do you understand? You're dead.'

The connection broke. It took Danny a moment to realise whose the voice had been: Callum Hacker's. But why? Danny had barely mentioned the Hackers in the article he'd written, the article that was still probably only in the process of being prepared for online publication. What was Hacker so angry about?

Then Danny remembered his was not the only article being written about the killings.

He opened up the computer and looked at the online edition of The Gloucester Herald.

His head sank into his hands as he read the headline.

GLOUCESTER RAPIST QUESTIONED IN COSTA KILLINGS
Link between Bredon Hill murder and Spanish serial killer
By Jim Durkin, Ray Taylor and Danny Sanchez

Danny had never thought that he would have cause to lament the practice of honour among journalists. Durkin had kept to the letter of their agreement and signed the article with all three names... and, in the process, he had not only embarrassed Danny, but endangered his life.

Danny only speed-read the article; he knew all the bloody details anyway. Durkin was a good journalist: nice crisp prose style, story solidly built on facts. Too many facts for Danny's liking. The article went into detail about Callum Hacker's homosexual tendencies and his prison sentence for male rape. The difference was that Durkin had 900 miles and the Bay of Biscay between him and Callum Hacker; Danny had about fifteen minutes of *autovia*.

At nine-thirty that morning, the staff of *Sureste News* began arriving, having been called in to the office for a special Sunday session. The story of the bodies would require all four of them to work. Danny told them about Callum Hacker and instructed them to keep the door closed and locked at all times. At ten o'clock, Danny phoned Paco. Danny could hear that Paco was driving as they spoke.

'I can't talk, Danny.' He sounded fraught. 'It's Alejandra.'

'What's the matter?'

'Lourdes can't find her.'

'Are you sure?'

'*Joder*, Danny, she's going out of her mind. Of course I'm sure. I've got to go and help her. I'm sorry.'

'Don't be sorry, *amigo*. Just find your little girl.'

Danny's story went online at eleven. The phone calls began at 11:15: the local Spanish newspapers first, then the UK nationals. By midday he was being called by journalists from France, Italy and Holland, all asking for contact numbers.

Danny had written the bare facts; that the instigator of a series of killings had been at large for years, using disturbed individuals to carry out his work. It was tempting to mention his suspicions of official attempts to stymie the investigation, but he had nothing concrete to back his theories up. That story could wait for another day. Right now they needed to put a figure on the number of bodies found, how long they'd been concealed and where they'd come from.

At midday, it was announced on the radio that Alan Reade had been caught. Danny shook his head. Now it was more important than ever that they flushed out the whole story; other journalists and police would be preoccupied with Reade's capture; Danny knew that it could provide only a false trail.

Danny's mobile rang. It was a number he didn't recognise. He decided not to answer it, then changed his mind.

'Señor Sanchez, it's Dolores Donaire, from the university. I saw your article this morning. I think we should talk.'

'I'd love to, but it will have to be by phone. I'm up to my eyeballs.'

'I've been consulting with a colleague to draw up a profile for Orson and we've arrived at a few conclusions. Have you heard of Dr Benjamin Spock?'

'Sure,' Danny said. 'Don't spank your children. That guy, yeah?'

'There's a little more to his work than that. Post-World War II, he conducted a study in which he established that sociopaths found it far easier to fool and control members of the opposite sex than they did people of the same sex; men could fool women, women could fool men. However, members of their own sex always found them creepy. Take the example of Ted Bundy; he was never short of female companionship but had almost no male friends.'

'I don't want to sound rude, but I really do need to crack on. How does this relate to Orson and his victims?'

'*His*. That's precisely my point; I've considered the matter carefully and I now think *he* is actually a *she*, Mr Sanchez.'

'Orson is a woman?'

'Don't sound so surprised. It was the rape angle that made me think of it. You pointed it out yourself. This individual is obviously intelligent, patient and extremely cautious. But why involve these "idiots", if you'll pardon the expression. People like Nicholas Todd, Ishmael Vertanness, Phillip Cohen? Misfits and losers, people who fill the profile of violent criminals so perfectly? What was it they brought to the equation?'

'Tell me,' Danny said, when the silence had grown uncomfortable.

'A woman cannot physically penetrate another person. She can do with an implement, but not with her own body. Think about it; this perpetrator has a strong necessity to control, to humiliate, to witness the suffering of others. Such deviant fantasies often grow from something that is lacking in the real world. I would hazard a guess that Orson had been the victim of a sexual assault or rape in the past. This has resulted in the need to dominate, to control. Perhaps it's a way of exorcising the demons. Having been the victim, Orson is now in control, is powerful.

'That's why I think Orson is a woman. All the other pieces of the jigsaw then slot into place. You asked yourself how on earth someone like Vertanness could get close to his victims? What better accomplice than a woman? Look at the example of the Wests. Girls got in the car with Fred because Rose was with him. Again, it would be likely that this woman had experimented with some form of "proxy-rape" herself; that's how she discovered how unsatisfying it is. It is often the way, Mr Sanchez; the abused becomes the abuser.'

He hung up. The truth dropped on him like hundred-pound weight. Christ, it wasn't Callum Hacker and it wasn't Tommy Cain. It was Cain's sister. She was Orson.

20

Orson stood before the mirror and stared at the dark eyes reflected there. There had been a little girl behind those eyes once, but no trace remained now. A person could be either sex on the inside. It was a question of willpower. A person's body was a vessel, nothing more. It was what you filled it with that was important.

Little girls were dirty. They were sluts. They were weak. Little girls could be poked and prodded and mauled. Orson had learned that lesson in Mamá's cellar, pigtails swinging as Tommy and Mamá's friends climbed atop and began the sweating and grunting.

The answer had been so simple. Nothing ever happened to Tommy. Orson would change, lock that little girl away in the cellar forever. From then on, she would become he. And he would be the one hurting, the one with power. He would make everyone pay, just like he'd made Mamá's cat pay as Tommy held it down.

Naked from the waist down, he stood before the mirror and pushed fingers into the triangle of pubic hair, then clamped them between his legs, felt the sticky warmth.

He pushed his breasts out, ran fingers through his hair.

It was useful, the way he looked. No one ever suspected. They loved to flirt with him. Oh, he knew what little boys wanted. He'd learned that lesson long ago. He enjoyed seeing the way other men stared at his long legs, his curves, not realising their danger. People trusted women.

Especially here in the new country. That was why he'd insisted on looking at the photographer's ID, this Paco Pino fellow. He knew where he'd seen the photographer before: among the crowd at the nursery, holding his little girl as they'd both enjoyed the clown show. Pogo had given her a lollipop. What could be safer? A female clown. Orson enjoyed the shows; he stood there beneath the make-up, knowing they could not see him for what he truly was.

He paused, wound the window down, beckoned to a man, asked him the question he'd asked a dozen times already. Paco Pino? The photographer. Yes, I know him. He lives down there on the corner. He's working now, though.

He parked outside the school, watched a group of children through the railings. He called one over, asked who the little girl with the dark brown hair was. Alejandra. That was her name.

He circled the block again, waited ten minutes, then approached the railings, called the girl by name.

'Hello there, Alejandra. Do you remember me?'

The little girl nodded enthusiastically. 'You came to our nursery with the clown.'

He smiled. 'That's right. I'm Pogo's friend. Your mummy's with Pogo now. Would you like to go and see them both?'

A pause. Then a nod.

'Just press that button there, sweetheart, and open the door.'

She had to jump to reach it. The gate clicked.

He wrapped fingers tipped with scarlet varnish around the child's hand, led her calmly across the road. Caution and patience.

But he was no longer smiling. He had work to do.

21

Danny phoned Jim Durkin. The journalist answered with a sigh. 'If you're going to shout at me, don't bother. I've already had death threats from Spain.'

'Jim, do me one favour and we're quits. Did you find out any more about Tommy Cain?'

'Yes. You were right. He was in prison. Still is, in fact.'

'What about the sister?'

'Yes. Ricarda Inmaculada Cain, better known as Ricki Cain.'

Danny mouthed the name, wondering why it sounded familiar. He heard Brian Kimber's voice. Adrian's girlfriend. Nicki Jane.

Or something like that.

'Do you know what she looked like? Can you get a photo?'

'Why the sudden interest?'

'Can you or can't you?'

'I'll see what I can do?'

That was it. All the pieces fell into place. Ricki Cain, the girl Adrian Kimber was besotted with, the poor abused daughter of Inmaculada Cain, the sister of Tommy Cain. She'd been twisted all out of shape as a child. Now she was getting even. What was it the psychologist had said? "The abused becomes the abuser." Ricki Cain had made Kimber steal the details of Project ROUNDUP for her. And that was who Kimber had gone to meet on Bredon Hill – who would have suspected a nineteen-year-old girl?

Danny's phone rang.

'Paco, you'll never guess what –'

'Come to the Hackers' yard. Now. It's important.'

'What do you –'

'Please, Danny. Just do it.'

The phone went dead.

22

Danny pulled up outside the Hackers' yard, wondering what the hell Paco was doing there after dark. The gates to the builder's yard were open. Danny walked towards the warehouse and pushed at the door. It creaked. A man's voice said: 'Come inside. Walk to the centre of the room.'

'Why?' Danny said without moving.

'Because if not I'll fucking kill the kid.'

That was a woman's voice, low, measured, cold. Christ, where had he heard her voice before? He recognised it, he was sure, that deep, almost masculine tone.

The warehouse stank. The smell made Danny feel light-headed as he edged inside. Paco was slumped in the centre of the room, blood trickling from his forehead. Danny walked towards him and realised that two figures were lurking in the darkness to one side of the door.

The woman's face was masked by shadow. Danny heard a squeak, saw the infant figure. She was restraining the child, who was trying to squirm away from her. The blade at Alejandra's throat glinted. Her eyes were wet with tears, but she made no sound; the situation was beyond her ability to comprehend.

Ricki Cain walked forward, carrying the struggling child. Behind her loped a young man who was also brandishing a knife.

Danny recognised Craig Thorndyke's blanched, ravaged

features. He saw what Toby Ibañez meant about him being creepy. His eyes were jittery, unsettled, his mouth scabbed. A length of rope was coiled around his hand; his lips were wet with spittle.

Ricki Cain motioned Danny towards the centre of the room and addressed Thorndyke. 'Tie him up.' When Danny hesitated, she poked the knife into the child's throat. 'You don't have a choice.'

She was right. Danny didn't.

He sat with his back to the post. Paco's hands were pinioned behind him, held by cable ties. His forehead was smeared with blood. Danny's arms were now similarly restrained. The cable ties bit into them cruelly.

Craig Thorndyke knelt beside him and pressed the hunting knife to his throat as Ricki Cain headed for the door. Thorndyke's eyes were feverish, his expression brutish. 'Not long now. Do you realise the fun we're going to have?'

Danny's head reeled. Something in the warehouse stank, a strong, chemical smell, like petrol. Danny sniffed the air again.

Not *like* petrol.

It *was* petrol.

His eyes shot to the wall and took in the empty brackets where the two fire extinguishers had once sat as Ricki Cain disappeared outside.

'Thorndyke, watch the door.' Danny wriggled in desperation. 'Don't let her close the fucking door.'

Craig Thorndyke smiled. 'You must think I was born yester-'

Thorndyke spun round at the sound of breaking glass, gaped as flame from the petrol bomb engulfed one corner of the room. The metal door slammed. Danny heard the rattle of a chain holding it shut.

Thorndyke ran, yanked at the door. It opened inwards perhaps an inch.

Danny heard the sound of a car starting. The fire raged,

racing up either side of the wall. She'd rigged the place to burn. Not that it needed much help. Flames licked the piles of wood. Something exploded. The heat was intense. The dense smoke was suffocating. . The air was already difficult to breath. The stench of burning plastic filled Danny's nostrils. His eyes stung .

Craig Thorndyke stared dumbly as the orange flame surged along both walls of the outhouse. In a matter of seconds it had circled them. He hammered at the door, voice shrill. 'You bitch! Ricki! I'm still here! Don't leave me!'

The flames sucked upwards hungrily.

Craig Thorndyke was smashing at the metal door with a plank of wood. The sound echoed above the crackling of the flames, drowning out Danny's cries as he screamed to get Craig Thorndyke's attention. 'There's another way out.'

'What?' Thorndyke's eyes bulged with panic.

'There's another way out.'

'Where?'

'Untie us.'

Thorndyke pressed the knife to Danny's throat. 'Where is it?'

'Either you cut the ties or you cut my throat.'

Thorndyke ran round the perimeter of the warehouse, arm raised against the heat.

'Where is it?'

Danny shook his head. 'Cut us free or we all burn together.'

Thorndyke screamed as a burning timber toppled to the ground at his feet. His eyes were bulging with panic. He knelt, cut Danny free.

'Where is it?'

'Cut him free, too. Quickly.'

Danny helped Paco to his feet. They stumbled towards the back of the warehouse. Danny felt his way along the wall, trying to remember the whereabouts of the hole made for the rottweilers , trying to work out if it was big enough for a man to get through.

It was.

Sheets of flame rippled across the ceiling as Danny pulled Paco through the dog-flap. Somewhere plastic was melting. The air was thickening with choking fumes. Craig Thorndyke followed on his hands and knees.

It happened quickly. One moment they were outside, rolling in the dust, scrabbling to run from the intense heat, sucking at the clean air, three survivors each glad to be alive.

And then Paco got his breath back.

He raised his head. His eyes shone as he stared at Thorndyke.

'Hijo de puta.'

Paco charged.

The two men crashed together, Paco's hands stretching for Thorndyke's scrawny neck. Paco got within inches, then blew air. He seemed to deflate from the legs up as he suddenly stood still, grunted, then staggered backwards, clutching his stomach, a dark stain spreading across the fabric.

Craig Thorndyke turned towards Danny, the dripping blade still in his hands. Heat had singed his long fringe, burnt his eyebrows. 'Your turn, prick.' He ran at Danny.

There was no time to think. Danny grabbed sand, flung it in Thorndyke's eyes.

Thorndyke's hands shot to his face. He staggered past Danny, who stood up, grabbed a stone and hit him with full force across the back of his head. Craig Thorndyke tumbled to the ground.

Danny fought the impulse to land him another blow.

Paco was trying to sit up. He got halfway, let out a whimper. His hands were sticky with blood. Danny knelt beside him. He took him by the ankles, dragged him away from the burning warehouse. Paco screamed.

Danny seized his mobile, called for an ambulance, folded his jacket, put it below Paco's head, told him to keep still. Flames and smoke billowed from beneath the edges of the metal roof, huge flickering orange tongues that rose five, ten metres above the building, edged with roiling plumes of smoke, grey-white against the black of the night. The whole yard was illuminated with an eerie orange glow.

Paco kept trying to sit. Waves of blood spilled from his wound every time. It took Danny a moment to realise that the grunts were actually Paco speaking. He leant his head close to Paco's mouth.

'Find . . . my . . . daughter.'

Alejandra.

She was still with Ricki Cain.

Neighbours were emerging from nearby houses now, Spanish housewives in slippers and dressing gowns. A middle-aged man ran across to them, pulling a t-shirt on over his head as he did so.

Danny beckoned to him and explained the situation as quickly as he could. The Spanish man stayed with Paco as Danny tied Craig Thorndyke's hands behind his back, took the knife. He wiped the blade clean of Paco's blood on Craig Thorndyke's t-shirt, headed for his car.

The old man shouted at him. 'Hey, where are you going?'

People watched as Danny drove through the crowds gathering at the gates of the building yard. There was a dull booming sound: part of the roof had collapsed. Danny sped off down the road.

As he did so, a white van screeched to a halt, jerked itself round and began to follow him.

23

Danny called Tony Ibañez's number as he drove.

'Mr Ibañez, I need some information. Your worker, Allison. Where does she live?'

'I can't give you information like that.'

'Did you hear about the house the police found yesterday loaded with dead bodies?'

'Of course.'

'It was Allison. Only her name's not Allison. It's Ricki Cain.'

A pause. 'Is this a joke? It's in very poor –'

'Listen, she just locked me in a burning building and kidnapped my friend's five-year-old daughter. Now give me her fucking address so I can contact the police or I swear I will see your name is spread over every paper from Birmingham to Benidorm.'

Ibañez was quiet. Then he said, 'She lives in Los Membrillos.'

That figured.

The truth had hit Danny when he'd heard Ricki Cain's voice. He'd recognised it immediately, yet couldn't place it. Of course not. The only time he'd heard her speak she'd been speaking French, sitting in the back room of Shelter All. That was how she found her victims. Christ, she had a direct phone line to them. She could sit there at night, asking them all sorts of personal details. Who knows you're here? Have you told your family where you are? Are you a runaway?

When did you last speak to your family? And whenever she located one of life's waifs and strays, someone that would not be missed, she arranged a meeting with them. And then they disappeared. Only they didn't disappear, because in order to do that someone would have to miss them. Ricki Cain had been careful never to choose anyone with friends.

The address was not easy to find, but as Danny approached the area he began to recognise it. It was close to the house, the one where the bodies had been found. Christ, it was right above it.

He turned into the dirt road.

A palm tree stood in front of the house. As Danny's headlights swung round, he saw that the bonnet of Ricki Cain's car was wrapped around it. Both front tyres were blown. Shards of broken headlight sparkled on the floor. The boot of the car was open. The two fire extinguishers from the warehouse were in there.

Ricki Cain stood beside the house, calling, whispering. Barks and snarls sounded from within the house, accompanied by the sound of ripping and gnawing. Then Danny heard the scream.

Alejandra was inside the house.

Danny ran to the front door, shoulder barged it, fell backwards. The door was too solid. He might as well try to break through the wall. All the windows were barred.

Ricki Cain's expression was completely calm as Danny approached. Correction; her face was devoid of any emotion. Her eyes were like those of Ishmael Vertanness: blank, dark, soulless. Three vertical scratches ran down one cheek, bleeding. She touched a hand to them. 'Little bitch scratched me.'

'Where is she?'

'She's fine. She's inside.'

The meaning of her sly smile took a moment to compute. 'You left her inside with dogs?'

'Not just any dogs. The Hackers' dogs. I'm that "former

cleaner" you mentioned in your article. Now give me your car key.'

'You bitch.'

Danny took a step forward, brandishing the knife. Ricki Cain stepped back and laughed, spinning the house keys on her finger. 'One more step and I throw them into the darkness. Now give me the keys to your fucking car.'

A piercing cry sounded within the house.

'*Keys.*'

Danny threw the car key at her feet. Immediately she tossed her house keys in his direction. Of course. She wanted him to have the keys; it was the only way to ensure he was too busy to stop her from leaving.

Danny ran to the front door and fumbled the keys into the lock as Ricki Cain drove away in his car. The deadbolts turned. He opened the door a fraction, heard paws scrabble at the linoleum. A slavering mess of pink, black and white appeared in the gap. The dog's jaws. Something large and heavy hit the door.

He heard Alejandra scream again. He ran to the bedroom window, looked through the bars, saw what was happening. The door to the bedroom was locked, but someone had kicked a hole in the flimsy wood, a hole large enough for the dogs to get purchase. They were ripping their way through it one piece at a time. Alejandra was huddled in the far corner below the window. That was what the whispering had been, Ricki Cain calling to the dogs, whipping them up. They had the girl's scent now.

The door rattled in its frame as another huge piece was torn off.

What could he do? He would have no option but to sacrifice himself, take his chances with the knife against the dogs. Not that he had any real chance. They'd tear him to pieces. Still, there was a slender hope that he might survive; without his help, Alejandra had none.

He hefted the knife, prepared to enter.

And stopped.

The fire extinguishers.

He ran to the smashed car and picked up one of the extinguishers, ran back to the front door and threw it wide open. The dogs hurled themselves at him. They had crossed the floor of the house in seconds while Danny was still fumbling with the top of the extinguisher.

Danny heard paws scrabbling on the linoleum; the world filled with white.

The explosion of dry powder came so suddenly that it caught Danny by surprise. He stumbled backwards, a wheezing exhalation of powder blasting in a crazy up-down, side-to-side pattern as he struggled to control it.

He heard something thrash and snarl close to him as he advanced into the cloying mist, still blasting the powder from the extinguisher, following the wall to guide him.

When the mist had cleared slightly, Danny that saw the first of the dogs was immersed in the stuff: its eyes, nose and mouth were caked in a thick film of white power. The second dog was less incapacitated.

It paused, sensing movement. Danny was two feet from the bedroom door when it pounced.

'Alejandra, unlock the bedroom door,' Danny screamed as the dog's jaws came together behind his leg, tearing at his jeans. The dog was so powerful he could feel himself being shaken from side to side as it worried at his trousers. Danny crashed to the ground. The blinded dog thrashed wildly, sensing prey. Danny fumbled his belt buckle open and kicked himself out of the jeans. Jaws snapped at his naked legs. He turned, blasted the fire extinguisher again.

'Alejandra, unlock the door.'

The other dog had become a thundering juggernaut, crashing around in the kitchen as it snarled and slavered, its hearing the only sense it had left.

'It's open.' Alejandra's voice sounded pitifully small behind the door.

He pushed at it. It didn't budge. Danny was so terrified, it took him a moment to realise the door had opened towards him. Both dogs came for him as he hurtled through it. Danny slammed the door shut and ran for the dresser, dragging it across the room to form a barricade. The door trembled and shook as the dogs battered it.

Danny leant his fourteen stone frame against the dresser. For the first time in his life, he was glad to be overweight.

24

Callum Hacker wrenched the van round, creating a cloud of dust, his teeth clenched. He'd lost the bastard. He pounded the dashboard with his fists.

Where the fuck had that prick journalist gone? That was the trouble with these stupid Dago roads, too many fucking curves and bumps. Still, he'd find him. Dean and Adam were at the warehouse dealing with the fire, but as for Callum? He didn't give a shit about the business. Settling accounts was all that mattered.

Sanchez.

He was going to kill him. He'd seen the article. No one called Callum Hacker gay. Or perhaps he'd teach him the other lesson first, hold the bastard down and let him have it. He'd get that lying prick back in Gloucester, too.

Then he'd kill him. He'd always known he could do it. He'd come close in prison, a bed sheet wound round some cunt's throat, watching the veins bulge in his throat as his face reddened to purple. Tonight would be the one, though. There were no prison guards to worry –

The car appeared from nowhere. One minute the road was empty, the next two head lights appeared. It came from a dirt track leading to the main road. He could see the dust it had raised in his –

White Golf. Black Stripe on the bonnet.

Callum put both feet on the brake. He heard the tyres

screech, did a three-point turn in the middle of the road. Two red lights twinkled ahead of him. He had him. Now he fucking had him.

He pushed the van as hard as it would go: 130 km/h. 140. 150. He was gaining on the bastard.

He switched his full beams on. He wanted the cunt to be scared. He laughed as he saw a hand waving from the window, telling him to pass.

'Have it,' he screamed, lurching forward to add extra impetus as the van smashed into the back of the Golf. The car zig-zagged across the road. He smashed into it again, laughing, as the two vehicles weaved across the road. The Golf emitted furious beeps as Callum Hacker drew alongside and swerved into the side of the vehicle.

'Think I'm fucking gay, do you? Call me a faggot, would you?'

He watched in satisfaction as the other car spun round on its front wheels and rolled along the centre of the road. He kept his eyes glued to the driving mirror in order to watch as it rumbled over the edge of the road and disappeared into a gorge.

The rock wall loomed up from nowhere. One moment, there was road, the next it curved away sharply to the right. The sound of shattering glass was the last thing Callum Hacker remembered as the air before him solidified into a sledgehammer and swept him up, backwards and away.

25

Three days later

Danny sat on the edge of his patio. He wasn't drinking wine tonight. Tomorrow was deadline day and it would be a busier one than usual.

Ricki Cain was dead. He made damn sure of that with the Guardia Civil's press officer: Yes, the body pulled from the wreckage of his car was definitely a woman in her late thirties. He told the police everything he knew about her, about the murders she'd instigated. Police searching the house could find only one thing to link her with the crimes: the remains of a melted mannequin doll that had been burnt in the garden, its chest and genitals hacked to pieces, its face smeared with make-up.

Paco Pino would be OK. (The blade had missed his vital organs, 'thanks largely to the five or six centimetres of fat it had to pierce first,' the doctor had said, only half-jokingly.) Someone else who had reason to be glad of an over-indulgent diet.

Alejandra bounced back a bit, but she didn't seem to bounce quite as easily or as high as before it had all happened. There was a silent, secretive side to her now, Lourdes said and she'd had to start wearing nappies again.

Danny told the police what he knew of Craig Thorndyke's involvement. When they investigated further, they found that Thorndyke hadn't just been brought over from England because of the drugs. He had other credentials: a previous conviction for violent sexual assault on a school friend, committed at the tender age of fifteen.

The two Hackers – father and son – had ended up in hospital together. Charlie Hacker's fractured skull healed. Callum Hacker's injuries did not.

The fact that he was pulled, still breathing, from the wreckage, of the vehicle after his van had careered down fifty metres of a ten-in-one gradient before crashing at the bottom of a rock-filled gorge was testament to how strong he was. Forty-eight hours later, his life support machine was switched off.

Police found thirteen bodies in the walls of the house, all of them belonging to immigrants. Toby Ibañez was questioned, but it became clear that he had nothing to do with the crime. However, the adverse publicity that Shelter All suffered sounded the death knell of the NGO. Accounts of those long nights that Ricki Cain – aka Allison – had spent alone manning the phones, quietly choosing her victims, spread like wildfire among the immigrant communities. Toby Ibañez was left with a charity to run that had no customers.

Danny sipped his water, listened to the sounds of his mother banging around in her bedroom. Tomorrow would be a day of many phone calls. There was still one more phone call that he wanted to make today.

He dialled the 0044 dialling code, waited to be connected.

'Hello Marsha,' he said.

'What do you want?'

'I still owe you a night out.'

Marsha's voice was cold. 'That's going to be a little difficult, don't you think?'

Danny had wondered what to say, but now that he was speaking the words came easily. 'That's why I'd like you to come and stay a weekend in Spain. I'll pay the flights.'

Silence. Then, 'Are you serious?'

'*Por supuesto*. That means "of course" in Spanish.'

'Show off.' Her voice had thawed. More silence. 'Danny. I don't know what to say.'

'Say "yes" then. What have you got to lose?'

More silence. 'Can I think about it?'

'As long as you think your way to agreeing, you can have all the time in the world.'

She was enjoying herself now. 'Trying the old hard-sell technique, eh? I will begin the process forthwith. But I'm not promising anything.'

'I'll call you in a couple of days then.'

'I'll look forward to it, Danny.'

They hung up.

Right, one problem resolved. Now for problem number two. Danny Sanchez walked inside, knocked on the door of his spare room.

'¿Mamá? Have you got a moment? There's something we really need to talk about.'

ACKNOWLEDGEMENTS

A huge thanks to Salt Publishing for having the courage to commit to my publication.

Thanks to Peter and Rosie of the Ampersand Agency for believing in me.

Thanks to Jim Simpson, whose advice on nineties' police procedure was invaluable.

Thanks to Richard Torné, my editor at *Costa Almería News*, who first gave me the chance to write and provided the initial inspiration for Danny Sanchez.

Thanks to Françoise, Ian and Damyin, whose comments and advice during the writing of the book were greatly appreciated.

Thanks to Richard, Russell and Helen for putting up with us.

Thanks to my AA sponsor, Paul, for talking sense.

Thanks to Linda Bennett for her editorial wisdom.

Finally, I would like to say a word on Len and Helen Prior, the British couple whose house in Almeria was demolished by judicial order in January, 2008. I covered this story while working as a journalist and the incident provided indirect inspiration for the opening of this novel.

I would not want my work of fiction to detract from or cheapen the misery the Spanish authorities have forced the Priors to endure. As I write this (February 2013) Len and Helen have still not received a penny of compensation while petty-minded Spanish officials from the local and regional government continue to bicker. If this book serves to draw wider attention to the shabby way in which the Priors have been treated, especially by the Junta de Andalucía, it will have more than served its purpose. Caveat emptor.